Prescription for Mayhem

B. Steven Mohnarke

STRIKING IMPRESSIONS

Hawthorne, California

Summer, 1997

STRIKING IMPRESSIONS

P.O. Box 926 Hawthorne, CA USA 90251-0926
(310) 644-6796

Library of Congress Cataloging-in-Publication Data

Mohnarke, B. Steven
Prescription for Mayhem : drug legalization / B. Steven Mohnarke
p. cm.
ISBN 0-9639422-3-9
1. Drug legalization—Fiction.   2. Drug abuse—Traffic—Fiction.
3. Drug traffic—Fiction.   I. Title
PS 3563.O437P74 1997   831'.54

Printed in the United States of America
by McNaughton & Gunn, Inc., Saline, Michigan

First Edition

Publisher's note

By agreement with the author, we would like to inform the reader that Mr. Mohnarke has asked us not to forward to him any correspondence of a non-business-related nature. He is currently very busy with many projects, and says he does not have any free time to respond to letters. We hope that the reader will keep this in mind should they decide to contact us after reading the novel, for their letter will not be forwarded.

We are also obliged to inform the reader that Mr. Mohnarke has stated that he is not currently available for *any* interviews, debates, book signings, testimonials or appearances relating to this book or its content.

Joe Roberts
President - Striking Impressions

Dedication

To my friends:

Andy, who used drugs to get women into bed.
Josie, who couldn't start the day without a joint or two.
Ellen, who overdosed twice.
Bob, who used to feed women drugs and liked to watch them go crazy in public.
Phil, who was an alcoholic at eighteen.
Ed, whose drug habit cost his father his job after twenty years with the company.
Max, whom I saw operate on a patient while drunk.
Tom, who had to have a joint before going to sleep.
Jon, whose cocaine addiction almost cost him his wonderful wife.
Peter, who used drugs to forget how badly women had burned him.
Louis, whose alcoholism caused his stomach ulcer at twenty-three.
Mike, an alcoholic.
John H., who smoked joints to forget his wife's affairs and his impotence.
Doreen, who used drugs to forget that she was beautiful.
Judy, whose cocaine habit helped her forget how miserable a person she thought she was.
Pat, a fine man who overdosed and committed suicide because of alcoholism and unrequited love.
Chris, an ex-alcoholic.
Hop, a longtime alcoholic who just experienced his first heart attack.

Acknowledgments

First editing was by V. B., second editing was by L. Z., and final editing was by J. S. Thank you all for taking my incoherent words and making sense out of them. Thanks also to those that read the final manuscript.

Prescription for Mayhem

Introduction

June 3, 2035
Washington, D.C.

My very dear fellow Americans,

Historians recorded the years between 2027 and 2029 as the most important years since our country was founded. Americans experienced the most powerful, and I may add, worst, "revolution" ever known. More lives were lost during those painful days than in any of the prior wars.

Now that the hoopla has died down about the events which took place nearly eight years ago, people are looking back and are asking how, and more importantly, why this all came about. Since the office of the President is where the buck is supposed to stop, they came to me.

I had a part in all of this. I don't want to ask for credit, nor a condemnation. At the time, I was the Speaker of the House of Representatives. It was then and there that this story began.

Some historians have tried to hold me, John Jones, responsible for the beginning of the revolution, or Sam Bunker and a few other members of Congress. To be honest, I don't know that any one person started the ball rolling. Just like a pile of garbage that accumulates, the stink got so bad and the pile got so big, that some of us got sick of the garbage and took action, which you'll be reading about shortly.

In the creation of this book, I've been influenced liberally by the writings of Congressman Samuel Bunker who was chairman of the *Guidance and Direction Committee* that was instrumental in the "revolution." Now Sam, a dear friend and fine representative of the people isn't here to defend himself.

He was murdered by a Mafia hitman four years after the committee disbanded in 2032. I do miss him dearly and think of him often.

Some of the other members of the committee are also gone. Steve Harning had a fatal heart attack and Bob Emerson was killed while serving a jail sentence. The other members did not keep journals and in talking to them privately, they really don't want to remember the committee. It's still too painful. Considering the job they were called upon to perform and their skill in executing it, we owe them the privacy they desire.

So, Sam's story is included here. I neither applaud nor admonish him for his narratives; it is his, and a reflection of him. Along with Sam's writings are reports from the governmental Social Service agencies. These reports focus upon one of the worst cities affected – Los Angeles.

These reports will help offer a glimpse of what life was like in the Los Angeles and Hollywood areas during that time. These reports are presented as case studies and include compiled analyses from all walks of life. This cross section is represented by a postman, plumber, secretary, policeman, artist, doctor, and welfare recipient.

I've interspersed these case studies with Sam Bunker's journals. These are not just running reports of the committee meetings, but also his astute speculations on organized crime and their response to this "revolution." I hope this gives you a feeling of what went on in this turbulent period and allows you to understand its nuances and repercussions. This was not an easy time for anyone. Some say that April 26, 2028 and the next six months were the closest thing America ever experienced to hell on earth. Some people still say that the problems are with us.

Lastly, the most important thing for you to do is to think about the event. Turn it over in your mind's eye and see how it affected the people of the world as we know it today. That's it! Just think about it. If you'll do that, you'll be doing Sam Bunker, and me, the greatest honor you could bestow upon us.

May God bless you, now and in the future.

With the utmost sincerity,

John Jones - 48th President of the United States of America

Chapter One

February 1, 2027

It hit. The gavel hit the wood and echoed through the hallowed chambers of the House of Representatives. The dull sound was barely heard above the din of the crowd. The Speaker of the House of Representatives raised the gavel again and struck the wood, but no one was listening. For a third time he struck the gavel against the wood, this time with a vengeance.

"Damn it to hell," the Speaker said loudly into the podium microphone. "When I say come to order, you goddamn better come to order!! Bruce," he snapped to the Representative from Michigan, "sit your fat ass back in that chair before I find you in contempt and ship you back to Detroit!" The sounds in the chamber began to recede as his voice boomed on. "Bill, put out that cigarette. You know damn well what the rules are! If you feel like smoking, get your ass out in the anteroom; but don't, for Christ's sake, let down your few million tobacco-growers!" All the cigars and cigarettes went out and the six-hundred-odd men and women looked at the speaker's podium and the speaker, John Jones of Kentucky.

The honorable John Jones was a hefty man around six feet tall. He had a winning smile and spoke with a slight Southern drawl. His thinning hair was black, his temples gray, befitting the post of Speaker of the House. Everyone knew he had a big heart. In public, Jones spoke well but seldom spoke. He swore a lot to his friends but never lied. These traits endeared him to his colleagues, who always knew his position on political issues.

As the noise died down, Jones looked out at his colleagues and noticed that the press gallery was empty. "Good," he thought. The last thing he wanted was a bunch of pissant reporters trying to get their names in the news. It was his order that barred the press and the public from today's special joint session of the Senate, House, Cabinet, and Supreme Court.

"Well, that's a start," he thought. He looked from the rostrum toward the main floor. "These SOB's represent over three hundred million Americans," he thought. "Shit," he muttered under his breath as he neatened the pile of notes for his speech. He looked up from the podium to face the group, loosed his tie and collar a bit, then pulled the crotch of his tight pants so that he wouldn't have to squirm as he spoke. He always felt out of place in a suit and tie. He cleared his throat and waited for the room to quiet down.

"Oh, boy!! Are we in for it now!!" thought Sam Bunker, the Honorable Congressman from Kansas. Sam had been a Congressman more than thirty years, and he had seen it all. He knew from past experience that whenever John Jones cleared his throat before talking, all hell was sure to break loose. He sorely wished he had gone to the bathroom, because it looked like this was going to be a long, long meeting.

Sam yelled for a page to come over. The page was a crew-cut red-haired boy of sixteen with freckles and glasses. His face was ruddy red from the tight collar of the page's blue, red and white uniform. The bell boy's cap, part of the uniform, made the boy feel ill at ease.

"Boy," Sam said. "Here's twenty bucks. I want you to run over to the cafeteria and have the fellas gimme a thermos of coffee and a quart of Irish whiskey, in a brown bag, of course. And hurry!" he said as he watched John Jones move about the podium like a rooster getting ready to crow.

The page looked at the money in his open hand. "Things should be different here," he thought, putting the money in his pocket.

"Boy," Sam Bunker said flatly, his bladder sphincter constricting and causing him to shift around in his seat, "Tell them it's for Sam Bunker, Okay? Remember, a thermos of coffee and a quart of Irish whiskey. Now move it, or I'll guarantee that next year every tax return from your home town will be audited!"

With that, the blue-eyed page ran out of the council chambers as if the devil was on his tail. Sam smirked and rubbed his two-day-old whiskers. Sam had a characteristic face; thick glasses with plastic bifocals, white hair combed back, and distinguished wrinkles. He was five feet eleven tall, and if he stood straight, he appeared as though he could support the world on his shoulders. He was considered honest by all his constituents and members of Congress.

And he would break his back for people, unless they stabbed him in it, and then Sam would attack them like a lioness defending her cubs. People respected him because they always knew exactly where he stood on issues, even to the point of Sam's occasional lack of tact.

Sam saw the page sprint from the House chambers. Sam liked youngsters. He felt that boys like this page made America and Americans look good. Sam adjusted his bifocals and glanced at the desk in front of him. "Huey Long talks too long," was what some senator had etched into the wood of the desk a long time ago.

The boy ran through Statuary Hall, then through the Main Rotunda and past the Senate Rotunda to the Senate side of Congress. He ran to the grand staircase and then sped towards the Senate cafeteria, which was open. Sweating, the page ran into the cafeteria, taking off his page hat and fanning his face and sweaty neck.

"I need...I need...I need..." he muttered between breaths.

"Young man," the manager said like a father would, "slow down and relax. That's better, isn't it?" The page leaned against a wall, catching his breath. "Now, young man, what do you want?"

"I need a thermos of coffee and some Irish whiskey for Sam Bunker," the page uttered between breaths as he reached into his pocket for the money Sam Bunker had given him. The boy took out the money and held it toward the manager.

"Holy hell!" the manager yelled as he jumped up and turned his head away from the boy. He began to shout orders to the rest of the crew. "Hey everyone! Sam Bunker wants some Irish coffee. Get the extra coffee maker going. Start making sandwiches." His head jerked from one side to another. "Call Sue, Candy, and Linda and have them come in today. We'll need all the kitchen help we can get."

The page looked quizzically at the cashier and the cafe workers scurrying around. "Weird," he thought, putting the money back in his pocket until the manager returned. "Maybe it has something to do with the weather." He scratched his head before he replaced his cap.

"Here you go," the manager said, quickly handing the page a large brown paper bag and started moving away from the cash register.

"Excuse me, sir," asked the boy shyly, remembering that his biology teacher at Hamilton High, Mr. Don Teeford, said it was no sin to ask questions about things he didn't quite understand. "But I don't understand what happens when you mix whiskey with coffee? Is there a problem doing that in Congress?"

"Young man," the manager quickly replied, "you don't know this, but Sam Bunker's father, God rest him, was also a Congressman. Sam Bunker, Sr. always asked for Irish coffee right before Congress decided big things like the Korean War, the Cuban Crisis, the Civil Rights Amendment, Vietnam, and whatever else was important in the last half of the twentieth century. Sam Jr. has been doing the same damn thing. Takes after his old man." He then looked at the bewildered boy and explained, "Sam Bunker makes his Irish coffee every time there's a national crisis."

The page held the paper bag in one hand and started digging into his pocket again for the twenty dollar bill. The manager said "Forget it," as he ran to the phone to call his broker about selling his stocks, and then to call the Press Club for his usual five hundred dollar tip that something was up on the Hill.

The page walked slowly back to the House, carefully holding the coffee and whiskey so it wouldn't spill. All the way back, he wondered if what was happening would become a national crisis. It sounded scary. Why would the cafeteria manager be so excited? Suddenly, he was scared and felt the urge to go home.

As he walked toward the chambers, he saw security guards gathered at the chamber doors. He passed them at the entrance and heard them talking.

"Once again, Jack," growled one guard, "once the Speaker begins, no one, especially no one from the press, gets in. This closed session is important! If one word of this leaks out, it'll be our jobs. They'll do it too, those cold-hearted assholes," he said between clenched teeth, his palm resting on the butt of his revolver. "So, no one gets in but members of Congress."

The page walked to where Sam Bunker was seated and carefully rested the bag on the desk in front of him. Sam looked at the boy. The boy was trembling slightly.

"Thanks a lot," Sam smiled as he looked at the boy. The boy looked uncomfortable in his page's uniform. "It looks like that collar's killing him," Sam thought. Sam imagined the boy to be more at home on a tractor or on a trash can lid, sliding down a snowy hill in January rather than working in the halls of Congress. It reminded him of his youth and gave him an inner glow.

"Keep the change," Sam added, as he saw the boy reaching into his pocket. Sam observed that the boy looked nervous. "Maybe he can sense that something is up," he thought. "I guess we all can. Dad was right. Being a Congressman isn't a great job. He said I would been better off doing something to make me happy; like being a pimp instead."

"Everything is OK," he quietly whispered to the page with a sigh. "Now get out of here: Take the day off. I have a feeling that you won't be able to get back in anyhow."

The boy made his way out of the chambers, wondering how he would spend his twenty buck tip. Maybe he'd go to Arlington Cemetery and look around, or possibly the Air and Space Museum. Now that he had the whole day to goof off, with pay, he didn't care about Congress anymore.

As Sam watched the boy leave, he thought that the lad had a look people have when they know something important is about to happen, but they know they won't be able to do a damned thing about it. He looked into the bag and began cursing to himself as he realized the page had given him a pint of whiskey instead of a quart. "Wait till I get my hands on that brat," he thought. He started mixing his Irish coffee under the desk.

"I'll skin him alive," he said to himself.

Sam stood up to quickly run to the bathroom, but the gavel sounded one last time. John Jones said solemnly, "Gentlemen and ladies, let's get this meeting going. We have a lot of business to cover."

Sam sat back down slowly and groaned as he felt his bladder sphincter contract in pain. If he only had balls enough to stand up, unzip his fly, and pee all over his desk! He didn't care what his so-called colleagues thought. "I've been trying to make this country better for thirty years," he thought, "and all I've done is bash my head against the wall time and time again."

He looked at the pint that should have been a quart and shook his head "No," muttering to himself. "This damn country has been going downhill for the last twenty-five years and it's about time for the damned nation to hit rock bottom."

He took a sip of the Irish coffee and hoped he'd be good and drunk before the morning was over.

Prescription for Mayhem

Chapter Two

John Jones looked up from the podium at the Senators. The Representatives, Cabinet members, and Supreme Court justices also sat before him at the Special Session the President had requested. The members of Congress were uncomfortable, not knowing why this special meeting had been called. "The worst is yet to come," thought Jones. The paneled doors were closed with the Congressional police outside, assuring privacy for the meeting.

John Jones took a deep breath, adjusted the crotch of his pants one last time, and said to himself, "Here goes nothing.

"I hereby call this Special Session of the Congress of the United States to order," he roared as he banged the gavel on the platform. He waited until the Chaplain of the House gave an introductory prayer for the session. When this was over, Jones began.

"Members of the House of Representatives, Senate, Supreme Court justices, and Cabinet members; under Article two, Section three of our Constitution, the President of the United States can call an emergency session of Congress when he deems it necessary. This is the fifty-first such session to be called in our history.

"I apologize for the President's not being here today, but as you know, he's in the hospital for an emergency gall bladder operation and should be up within a week. The Vice-President is heading a peace conference in Libya, so as next in line, it falls upon me to chair this meeting. This is the first Special

Session called since we celebrated our Bicentennial-plus last year on July 4th, 2026. That was when we celebrated our two-hundred-fiftieth year as a nation, and a glorious year for the fifty-five states in our Union.

"The Bicentennial-plus celebration was exciting, with a party at the White House that topped any other one I've ever been to, or can ever imagine in my legislative life.

"Laura, my wife, and I got to the White House at eight o'clock or so, a little while after sunset. It sure was a pretty sight, believe you me, with fireworks exploding, lighting up the sky. With every explosion, our chauffeur, Jeff, kept peering around, worrying that some assassin was out to get me. Then again, you know how those Secret Service men are," he added as a small chuckle rippled through his audience.

"There were about a hundred and fifty people there and it seemed to me they had all been doing some heavy drinking. We could hear them while we drove up to the entrance of the White House. Jeff stopped the car at the entrance. The Vice-President himself opened the car door to let Laura and me out. He makes a hell of a better doorman than a Vice-President, but you Senators already know that." More chuckling and a few belly-laughs came from the members in the chamber.

"When we walked into the reception hall, I had a couple of drinks and was soon ready for anything! Even a meeting with the Ways and Means Committee! I've had drinks before, but these must've been the smoothest Hurricanes I ever had north of the Mason-Dixon line.

"Laura and the first lady started talking about the latest fashions and recipes, even though they both have cooks and designers. And..."

A new Congressman from Berkeley, California stood up and interrupted Jones. "I rise to a point of order, sir."

"Yield to a question," Jones said quietly into the microphone. "This better be good," he thought.

"What is the point to all of this? This is supposed to be a meeting involving an emergency situation. I..."

"You're out of order, sir," John Jones bellowed with authority. "Shut up and sit down...now!" he yelled as the Congressman sat down.

The Sergeant-at-Arms' neck hairs bristled at the way Jones addressed the Congressman. But he knew that in a Special Session the President could throw out *Robert's Rules of Order* and parliamentary procedure altogether if he wanted. And Jones was representing the President. Some members looked at the Sergeant-at-Arms for action, but he did nothing.

"And you listen," he said, in a quieter voice, his face still red. "You new kids are sure cocky. Just 'cause you represent a couple hundred thousand or so doesn't mean beans around here. We are the country! So don't give me any of your goddamn snootiness. I'm getting to the point in my own fashion and in my own good time. I'll be goddamned if you tell me what I'm going to do."

The Sergeant-at-Arms winced at the venom behind the words.

John Jones added very softly to the Congressman, "You'll find out that you can get more done if you work with us and pretend that we're equals." After taking a breath, he spoke in a whisper and knowingly said, "You don't know how much that outburst of yours will cost your future career in the minds of these people.

"Now, where was I?" John Jones asked as he shuffled the papers and scanned the people in the chambers. He signaled the Sergeant-at-Arms to check why Sam Bunker had his head cradled between his arms.

"Oh, yes," Jones remembered what he was saying, "The party was a great success. We had a wonderful time. And it was memorable, too. The most memorable moment was when the President's four-year-old son, Brian, came out of his bedroom. He was frightened by the fireworks and ran to his father's lap. He had on little yellow pajamas decorated with teddy bears and was hugging a big teddy bear. I'm convinced that if the President had only held up his son to the TV cameras and done nothing else, that would have been enough to elect him."

"The boy stopped crying, and was now sniffling when he asked why everything was so loud. I remember the President telling him that everyone was celebrating America's birthday and this was a birthday party. The little boy sat on his father's lap for a few minutes, looking out the veranda window at the fireworks over the Potomac. He looked back at his daddy. "Daddy," he squeaked in a quiet voice, "Do you love America?" The President seemed startled for a second and the whole room became quiet. The President looked at his son and proudly answered, "I sure do." The President then turned to look out at the bag lady living on the streets in front of the White House. I know you all have seen her. She's the one who swears that she's protecting the President and the nation.

"Shortly after that I heard the President asking his Cabinet members if they loved America. Silly question, huh? Or is it? One of the things I want to ask you all is do you love America? Do you? Sure it's comfortable being a member of Congress and having everybody assume that we love America. Hell, whenever we're feeling low we can give ourselves a salary raise. I guess that only happens in America." Giggles came from the House floor.

The Sergeant-at-Arms stood over Sam Bunker and took the brown bag from the side of his chair. Sam couldn't be roused. The Sergeant-at-Arms looked at John Jones and made a motion with his hand toward his mouth like he was drinking something. He moved his hands towards his nostrils and pinched them as though he smelled something foul. The Sergeant-at-Arms hadn't seen the puddle of urine underneath Sam Bunker's chair but he sure smelled it. John Jones nodded his head and signaled the Sergeant-at-Arms to leave Sam where he was.

"The *only* reason for this Special Session, and the *only* question to be addressed today is," said Jones, taking a long pause, "Do *we* love America enough to do something about its terminal condition? America is sick! America is dying! Do you remember the commitment you gave to someone you loved? If you're like me, it was a long while ago. But if you love someone you take care of them whether rich or poor, in sickness and health, forsaking all others, for better or worse, until death do you part. Sounds familiar, doesn't it? I'd like to talk about these threats to the country we love. For if we don't fix these threats here today, our country will die as surely as if we put a bullet through its heart.

"For richer or poorer. Folks, America isn't a rich country any more. Our imports exceed our exports. We've become a user nation, and have money problems. We owe everyone and no one sees an end in sight.

"In sickness and in health. We've become victims of laziness and greed. We don't compete when it's easier to have someone else produce goods, if we get a percentage when it's sold. We do that. The underpaid Mexican laborers we have in this country are doing the real work, even though we kick and scream that they're taking away jobs from Americans.

"Forsaking all others. We Congressmen are prime examples of this. I've heard more sex scandals in the last five years than in the last twenty years combined. Have we forgotten that we represent millions of people? Sometimes I wonder. For those who say we don't make enough money, there are stories and hard evidence of grafting among us. We're tainted and there seems no way of separating the chaff from the wheat.

"For better or worse. Our country is plagued by illiteracy. We have gangs, criminal acts, and ecological problems beyond the wildest imagination of a corrupt society. Americans still have problems getting food, clothing, shelter and medical care. We have the homeless, the hungry and the haunted. Let's face it! We're morally and financially bankrupt. Some say we should kill the horse and put it out of its misery!

"Until death do us part. As representatives of the people, we've failed. Failed miserably! Each one of us," John Jones said as he pointed his finger around the room. "America is deathly ill. And if we love her, truly love her, can we stand by the sidelines doing nothing and watch her die?" Jones shuffled his papers.

The room was deathly still. Each person was alone in their private thoughts. The silence was heavy. The only sound that could be heard was a soft snore from Sam Bunker, whose head was now tilted back, his mouth open.

Prescription for Mayhem

Chapter Three

"I've got them," John Jones said to himself. "I've got those bastards right where I want them," he thought as he looked around the chambers. John thought of his ten-year-old daughter, his only child and the joy of his life. She had been attacked and killed by a nineteen-year-old heroin addict less than one week after the Bicentennial-plus celebration. The addict took her lunch money and then brutally raped her. The crazed junkie then took a knife and slit her open from her vagina to her throat.

John Jones mourned for two months, asking the heavens, "Why? Why? Why would anyone kill my only child?" Then he changed his words to "Never again." He had to do something. Anything. Last October he talked with the President and everyone else he could find about the country's problems. The President, Supreme Court, and others agreed that desperate times warranted immediate actions.

"The President should be speaking today at this Special Session," thought Jones. "He's much better at this than I am." Then he reminded himself that he was doing it all for his daughter.

"Goddamn it," he shouted loudly enough to echo off the chamber walls. "What do we do? Legislate? We've enough useless laws on the books to wipe our butts until the next millennium. We've got to do something and we've got to do it now!"

"Mr. Chairman..." spoke Senator Michaels as she stood up.

"Chair recognizes Senator Michaels," said Jones, sitting down.

"I raise a question."

"Yield to a question," replied Jones.

"What can we do?" she asked as she sat down.

Jones stood up. "From talking with the President and the members of the legislature, we concluded that we've got to try something that has never been done in the history of Congress. We have to sacrifice something that is near and dear to us all."

He paused for a moment. "It's power," he concluded. "The power we've had entrusted to us from the millions of Americans. The power we've abused. We've got to use that power for good!

"To do this task," he continued, "the President and others have come up with a solution. What we need is a few women and men to guide us. We must entrust them with the power necessary to accomplish the job of fixing the problems that are killing America. Do I hear a motion that we create a new committee with the power to drag us back to life?"

"Mr. Chairman," spoke Representative Hoffman as he stood up.

"Chair recognizes Representative Hoffman," said John Jones, sitting down.

"I so move that we create a new committee to fix the problems bothering America through legislation, with the power to do so."

"Second," came a voice as the Representative sat down.

"Objection!" cried Senator Harris.

"Chair recognizes Senator Harris," said Jones.

"What exactly is the problem? It's too vague and needs to be clearly stated at this point. I further object to the consideration of the question."

"You are out of order, sir," said Jones firmly. "The only purpose of this meeting is the consideration of this question."

"Objection," came from the Majority Leader of the House, not pleased with the prospect of giving up his personal power.

"Chair recognizes Representative Enoch," Jones said.

"I move we lay the question on the table."

"You are out of order, sir," said Jones pointedly. "This cannot be postponed, as it is the only business of the day."

"Objection," came from the Majority Whip of the Senate.

"Chair recognizes Senator Sarver," said Jones, getting a bit tired of the animosity.

"I move that the question be referred to a committee."

"You are out of order, madam," Jones said diplomatically. "We have been given a presidential request to complete this task as a committee of the whole. It cannot be further delayed."

"Point of order," came from Representative Salt.

"Chair recognizes Representative Salt," said Jones as he sat back to hear the oldest man in Congress speak. It felt good to relax for a few seconds and hear his old friend speak.

"There is a conflict with the rules of order and standing rules. There is a motion on the floor to form a new committee with the power to legislate laws by representing the Congress with a two-thirds majority vote, even though a majority is not present. This clearly violates standing rules of Congress. And to vote on amending standing rules needs a day's prior notice," he said.

"Point of order sustained," said Jones, grateful that his friend brought it up. "The notice for the possible amending of standing rules among other changes was included in the notice for the Special Session. Thank you for reminding me. We have to first address the standing rules before a committee can be formed. Representative Salt, would you like to put that in the form of a motion?"

"I thought you'd never ask," said Representative Salt with a quavering voice. "I've wanted to do this for the last fifty years that I've been here. I move that we amend the rules which interfere with the formation of this committee such that the proposed committee can legislate laws similar to that of a two-thirds majority vote of Congress, without consideration of the membership at large."

"Second," came from the floor.

"This cannot be debated," spoke Jones, knowing that this was probably the first time in over a hundred years where the rules of the Constitution were in danger of being changed. "Think carefully," he said as he brought forth the question. "The nation rests on this. As many as are in favor of amending the standing rules say Aye."

A tremendous roar went through the chamber.

"As many as are opposed say Nay."

Few voices were heard.

"The motion to amend the rules for consideration of a committee such that the proposed committee can legislate laws similar to that of a two-thirds majority vote of Congress, without consideration of the membership at large, has passed. We still have the motion on the floor to create a new committee to guide and direct America through our problems by legislation. The question is open to debate," Jones said quietly.

"Chair recognizes the Chairman of the Ways and Means Committee," John Jones acknowledged to a man standing up.

"I have a point to make," said Howard Pewsner, head of the Ways and Means Committee. Pewsner was not anxious to relinquish the power he had gotten from his many terms of kissing asses in Congress. "How do we know that this will be successful? Maybe we're rushing into things." Pewsner sat down.

"Chair recognizes Senator Tom Baker of the Education and Welfare Committee," Jones mouthed.

"Howard," vocalized Senator Baker, "I understand that you don't want to give up the power you've earned. None of us do, but I acknowledge that we've all failed. You've failed and I've failed. Do you hear that? America is sick. Very sick. And dying, too! Can't you see that? We need to do something different, as Chairman Jones said, and we must do it now!" The Chairman of the Ways and Means Committee sat quietly for the first time in his life.

"Mr. Chairman," said Representative Brooks, standing up.

"Chair recognizes Representative Brooks," John Jones replied.

"My only concern is that such a committee be representative of all the committees we have in Congress. It's okay for this committee to be small, but we should try to cover our bases."

"Would you like to put that in the form of a motion?" Jones asked.

Representative Brooks stood there, thinking for a moment, then decided to place no limitations on the committee. He wasn't sure if thirty- nine people, one member from each committee, could do any better than six hundred. He shook his head no and then sat down.

"Is there any other debate?" asked Jones.

Once again, the chamber was silent.

"Do I hear the motion?" John Jones said convincingly.

"So moved."

"Second."

"As many as are in favor, say Aye," John Jones asked. The halls echoed with affirmation.

"As many as are opposed, say Nay," Jones continued. About thirty people stated the negative.

"Abstaining?" Jones spoke. A few voices could be heard.

"The motion passes," John Jones said.

"Mr. Chairman?" said Representative Bailey, standing up.

"Representative Bailey," said John Jones toward the man who first showed him the ropes when he came to Washington.

"I move we reconsider the vote."

"The motion has already passed," replied Jones slowly, trying to figure out what his friend was getting at.

"I know that, Mr. Chairman," Mr. Bailey respectfully said. "But what we're doing is unique. We all have to agree with the motion or it will fail, along with the country. This should be unanimous. I'm asking you all to reconsider the vote. Those of you who oppose it, let us know now, or forever hold your peace."

"Second," came from the floor.

"The motion to reconsider the vote is on the floor and now open to debate," Jones said, ready for another debate go-around.

No sound echoed from the floor.

"Is there a motion for the question?" asked John Jones.

"Moved for the vote," Representative Hoffman loudly said.

"Second," Representative Bailey proudly voiced.

"Those in favor, say Aye." The answer resounded from the halls, stronger than before.

"Those opposed, say Nay." No response came from the chamber.

"Abstaining?" No response came back.

"The motion is unanimously carried," said John Jones, breathing a sigh of relief. "We now have a committee determined to get the country back on its feet, headed in the right direction. The committee will consist of members chosen from the existing Congressional committees. I will make a first cut of a selection, and send each of you a copy. Should you disagree with the selection, let me know, and the final cut will not be made until there is absolute agreement. All correspondence will be monitored and handled by the Sergeant-at-Arms."

Sam Bunker suddenly belched so all could hear. A second moment later his belch was followed by the loudest fart ever heard in the hallowed chambers. The Congressmen around him began to fan the air and laugh sheepishly.

"Ladies and gentlemen," John Jones said, smiling, "On that note, or rather, on those notes, I declare this Special Session of the United States Congress adjourned. I'll keep you posted on the committee." With that John Jones struck the gavel on the podium.

The congressmen and senators started to make their way out of the chambers, most aware that they still had time to make lunch at Sans Souci. A few of them came up and slapped Jones on the back.

"Best speech I ever heard."

"I hope this thing works. This country stinks."

"Thank you, John," said a Supreme Court justice. "It sure was needed. Have you any idea who you want on the committee?"

"I think I have an idea," smiled Jones, who was looking at Sam Bunker as he was talking. Sam was awake now and holding his head. He felt as if the world was spinning. He grabbed the nearest wastebasket and puked in it.

"Sam," John Jones thought, "your headache is just starting."

Chapter Four

Three months later
May 11, 2027

"Where have you been, Sam?" asked Tom Baker. "After all, this is our first meeting!"

"I was at the Lincoln Memorial," Sam Bunker said dryly. "I always go there to get inspired."

"What inspiration did you get?" asked the Chaplain of the House, waiting to bless the meeting.

"I saw Abe's right foot leaning forward, like it just squashed a cockroach," Sam surmised. "I knew exactly how that bug felt."

"That still doesn't explain why you're late."

"I couldn't find this damned room," Sam nervously said. "They said it was the room right next to the Prayer Room. I've never been in the Prayer Room of Congress before. How did I know it was just west of the Rotunda?"

"That doesn't explain why you're late," the Chaplain admonished.

"What're you doing here, Reverend?" asked Sam, changing the subject.

"Mr. Jones asked me to give a blessing before each session," the Chaplain replied. "He said he wants to cover all his bets."

Sam looked around him. He was in a small room with only one door and no windows. The room was paneled in oak, and cozy. There was a glass chandelier in the center of the vaulted ceiling, a bookshelf with nothing on it, and an old mahogany conference table with six chairs around it.

"This place doesn't have any windows," Sam surmised. "It's just like a prison."

"Neither do the Congress chambers," reminded Tom Baker. "I was told we would be in an interior room so that we couldn't be monitored by anyone."

"How considerate," Sam said wryly.

"There will also be armed guards assuring your privacy. They, of course, will be wearing earplugs," uttered the Chaplain.

"As I said, they're too considerate," Sam remarked even more sarcastically.

"Please bow your heads with me in prayer," began the Chaplain as they started the first meeting of the newly formed *Guidance and Direction Committee*.

The people bowed their heads.

"Dear Lord. Hear our pleas. We have been appointed to direct and guide this country based on freedom to follow your path, narrow though it is, towards enlightenment and fulfillment. Guide our steps.

"Put your guiding touch on Thomas Baker, of the Education and Welfare Committee. Please help Bob Emerson, of the Banking and Currency Committee. Show your path and guidance to Steve Harning, of the Judiciary Committee. Also, please heal him. He is still having difficulties from the bypass operation he had three months ago. He is needed, Lord, to be your hands and voice. He has served you and this country for many years. Thank you, Lord, for Steve. And, we pray for Frederica Wright, of the Government Operations Committee. Bless Frederica by helping her recover from the complications from the cataract surgery, and the loss of her eye.

"And, Lord, last, but not least, we pray for the touch of the Holy Spirit on the mind and tongue of Samuel Bunker, of the Ways and Means Committee. He is the appointed head of this committee, so please guide and direct Samuel as you see fit.

"We thank you for the blessings you've bestowed upon us and the challenges you've placed before us. We pray in the name of your Son, Jesus, who died for us, who showed us how to be a servant and how to love you and our neighbors. We pray in His name. Amen."

"Blasted ministers," thought Sam Bunker. "You give them a minute for a blessing, and they turn it into a ten-minute sermon. Maybe Jones should've invited the Senate Chaplain instead of the House one. Well, my first act as head of this committee will be to talk with the Reverend and make sure he doesn't speak without a two-minute constraint. How did I ever get to be the head of this group anyway? Did I ask for it? No! Do I want it? No! I'm still not sure why they wanted me or what's going on! I'll never fall asleep in Congress again!"

"Sit down," Sam quietly spoke to all. The Chaplain left, closing the doors behind him. The seat at the head of the table was left for him. Sam looked up at the people before him. Four pitiful people stared back at him. It would be their job to make the nation fruitful again. He didn't know if they could do it. He didn't think so.

Sam remembered being called into John Jones's office the next day after the joint Special Session adjourned. He remembered that it wasn't a request, but an order. He figured that John Jones was going to slap his hands for falling asleep, drinking, farting, pissing and puking during the Special Session and tell him not to do it again. Wrong.

After Jones consulted with Sam on what the new committee was supposed to do, he said that he was going to suggest Sam to chair it. John Jones didn't say why. He just kept saying that Sam would probably be the best man for the job, despite Sam's objections.

"And what about these representatives?" Sam asked as he looked at the preliminary list of the members chosen from Congressional committees. "Do you know how many committees we have under this stinking dome? Let's see, we have twenty-two or twenty-three committees in the House. And we have sixteen more committees or so in the Senate. That's thirty-nine people. Goddamn it, John! If you think that thirty-nine people can decide things, take another good look where you sit, 'cause that's what you're thinking with. Thirty-nine people couldn't legislate their way out of a driveway. It just won't work. You've got to cut it down. And while you're at it, try to see if someone else can chair this turkey shoot. I don't think I'd be the best one for the job."

Sam would remember for the rest of his natural life the cussing he got from John Jones. Jones used every word he knew. He even invented a few. The bottom line was that Sam was going to do what he was told with no objections, unless he "goddamned died." Then they were going to put his corpse at the head of the committee table for a week just to be sure, or at least until the smell got bad.

Jones did agree that he would think about fewer people on the committee and get back in touch with Sam. After a little consideration, John Jones personally called each of the six hundred members of Congress and told them that the committee would have to be pared down, because thirty-nine people would be too many. It took some finagling, but each member signed a form stating that five or six people would be fine.

After many changes, Jones had the committee he wanted. Six of the strongest and most dedicated people in Congress, who epitomized the American ideal. These six people would have enough power in their twelve hands to rip the face of the earth apart if they wanted to.

John Jones knew them all well. He knew Tom Baker, an outstanding Senator with a sharp concept of right and wrong. Tom would be the expert in the Education and Welfare aspects of the committee. Tom, with his boyish grin and the distinction of being the biggest prankster in Congress, loved to have practical jokes played. John personally remembered how Tom had once wired up his microphone so that every time he talked, he got a shock. Once he found out Tom had done this, he thought it pretty funny.

John Jones respected Senator Robert Emerson. Bob was from a good Nebraska family. He was filthy rich, and totally uncompromising in his convictions. Bob was a financial wizard who ended up giving more to charities than he made for himself. He was a humanitarian.

Jones knew the committee needed Representative Steve Harning. Steve had been in Congress so long that everyone felt he would always be elected without running. Steve was a fine man but had a weak heart. He was more involved in the social advancements made by Congress than anyone else. Steve was one of the most powerful men in Congress, not because of the Judiciary Committee he headed, but because he knew and had relationships with all the judicial arms of government. He knew each member of the Supreme Court personally, most of the three hundred federal court judges, and even many of the policemen around D.C. Steve once told John Jones that he had always wanted to be a cop. He had begun at the police academy, but gave it up when he was accepted into law school instead.

Frederica Wright was a perfect example of a bookworm. She wore thick glasses and a plain dress. She was thin and spoke with a soft lilting voice. She could whine when she wanted to, but Frederica knew the government inside and out. She understood the system, and since the system was so large, anyone who understood it could manipulate it. Since she was on the Government Operations Committee, Frederica fit in perfectly.

Congressman Emil J. Wardlaw was perhaps the slickest of the Congressmen. He had his hands in all kinds of things, and knew the best ways to get things done. Although on the Appropriations Committee, Wardlaw had an uncanny knack of circumventing committees. He was an excellent public speaker who managed to get along with everyone.

Sam was given the chance to review the list before it was made public in early April. He looked over the list and grabbed a few papers from a locked drawer. He made two phone calls, and then told his secretary where he was going. He went over to Emil Wardlaw's office.

"Get out," he said to Wardlaw's secretary as he walked into Wardlaw's inner office without knocking.

She looked at Emil, who nodded.

She left.

"Sam, my old buddy," smiled Emil, standing up and going over to shut the door. "How are you doing? How's the wife and kids? Sit down and let's talk."

Sam stood straight. "Sit down," Sam spoke firmly.

Emil sat, looking at Sam, and wondering what this old man had on his mind. Emil didn't respect Sam nor those others like him.

"I wanted to let you know prematurely that John Jones nominated and approved you for the *Guidance and Direction Committee*," Sam said. "The list isn't coming out until next week."

"I'm honored," Emil replied.

"I'm not," Sam growled angrily. "I want you off the committee."

"I don't understand," Emil asked.

"I don't want you attending the meetings. I don't want you listed as one of the committee members. I want you to refuse the position."

Emil sat for a moment. The people on the committee were going to be the most powerful in the nation, with unlimited power above that of the President.

"And if I don't?" Emil softly voiced, noting how Sam's hands trembled from age. Sam always breathed with difficulty, and Emil thought he looked old.

"I'll tell them," Sam replied, just as softly.

"Tell them what?" Emil asked.

"You know," Sam said. "You've got quite a reputation in Congress. You're the person to talk to if you need things done. We call you the 'Arranger.' Quite a position for a person who has been here only five years."

"Thank you," Emil said proudly. "But are you going to tell everyone that?"

"Not quite," Sam replied with some bitterness. "Your voting record shows you're pro-big business regardless of their suspicious track records. You've lobbied for increased gambling in the states, and for prisoner rights. You've supported decreased sentences for pushers and pimps through the Prison Rights Amendment you shot through Congress five years ago. You've hidden your roots well. But there was something about you that I didn't trust, so I started digging through your background myself."

"And..." Emil asked, knowing that nothing would hold water in a congressional inquest.

"...And you're Mafia."

"You're crazy!" Emil laughed. "It's preposterous."

"Does the name Peter 'Dick' Alonso ring a bell?" Sam asked, smiling with an eyebrow raised. He looked directly at Emil. He saw that Emil recognized the name of the biggest Mafia defector in the last thirty years. The Mafia was still trying to find Alonso.

"I've heard of him," Emil said straight-faced.

"He nailed you. We just showed him a picture of you when you were younger, and he not only told us your connections, but told us some things about your past and your relatives that are now solid proof. He wrote it all down," Sam said, throwing pages one through three of a twenty-five page document on Emil's desk.

"You have until Monday to get out of Washington and I want you to take these people with you," Sam ordered, tossing a list of eight names of other members of Congress on the desk. "If any of you remain in Washington, you will be exposed instantly. The Attorney General has written orders with the presidential stamp, requiring you to obey those demands or face immediate prosecution. You know, once we found you, it was easy to figure out who else was involved. Flies always gather around shit! To make it final, you and your friends will resign your posts within the week. The only reason I'm doing it this way is to avoid another Congressional scandal and so we don't have the painful process of choosing any new committee members."

Emil looked as though he was about to say something.

"And what's worse," Sam added bitterly, "is that we're trying to make the country better, even for your kids. Don't say anything! No threats, no replies, no nothing."

With that, Sam turned and walked out. Emil sat in his chair, reached for the document and started reading the first three pages. He then knew that Sam spoke the truth and that his career was finished in Washington.

He grabbed the phone. "Uncle Giuliano," he said. "This is Emil. I'm fine, and you? I'm coming into town tomorrow. We've got a problem."

The next week, eight congressmen resigned their posts for various reasons. Sam, on the other hand, went out and got drunk.

Sam thought about the Wardlaw situation as he looked at his new colleagues.

"Well," he said, cheerfully. "I guess everyone's here. Having such a small committee makes roll call easy."

"Cut the crap, Sam," Frederica Wright replied in her usual voice, "and let's get down to business."

"Okay," Sam apologized, being thrown on the defensive. "First thing we do is dispense with formal parliamentary procedure. Anyone have any problems with this?"

No one spoke.

"Good," Sam replied. He paused for a moment, looking uncertain, then said, "Can someone please tell me what exactly our business of the day is?"

"Making America the land of the free and home of the brave," Tom Baker jokingly quipped.

"And how do we do that?" asked Bob Emerson, looking at Sam.

"You think I know?" Sam said. "I'm just the head of the committee, not the answer man."

"Why don't you make a list of things that need fixing, Sam?" Frederica Wright told in her whining voice, adjusting her glasses to see the group better.

"I can do that," said Sam quickly, getting out a paper and pen as he looked at the group.

"We need to raise money," Bob Emerson said with a sigh, as though he believed this meeting would be another waste of time. "The government is bankrupt."

"Raise money," Sam wrote down.

"We have to address illiteracy and the lack of motivation people these days have in order to make Americans more productive," Tom Baker said about one of his favorite causes.

"We have to eliminate drug-dealing and get rid of the Mafia," stated Steve Harning.

"Eliminate pushers and Mafia," Sam wrote down, then smiled. "Who knows?" he said, with a little grin, "That might happen. We also should have stronger laws protecting the innocent from violent and abusive crimes," Sam commented out loud.

Everyone nodded. He wrote it down.

"We have to make America strong, both morally and ethically," said Tom Baker, "to make it safe again."

"And no money-grubbing either," Bob Emerson added, wincing as he remembered all the times people succeeded in bleeding him for money.

Sam nodded.

The room was silent as everyone thought of things that America needed.

"Anything else?" Sam Bunker tiredly said.

No one had anything to add.

"The list," Sam Bunker summarized, "is to raise money for the nation, eliminate illiteracy and motivate Americans to be productive, eliminate drug dealing and the Mafia, address and eliminate abusive and violent crimes, and strengthen the morals and ethics of Americans; especially so that we're not money-hungry all the time. Is that it?"

No one added anything.

"In that case," Sam concluded, "This is a pretty easy list. We should be able to knock this out by next week and still have time to take the afternoon off."

Everyone laughed.

Chapter Five

One week later
May 18, 2027

The Chaplain gave a two-minute prayer timed to the second, and the second meeting commenced.

"Well?" Sam said, looking at his watch, "I hope you all did homework and came up with a solution. I know that I have some answers that seem pretty strange, and if I do, I'm sure you do. So let's hear your ideas."

"I'm a little worried about all of this," Tom Baker nervously spoke. "I'm having trouble finding answers, and the answers I dream up would have everyone breathing down our necks. The Supreme Court, federal courts, everybody. I'm afraid we'll be tied up in legal battles until doomsday."

"Not so," Steve Harning voiced authoritatively. "We were voted into existence by a unique legal event in Congress passed by a unanimous vote. Not a quorum, not a majority, but a unanimous vote. We have the backing of the full Congress of the United States and the President. Isn't that right, Sam?"

Sam nodded.

"I've already talked with my friends at the Supreme Court who were all at the Special Session," Steve continued. "They know what we're trying to do and have given vocal approval."

"Without overstating things," agreed Sam, "we have the power of the judiciary, legislative, and executive branches. We can accomplish anything we want. Should some person or interest group get in our way, we have the power to stamp them out. This is no time to be afraid; we've got the power of the nation at our fingertips, but let's be careful not to abuse it."

"Let's start with money," Sam began. "How the hell do we raise money for the nation?"

"Easy," Bob Emerson replied as though he was talking to his kids. "It's like the high school business courses we took. We increase taxes, increase exports, and limit imports."

"Does anyone want to increase taxes?" Sam asked.

"Not I," Bob replied. "My constituents bitch enough as it is about the cost of things without having their taxes raised. The average American gives a third of his time just working for taxes."

"I know," Sam said after reflection. "I know.

"Anyone else want to raise taxes?" Sam asked.

No one spoke up.

"Then how about limiting imports?" Frederica Wright of Government Operations asked.

"We could cut down the number of cars brought into the country!" Tom Baker said despondently, as though he thought that wouldn't be possible.

"We've tried controls before," Frederica added grimly. "They tried to limit importing cars from Europe and Asia while an agreeable trade balance was struck. It didn't happen."

"It's time that stopped," Sam Bunker spoke slowly, showing that he had thought seriously of the power the committee had and how he was going to wield it. "What if we cut all Asian car imports coming into the country within one month? We can limit the number of German cars coming in as well. The remaining car manufacturers in the world are pretty limited, and not worth dealing with yet, but we should also legislate so that they can't inundate us."

"As an additional aside," Frederica Wright added, sensing that inconceivable actions might be possible through this committee and getting into the swing of things, "the Japanese are particularly innovative about bringing cars into the U.S.A. without paying duty. They bring them in individually from Canada or Mexico. They also import the cars in two, three or several pieces, so that they are incomplete and assembled in the U.S.A. That's another way to avoid paying duty. If we eliminate the cars, we should also eliminate the parts."

"Good thinking, Frederica," Sam remarked. "That's a good point. Does anyone have any trouble with that?"

"I do," Tom Baker said. "What about the Americans who are buying foreign cars now? They won't be able to get parts for their cars and someone is going to be very angry."

"Well," Bob Emerson countered, as though he was addressing his Banking and Currency committee, "Why don't we add a twenty thousand dollar import tax to all brand new foreign cars sold in America? That way, if someone wants a foreign car, they can have it as long as they're willing to pay through the nose. We can make it mandatory for the foreign manufacturers to carry all replacement parts for ten years. That way, those buying new cars will have parts for at least ten years even though they won't be able to trade it in for a new foreign car when it's time to be replaced."

"Good point," Sam said, glad that Bob was on the ball and thinking. "What we have to do is to eliminate any new cars coming into the United States within a month or so, with a few exceptions; and increase the import duty to twenty thousand dollars over the car's entry sticker price for existing new cars. Now, let's plug up holes where cars are sneaked into the United States, assembled here, and arrange for the parts to be supplied for another ten years."

"Moved," Bob Emerson voiced, grimacing in amazement. He was still skeptical about the power they were supposed to have.

"Seconded."

"Ayes?" asked Sam. Everyone responded "Aye."

"So done." Sam stated. "Steve," Sam asked, "You've been on the Judiciary Committee longer than anyone here, and you know how to write a bill. Write these laws into existence."

"Be glad to," Steve Harning said proudly.

"There are other ways to limit imports," Frederica Wright added, "but there is nothing to replace them with."

"For instance?" Sam asked.

"Steel, for example. It's produced overseas or shipped there for milling. So are microelectronics and consumer electronics."

"Why not subsidize steel?" Tom Baker asked, reaching for the impossible. "You'd be giving people jobs, educating them and producing something valuable in the process. You'd even phase out more imports in the process."

"Sounds good," Sam said. "How about microelectronics? Does anyone want to ask his or her staff people to make a list of all the electronics companies in America, like Texas Instruments, Motorola, Hughes, Hewlett Packard, and others. They may not be aware yet, but if we limit imports by subsidizing consumer electronics divisions they'll be making a lot more electronic gadgets in days to come."

"While we're at it," Bob Emerson added, "we should limit food that enters the country too, or at least put a limit on the cost of things."

"In a second," Sam said. "Is there a motion for the subsidizing of steel and microelectronics?"

"Moved."

"Seconded."

"Ayes?" Everyone was in agreement.

"Good," Sam said. "Now, Bob, will you get us an import list for food and the things mentioned earlier so that we know who is exporting and importing what."

"I'll have my office staff get on it after this meeting," Bob replied, making notes.

"How about illiteracy and motivating people to be productive?" Sam asked, looking at his list.

"How much of the nation is illiterate?" questioned Tom Baker.

"About thirty to forty-five percent," Sam Bunker said with disgust. "I checked. All they do is watch TV."

"Is that high or low for the world?" asked Frederica Wright.

"It's the highest outside of Mexico and some other third world countries," Sam added with further disgust. "I looked it up."

"How do we change it?"

"We have to start with the children," began Tom. "They have to be literate. We can lock them up if we have to, but they have to be literate! If we create special schools with bars, if necessary, to keep them inside we can force them to be literate," said Tom, showing he had thought about the subject. "If they are stuck somewhere without TV, they'll be forced to read."

"I was kind of a brat when I was young," reminisced Sam. "What if they rebel?"

"I thought about that," Tom added. "For an alien, if any child is two years behind in their education, they will be deported."

"Deported?"

"And their parents too. Let's face it! Parents who love their kids will follow them anywhere. So, if a kid faces deportation, you can bet that a lot of families are going to learn."

"And what about the native-born Americans?" asked Sam. He was thinking what hell the southern states would go through with the literacy problem. "Where do we deport them to?"

"For every two years kids are behind in school, they must stay in a special school one year after they are eighteen years of age," Tom retorted quickly to Sam. "That way, we will have people with a good high school education by the time they leave school. Lack of an education would no longer be an excuse for bad manners."

"And adults?" asked Sam.

"Same thing," Tom said. "If they are aliens, they are deported instantly if they fall below a competent level. We can base this on the amount of time they've been in the United States. The immigration department could arrange the periodic testing."

Sam voiced nervously, "I guess we're not going to be a free ride anymore for anyone."

"Sounds good to me," said Bob Emerson. "Moved."

"Seconded."

"Ayes?" Sam asked.

"Everyone agreed, I guess," Sam reiterated, with reservations. "Steve, is this stuff legal?"

"Let me put it this way," Steve said diplomatically. "If they want to sue, they can, but they're not going to get an injunction against deportation from any federal judge I know. It's going to take seven years to get to court, even if the case is being heard. And all during that time they'll have to be in school or they'll be deported. We're going to force people to become literate, or they can be illiterate somewhere else."

"Motivation's next on the list," Sam read as he checked his papers.

Sam put his pencil down on the table and thought for a few seconds how much pain the literacy issue was going to cause people.

"I'd like to defer motivation for a while," requested Tom Baker. "It seems that all of this is tied together. Let's address it last."

"Anyone have any problems with that?" Sam Bunker looked around. "Okay, it's now at the bottom of my list," he said strongly. He took up his pencil and drew an arrow on the list, moving it to the bottom on his paper. "Then how about sex and violent crimes?" Sam asked.

"You're asking a kid who was molested and abused himself," Steve Harning, head of the Judiciary Committee, observed. "I've already thought much on this.

"For your information," Steve began, "in Moslem countries, if someone steals, his finger is cut off. If he steals a second time, his hand is cut off. If it happens a third time, they chop off the other hand. Theft is not a problem in those countries."

"We can't make it a law that if someone is convicted of stealing, their hands are cut off. Think of what the church would say," Tom answered strongly.

"Maybe we can't make it a law," Steve argued, "but we can give that option to plaintiffs if a thief is convicted. That way it's not our responsibility. This would definitely lower the theft rate quickly and in a case of molestation or rape, the thought of castration might be a strong deterrent. This eye-for-an-eye option could be made available to any person winning a case against any criminal committing the act in the first place. I always wanted to be a cop and eliminate filth. Maybe this is my chance."

"What about lawyers? Would they object?"

"Probably so," voiced Frederica Wright thoughtfully, "but as a lawyer myself, all they can do is obey the law and appeal a conviction after arguing it in trial. They don't make laws, they just distort them. That's why I'm depending on Steve to write new laws without the usual loopholes. They have to be iron-clad. The shorter the laws, the better."

"No problem," Steve smiled. "I have a personal stake in this."

"This is pretty strong stuff," Sam Bunker said, meekly.

"I know," Steve replied quickly but firmly, "but there's no other way. If there were another way, could you think of it?"

Sam looked down and frowned. He knew such a law would decrease crimes, but at what cost? He fantasized for a second about guillotines being built for public dismemberment, then shivered slightly.

"How about the death sentence?" Sam asked.

"That would be up to the plaintiff," Steve said. "If someone was murdered, those representing them would have the option to kill the murderer to stop him from committing such an act again. At least we ourselves wouldn't have to worry about death row or death penalties."

"I guess you're right," Sam said quietly.

"Moved," Steve stated strongly and proudly, with conviction.

"Seconded."

"Ayes?" asked Sam Bunker, feeling unsure and hoping there would be more debate.

Everyone said yes. Sam did also.

"The motion carries!" Sam exclaimed, nervously. He paused and looked at his paper. "Next, the moral and ethical revival of the American public."

"I move we shelve that for later. Place that next to the motivation question," Tom Baker said. "It's all combined."

"Any problems with this?" Sam asked.

"No?" Sam noticed when no one spoke, "then let's get on with the elimination of drug dealers and the Mafia. This is one of my favorite fields. I hate the Mafia!" Sam remembered the death of his first wife. The FBI said that the Mafia killed her.

"What are they involved in?" Bob Emerson questioned.

"Everything," Sam replied. "They control gambling, pornography, prostitution, and drugs."

"We can't do much about gambling," Bob Emerson said after giving it a quick thought. "People will gamble about what side of a wall a fly will land on if given a chance. There is no way to regulate it, outside of state control in specific areas for gambling to take place."

"Prostitution is the same way," Tom Baker spoke up. "No one can authorize government-owned brothels, for control or for profit. It has to be under state control. The church would be down our necks in an instant for legalizing prostitution. This is also related to reviving ethics. We should leave it alone for now."

"Anyone have a problem with this?" asked Sam.

No one spoke.

"Done," Sam said, with a swipe of his pen.

"But we can do something about drug pushers," said Frederica Wright. "We can make it harder for the pushers to be released if they are convicted. And we can confiscate all of their possessions and bank accounts."

"True," agreed Sam Bunker. "We can do that and more. But we're always chasing shadows. We're always sneaking about trying to catch someone else sneaking about. We're usually not that successful in catching the big guys. I've been told that the illegal drugs shipped into the nation each year account for trillions of dollars."

"Actually," added Frederica Wright, "You should be aware that your estimate is just the amount for drug sales. The nation's cost for monitoring and staffing undercover agents is also an enormous amount."

"Do you mean," asked Bob Emerson with disbelief, "that we have to solve this problem of drugs?"

"That's what we five are supposed to do!" stated Sam Bunker with a stroke of his head. "And there seems to be no end to drugs. We bust some guy, and four others take his place to supply the drugs."

"And, God, there is a demand for it," observed Tom Baker. "I wonder what the answer is. I sure don't know."

"It's getting late, folks," Sam Bunker noticed, watching his watch. "I just want to stress that what we're talking about is not to leave this room. Our discussions are private and are to remain so. I hope I've made myself more than understood. This also includes lobbyists of any kind. Those people have no souls and are motivated by self-interest only. Do not talk with them for any reason!

"I'm going to adjourn the group for the day," continued Sam. "We've done enough, and we'll convene next week. We still have to deal with the ramifications of our actions, such as increasing staffing of courts, prisons, police, and stuff like that. And we still have to talk about drug problems and the Mafia, motivation, and the moral and ethical strengthening of the nation. That's a lot to think about, isn't it?

"But before we call it a day, I want you all to think about the drug problem until we convene again. It's the biggest problem we have, and the hardest to solve. I've been thinking about it a lot all week. For the pusher and illegal manufacturer of drugs, we should have harsher penalties to make them think twice before making or selling drugs. It needs to be more than a slap on the wrist. The penalties should be so severe that no one would ever consider handling illicit drugs."

"So what if we remove the pushers and producers?" Bob Emerson moaned despairingly. "The law of supply and demand clearly states that as long as there is a demand, someone will produce the supply. We can't win."

"There is one way," Sam softly uttered, "and only one way it can be done to eliminate the manufacturer and pusher once and for all."

"And what's that solution?" quickly asked Tom Baker, showing that he was very interested in hearing the answer.

Sam Bunker spoke in almost a whisper, "Legalize drugs."

Chapter Six

One week later
May 25, 2027

Sam wasn't sure he should shoot the Chaplain. The Chaplain went a minute over his two minute limit and Sam didn't know why, but that Chaplain sure kept preaching from the book of Romans. When the Chaplain read the section, "If you are confident that you are a guide to the blind, a light to those who are in darkness, a corrector of the foolish, a teacher of the immature...are you, who teaches one another, do you not teach yourself?" Sam thought it hit home, although it was way too long. Sam believed that they needed a little humility.

Frederica Wright winced at the mention of eyes. She was angry with the doctors who operated on her. Before the operation, her vision was 20/40, but the doctors insisted that the cataract lens had to come out. They butchered the job. It bothered her that so many surgeons were anxious to cut people open, but that was how they made their money. At least she still trusted her pharmacist and her optometrist. But she was a lawyer and took solace from the fact that she sued the hell out of those clumsy surgeons.

"Well?" Sam demanded, as the Chaplain made his way out of the committee chambers. He watched the Chaplain pass the two armed guards stationed at the door. When the Chaplain left the chambers, Sam continued talking. "Have you been thinking about my suggestion last week?"

"I haven't been able to think of anything else," said Bob Emerson.

"Me, too," voiced Frederica. "I've been sleeping like crap for the last week."

"I don't feel well," commented Tom Baker.

"Me, neither," said Sam Bunker slowly. "Welcome to the club."

"Let me see if I have this right," Tom Baker questioned. "You want to make drugs legal?"

"Every last one of them," Sam said quietly but firmly.

"But people could kill themselves!" Bob Emerson cried.

"They are doing that now," Sam uttered. "And who are you to say that people can't kill themselves if they want to?"

"The Bible says that the body is holy, and that it should not be destroyed. I believe that is true," remarked Tom Baker.

"I believe that the human body is a miracle in the making and breathing," said Steve Harning, "But I also believe strongly that people have the right to end their lives if they choose to. And that includes drug use to get them there. Call it euthanasia, mercy killing, or whatever. If I get a clot in my brain, which I was told had a sixty percent chance of happening in the next two years, I would want the plug pulled so I could die. I don't want to live as a vegetable."

Steve thought of how feeble he was after his bypass, and how he had been struggling day and night to improve his strength. At times it hurt like hell just to lift his arm.

"This has nothing to do with drugs," Sam Bunker said nervously, thinking of his own aging.

"This has everything to do with drugs," Steve retorted, with his chest hurting. "Kids these days want to escape, try something new, buck the laws, or ....whatever. They should have a right to do anything they want to their bodies after they turn eighteen. If they're old enough to join the army and kill other people when Uncle Sam wants them to, then they are old enough to take their own lives."

"But they haven't been educated," pleaded Tom Baker. "They don't know what they're doing. It's like giving a child a loaded pistol."

"It's a damn sight worse to offer someone forbidden fruit with drugs," said Sam Bunker. "A damn sight worse."

"What about drug addiction?" Tom Baker asked. The thought of people with needles in their arms sent a shiver down his spine.

"People are addicted to sleeping pills, alcohol, sugar, caffeine, food, and you can just run down the list to your heart's content," Frederica Wright commented. "Are you worried about becoming addicted, or about what the people are already addicted to! Tell me, is addiction to alcohol truly worse than being addicted to caffeine?" she asked as she quietly sipped her morning coffee.

Frederica knew full well that it was impossible for her to give up coffee, for she had tried many times before.

Frederica then remembered back in time to her addiction to diet pills when in college. The pills wound her up so much she felt like she couldn't sit still. She frowned when she remembered the doctor who prescribed them for her.

"The problem with addiction can be corrected through education," said Tom Baker with a negotiator's voice. "If we could educate the public, we wouldn't have to worry about people being trapped by drugs. Once you're addicted, it's almost impossible to get free of drugs again. It's a waste of a life, in my opinion."

"Bob," Sam asked, seeing that the group was deadlocked. "How do you feel about this? Let us know and break this stalemate, huh?"

Bob Emerson looked at everyone for a moment, then reached in his pocket and took out his wallet. From that he extracted a card, turned yellow with age. He looked at everyone to make certain that he had their attention. He started to read.

"Who has woe, sorrow, contentions, complaining, wounds without cause, or redness of eyes?" Bob looked up and saw Frederica wince. "Those who linger long over wine. Those who go to taste mixed wine. Don't look on red wine when it sparkles in the cup. When it goes smoothly down; until it finally at last bites like a serpent and stings like a viper. Your eyes will see strange things and your mind will utter filthy things. Proverbs twenty-three."

"I'm an alcoholic," Bob said quietly. "And not a recovered alcoholic either."

Tom Baker looked at him in amazement. Bob Emerson was one of the richest men in the nation. His donations to charities made him a legend in his own time, and a godsend to millions of people in the nation, not to mention countless others he had helped throughout the world. He was a man who had everything.

"Sometimes I win," Bob lamented. "Most other times I lose, but I'll never end up in that pisshole Betty Ford rehabilitation clinic. It may help, but the publicity would be miserable," he said weakly. "I try to take things one day at a time. If I go home without drinking, it's a good day."

"I'm not an alcoholic," Sam said to himself. "Am I?" Sam knew he always had a drink for lunch and dinner, and an occasional Bloody Mary in the morning for a hangover, but he didn't think that made him an alcoholic.

"How did you start?" asked Frederica Wright, remembering the nights she was climbing walls from taking pills. That was when she almost committed suicide.

"It's not important. But I'm hooked. And, like drugs, I can always get booze, whether it is during a meeting of Congress, or smack dab in the middle of a dry state where alcohol is illegal. Where there's a will, there's a way. Isn't that what American ingenuity is all about?"

"Maybe I should give up alcohol," Sam admitted to himself, looking sadly at Bob. "But haven't I tried that before?"

"Do you think drugs should be legal?" Tom Baker asked Bob.

"I believe that everyone has it in themselves to make it in life or not," Bob replied. "I've never thought of myself as a guardian, telling people what to do. And that's what we've been doing! I think booze and drugs are no different. These substances should be used in moderation or else they can kill. But, like booze, I don't think it is our right to tell people if they can use drugs or not," stated Bob gently as he put the card back in his wallet.

"It's got to pass!" Sam thought. "We've got to make drugs legal! There is no other way!" Sam urged strongly as he addressed the group. "We can no longer afford to withhold from the American public what they want. We can't be big brothers any longer. The American nation has come of age and has to make choices on its own."

"Tabled for today are also motivation, morals, and ethics," Sam continued. "With drugs being legalized, motivation would be a factor that could bring us back to productivity. The people who are becoming rich through drug dealing would have to find something else to do. The morale of Americans could improve, giving people an opportunity to show how mature they are. It's like telling your kids they're old enough to have the keys to the car. As far as ethics are concerned, I don't think it's ethical to deny Americans something they want if it doesn't directly hurt others. Is it ethical for us to keep the nation away from the things that frighten us!?

"We've talked about drugs, and with their legalization, we could have trillions of dollars coming into the treasury through taxes. I'm sure Bob Emerson would agree that we'd be fools not to take the money from criminals and return it to the people.

"With education regarding drugs," Sam continued, "we've got to start with grammar school kids to show them what drugs can do to them..."

"I agree with keeping drug money out of the hands of the Mafia," Tom jumped in, cutting off Sam. "And I agree with the fact that we're not our brother's keepers. It's arrogant of us to tell our neighbors what to do. But we've got a lot of holes to patch up before we make this a new law. For example, what do we do about one of the largest lobbies in the nation, the Medical Association of America?"

"You know," said Frederica Wright. "I never had much respect for the Medical Association of America, the M.A.A. Doctors protect themselves, not the public. They're not going to give up the power to prescribe drugs, but the M.A.A. can be taken care of. We can do anything!" she said with conviction.

"How about the church?" asked Tom Baker. "Do you think they're going to like the fact that the American public may soon be able to get high, or low, as the case may be, whenever they want? Do you think the clergy is going to feel safe if we have pandemonium in our streets?"

"You're asking me," said Steve Harning quietly, calming the group, "if I would rather be a victim of someone trying to rob me to support an expensive drug habit, or would I rather see him walking down the street oblivious to everyone and bothering no one? What do you think?"

"Look, folks," Sam interrupted. "We've got a long way to go before we make this a law. We have to deal with the kids and that means that we have to make sure they're educated. We have to deal with the parents. We have to deal with suppliers. Someone has to regulate the drug industry, because they will invent different drugs to make a buck, then see later on what the drug is good for. Someone is going to have to deal with M.A.A. They're going to give us a lot of bull about uncontrolled drugs being harmful to the health of their patients."

"What's harmful," Tom Baker said anxiously, grasping at straws, "is that we're taking the control of drugs away from doctors and giving the control into the hands of the public. What about drunk drivers? There are too many drunks on the roads already! And what happens when we add in the fatalities from people driving after taking drugs?"

"Are we planning to do something about beefing up the police force so that we take care of the street scene?" asked Steve Harning thoughtfully. "And how about the courts? Who will try these abusers? We have to take care of that. And we should not forget the people who end up going to jail. Have we thought about changing the jail system? Let us also not forget the burden on society of rehabilitating people who are addicted."

"We've got a lot of things that have to be plugged up before we can do something with a bill," Tom said. "Can't we shelve this for a while?"

"No," said Steve Harning emphatically.

"No," agreed Bob Emerson.

"Absolutely not," Frederica Wright said strongly.

"We can't," stated Sam Bunker. "I know your concerns, but we have to take action now! If we delay, we'll be avoiding the power and trust of Congress and the people. We have to decide on this and we have to decide today!"

"I don't think it was a good idea to put me on this committee," said Tom Baker, putting his head between his hands. He thought of his children growing up and becoming addicts. He imagined the glint in the eyes of his five-year-old turning dull, and he shivered again.

"You know," Bob Emerson said solemnly, "I have kids of my own. If it were a question of them buying cigarettes, a bottle, or a drug, I would rather have them buying drugs at a pharmacy and not from some slimeball on a dirty street corner."

"Is it agreed that we do a lot of fine tuning before we set these changes loose on the world?" Tom Baker cried pleadingly.

Everyone nodded.

"Moved," said Steve Harning.

"What's moved?" said Tom Baker with a voice that wavered, sighing.

"Moved that we make drugs legal in the nation," Steve Harning replied, thinking of how this was going to affect his friends and family.

"Seconded," said Bob Emerson. He uttered a silent prayer that his children wouldn't become addicts and suffer the way he had over the years.

Frederica Wright thought about the tremendous cost to the government to try to keep the nation off drugs. From an economic and social viewpoint, Frederica saw no alternative but to say yes. She didn't want to think about the consequences or moral issues. They scared her.

Sam Bunker thought about it for a few seconds. There was no other way and it was going to be his group's decision if they passed it. He hoped their decision would be good for the nation.

Tom Baker wondered about the loopholes and knew there sure were a lot of them. He closed his eyes and uttered a quiet prayer. He then knew that he was going to vote and that he was going to vote "Yes."

Sam looked at each member of the group. "We have the motion and a second. We haven't been too formal, but this is the vote for the motion to legalize drugs. Ayes?" he asked, but didn't look up as he heard four hesitating voices say "Yes."

"Nays?" Sam asked, just to be formal.

"Abstaining?" Sam asked, giving them a last chance. No one spoke.

"The motion carries."

Chapter Seven

Jim Auchstetter sat on the terrace of his apartment in the Hollywood hills, watching the city sparkle below him. Although it was early in the morning, he sat in a chair, wearing only a T-shirt and shorts. He had a Michelob in one hand, taking occasional sips. A half-smoked joint was in the ashtray. He was preparing to relight it.

"Gonna be a warm one in Los Angeles today," he thought. He was glad he had the day off. The last thing he wanted to do was rip up another sewer line and stand knee deep in shit. He didn't mind being a plumber. There were always jobs to be had. The pay was union and pretty high for easy work. He had everything he needed and felt good about it.

Jim stretched and yawned. His back felt sore and he wondered where the pain came from. He knew that he hadn't worked hard enough to have pain, and his workouts at the gym never caused him any problems. He tried to keep his five-foot-four-inch body trim, lean, and mean. He shook his shoulder-length blond hair to take some of the stress out of his neck muscles.

After a few moments he smiled as he remembered that Cindy must have caused the muscle strain. Last night with Cindy had been wild. He had met her the night before at a new club on Melrose called The Hell Hole. He thought she was beautiful and had great tits. She was there with her friend Anne. He bought them a few rounds. Everyone joked around and he really hit it off with Cindy. They danced for a while and when the bar closed, he suggested they go over to his house for a few joints. Cindy was a little drunk and lonely and agreed to leave Anne behind.

Jim offered booze freely at his apartment and lit up a couple of joints. Cindy began to unwind and Jim told her a bit about himself. He talked about his favorite ball teams, the sports car he drove and his favorite rock groups. She marveled at his stereo, with its loud dance music, and was pleased that he seemed to be in the money.

"Want to get high?" Jim asked.

"Isn't this grass enough?"

"Nah, all this does is get you in the mood and relax you a bit."

After another joint, Jim said, "I've got something here that you'd love. It's great."

"What is it?" she asked, unsure of all this although she liked adventure.

"It's a lude," said Jim.

"A what?" she asked.

"A Quaalude," Jim said, showing her a pill he took from a medicine bottle labeled 'Bufferin.' "These are the best things to have. They make the world so mellow."

"I don't know," she said, looking at a white pill in Jim's hand.

"Don't worry," he added, smiling. "I'll just give you half a pill. That way, it won't do much of anything. You can tell me if you like it or not."

Jim took the pill he got from his pusher friend and cut it in half. He moved the half over to Cindy.

"I'm still not sure," she said, feeling some butterflies in her tummy.

"Don't be nervous. Here. Let me cut that in half. I'll just give you a fourth of the pill. That way, you could see how it affects you."

"I don't know," Cindy said, trying to get out of it. "I'm not used to drugs."

"Don't worry," Jim said confidently. "Watch me. I'll take a half." He swallowed half a pill.

"Now you," he said, and handed her the quarter pill with a beer chaser.

She had the pill in her hand but wasn't sure what to do with it.

"You don't have to be afraid," Jim confided. "Look at me. It didn't hurt me."

Cindy looked at Jim, who seemed fine. He felt no effects. Jim knew that the drug took a good twenty to thirty minutes to absorb. Jim felt great.

"So," Jim asked. "Want to take a chance and be a little adventurous?"

Cindy thought for a moment about her job. Her boss was a disgusting old man who'd been trying to get into her pants. She'd been turning him down for dates ever since she joined his company as a data management consultant.

Actually, she was a fancy filing clerk whom he had hired, probably planning to come on to her. She thought of her last progress report, which stated that she needed to show a serious attitude change or she would be fired. She felt it had been unfair and hadn't gotten over her anger.

She swallowed the pill, then drank a glass of beer.

"See," Jim smiled. "That didn't hurt, did it?"

"Yes, everything feels fine," she replied. Her body really didn't feel any different.

"Let's dance," Jim said, as he put a disco tune on his CD player.

They danced for a while and became hot and sweaty. Jim brought out another beer for her and they sat down.

"How do you feel?" he asked.

Cindy thought for a second. "I feel wonderful!"

"Take the other quarter of the Quaalude. The first one didn't really do anything."

Cindy hesitated, but took the second quarter of the pill. She began to feel better and they danced again. They sat down only to catch their breath.

Resting on the couch, Jim put his arm around her shoulder and began to gently massage her neck. Then he told her how pretty she was. Cindy listened to every word, glad to be appreciated by someone like Jim. He leaned over and kissed her. She responded by drawing him closer to her.

A short while later they were in his bedroom and he was undressing her.

"My God," Jim reminisced fondly, fighting off an early morning erection. "She bounced like she had springs in her butt. I've just got to call her again!"

His only problem was that he had too many girlfriends already. He was seeing two or three steadily, with five or six others for one-night-stands. "Balling buddies," he called them. "Life should be so rough," he said to himself. He laughed as he thought how good life was when his biggest decision was deciding which girl should share his bed for the night.

He got up and stretched, not sure what he would do for the rest of the day. He could go to the gym and work out, wax his car, clean up the place a bit, or just vegetate and watch television. He really wasn't in a hurry to do anything.

He heard the mailboxes downstairs being opened. He took the letter for the gas company payment from the kitchen table. He grabbed his keys and ran down the stairs toward the postman.

Craig Osborne had just finished placing all the apartment mail in the slots. He heard someone running and turned to see this short jock with long hair coming towards him with a letter. "That guy would make a great postman, because the mail would always get through," he thought and smiled.

Jim held out the letter to Craig, feeling the blood rush to his head from the beer and grass.

Craig took the letter, looked at the return address and made a quick check to see that a stamp was on it. He opened up the mail boxes again, and took out Jim's mail and handed the mail to him.

"Your mail, Mr. Auchstetter."

"Thanks."

"My pleasure. I'm Craig Osborne, your regular mail carrier on this route. Pleased to meet you," he said, as they shook hands.

"You're our regular mailman?" Jim asked, as he turned his eyes toward his mail to see if there was anything worthwhile in it. So far, the only thing that looked the least bit interesting was the latest lingerie catalog from Frederick's of Hollywood.

"Yep," said Craig. "I've been delivering this route a while now. When I sort mail, I try to figure out what type of occupation the person has."

"No fooling," replied Jim, frowning as he realized that a late charge was tacked onto the payment notice for his sports car.

"And," said Craig, "I figure you're in the contractor business, getting all those magazines about home building."

Jim then looked up at Craig. Craig was a good six inches taller than Jim was, had a good smile, crooked teeth, and not much else. Jim observed Craig's thinning hair, combed carelessly. His postman's uniform showed no muscle definition, and he had a little paunch. He wore squarish glasses that looked as though they were strong.

"You're close," Jim said. "I'm a plumber. Damned good one if I say so myself."

Craig looked a little disappointed.

"Damn!" Jim swore, noticing a form letter from his senator, "that's the last thing I need! A letter from some clown in the government. All they want is to get re-elected and raise taxes. They never care about us small guys. My taxes are high enough as it is. I don't trust any of them."

"I know what you mean," said Craig, thinking of his job being subject to the whims of the government. Still, the union seemed to be doing its best with his benefits. "In the paper this morning, they published a rumor that the local city government is putting together new legislation on drug control."

"I could care less if they sell drugs to kids as long as my taxes don't go up," Jim spoke loudly. "I'm tired of floating the government for nothing in return. What do I get out of this?"

"Your mail, for one thing," Craig smiled.

"Damn," uttered Jim. "All I get in the mail are bills, and junk mail from people who want money from me. Maybe what we need is a new government. Yeah, that's it!" he said sarcastically, rolling with it. "We can turn the tables, so that the Mafia is in control of the government, and all the elected jerks in Sacramento can sell nickel bags to the kindergarten crowd. I can see the campaign slogan for the Mafia now, 'Get stoned. A pharmacy in every medicine cabinet. Trips for the rest of your life.' It'd be a helluva lot better for me if that came true."

"Things could be better," Craig admitted, not really paying attention.

"You damn well know they could," Jim said. "The best way is to forget about it and get yourself plastered." Jim then remembered sadly that his dealer upped his prices for everything a few months ago.

"I'd like a little more money and some tuition reimbursement benefits myself," Craig said dreamingly. "I'm going to school nights for a bachelor's in history."

"Americans are too stupid to see what they're getting into," Jim muttered, listening only to himself. "They can't change a simple cold water valve with channel-lock pliers, and they'll pay dearly to have me come out and do it for them. They're all suckers waiting to be taken to the cleaners."

Craig thought about some of the mindless, stupid things he had seen on envelopes and at work, and had to agree with Jim that people weren't thinking much of the time.

"If the public's too stupid, the churches are the same," Jim continued. "All they want is for people to follow them like sheep so they can take their money away from them. They don't care about anyone either," Jim spat out. He then gave Craig another once-over.

"You married?" Jim asked Craig.

"No sir." Craig blushed a bit. "You?"

"Nah," said Jim. "I'm having too much fun running around with lots of sexually starved women."

"I guess so," Craig replied, not really hearing, as he was trying to sort the mail for the next few apartment houses. "I'd better be moving on. I've got a few more places to deliver before I go to the high-rise office building." Craig's head nodded toward the tall building down near the bottom of the hill.

"Nice talking with you, Mr. Auchstetter," Craig said. "Have yourself a good day." With that, he walked away slowly, thinking of a meeting he was supposed to go to later on that evening at church.

"Nice guy," Jim thought, "but harmless." Jim watched Craig walking away with his mailbag and felt that the guy had nothing going for him. No looks, not quick on his feet, and probably an easy guy to walk over.

On the way up the steps to his apartment, he wondered if Craig was the type to ever do drugs. "Nah," he said to himself. He laughed as he realized that Craig probably wouldn't know which end of a pill to swallow. Jim enjoyed being adventurous and doing what most people were afraid to do. It made him feel good to be in control of things most people ran away from.

As he watched Craig heading up the stairs of the next apartment house, he saw a Doberman growl and jump towards him. The postman calmly shot some mace into the dog's eyes and continued on as if it was all was in a day's work.

"The guy's got courage," Jim thought, as he walked back to his apartment. He was planning on writing Cindy's name in his address book. He debated with himself who to call for tonight. He thought about calling his steady girlfriend, Karen, but he knew that she would give him the same old stuff about how lonely she was, and how he should spend more time with her. Maybe there would be a ball game on TV. He knew he could stay home, invite a few guys over, and have a much better time than listening to his girlfriend whine.

Chapter Eight

The twelve-floor office complex of Thalberg, Chaney, and Fairbanks was at the bottom of the hill. It was the largest actors' agency in Los Angeles. They handled most of the big stars' management, public relations, and publicity. Their price was high, but actors were expected to be extravagant and would do anything to keep their names in the public eye.

As Craig entered the high-rise, he was abruptly pushed out of the way by a pretty young woman in a red floral outfit. She was running into the building. Craig's shoulder hit a wall and he winced as she ran past him. He looked at the five sacks of mail that were to go in the building's intra-office mail room, and rubbed his sore shoulder.

"I'm late," was the explanation Mary Lane shouted to him as she ran into the building. She should have been at work ten minutes ago but she had worked late last night. She had to revise some promotional material for a new actor. Now she had to review the galleys for a press release tomorrow morning. As a relative newcomer to Thalberg, Chaney, and Fairbanks, having only been there nine months as an assistant publicist, she knew that she had found her niche. She worked hard and spent her spare time thinking about how she could do even better. When someone asked her to do something, she did it enthusiastically.

Just last week Mr. Joe Chaney, himself, had said that Mary was "doing a great job, and will go far in the firm." She loved encouragement, and was determined to do better than anyone else.

But today, Mary was tired. She'd smoked a few joints to unwind when she got home last night and taken a Valium to relax. The next thing she knew, she passed out on the couch. During the night she woke, undressed, and got into bed. However, she forgot to set the alarm. She woke at nine o'clock. She raced into gear, taking only moments for the regular wake-up joint she had been smoking every morning for twenty years. She raced into the shower, dried hastily, and did her hair. In her red floral blouse and skirt she ran to her car.

At each stoplight, she moved the rear view mirror so that she could put on her make-up and curl her lashes. She cursed each stop sign for slowing her down.

As she parked her car, she took one last look in the mirror. She ate a breath mint so that no one would be able to detect the smell of marijuana and put on a spritz of perfume for good measure. She darted into the office, almost colliding with that stupid mailman before she reached her desk.

It was ten-thirty and no one gave her a second glance. She looked at the desk in front of her and noticed that there were no new morning calls for her, and breathed a sigh of relief. Then she remembered that her boss was going to be at a press conference at the Hilton and wouldn't be in until afternoon.

Mary walked to the ladies' room to get another look at herself. Her make-up was on well, despite the impatient drivers honking behind her. Her brown hair was bouncy and natural looking. Her skirt and blouse were on right, but she had to adjust the shoulder pads. Her lipstick was the right color and her shiny, white teeth gave no indication of her smoking. Unnaturally thin, she made sure that her padded bra fit right, and straightened her skirt one last time. She walked to the water cooler and took two pills from her purse. She gulped down a glass of water before her morning cup of coffee and swallowed the pills.

It was going to be a matter of time before the two pills took effect. The first was a diet pill to help her lose three pounds. She felt she was overweight. The second, Elavil, was the important one. It was a great antidepressant that enabled her to keep going through the day. The six or seven cups of coffee she had each day didn't bother her a bit, except for those necessary trips to the bathroom.

"Whatcha got going today?" asked Mary's next door office mate, Cheryl.

"I have to get these release galleys read by two o'clock, call up the actor to come in for an initial consultation and review, and make sure the bosses' plane tickets are ready for the New York movie premiere next week." Mary became quiet as she looked down at the list of things she had to do that day. She was sure she'd be up half the night completing it.

"Want to go to a party tonight?" Cheryl asked. "One of the guys in accounting asked me, and I told him yes."

"I'm not sure," Mary answered, examining the list of work assignments in front of her. "I'm not really dressed for a party."

"Sure you are," Cheryl replied. "You look great in that outfit. You're a knockout."

"I'm fat and you know it."

"Bull," Cheryl said. "You're skin and bones and any mirror will confirm that."

"I'm probably going to be too busy," Mary sighed. "I've got a bunch of work to get out today."

"Who cares?" Cheryl retorted, filing her nails. "You might meet someone there. You told me you don't have a steady, didn't you?"

"Yes," Mary quietly said, embarrassed. "I don't have a steady."

"Why don't you bring that guy you brought last time?" Cheryl asked.

"Which guy?" Mary replied.

"The one with the black hair and the X-ray eyes. You know, the one you brought to the Christmas party."

"Oh, that one," Mary said quietly. Cheryl remembered Carl Friedman, the man Mary got all of her drugs from. He was a tall man, very quiet, who smiled infrequently. He had piercing eyes that told you he was afraid of nothing. She saw Carl on and off, whenever she needed drugs. The usual way she'd see Carl was to call him, invite him over to dinner, take him to bed, and then tell him what she wanted. Within a few days, Carl delivered what she wanted. Although he charged her, saying he never mixed business with pleasure, she always got her drugs.

"I see him on and off," Mary admitted.

"Oh, married, huh?" Cheryl asked, hoping for some gossip for the other girls at lunch.

"No, it's not that," Mary laughed, thinking how Carl always gave her a little scare when she thought about him. "We just may not be right for each other."

"But you did bring him to the Christmas party."

"He was handy," Mary admitted truthfully, then remembered that she had wanted to go with someone, but wasn't dating anybody at the time. She had to plead with Carl to do her the favor of coming along. It wasn't his kind of party. "Too highbrow and snooty," he complained. But he went, and didn't even charge her full price for the sleeping pills she needed for the next few weeks.

"Maybe you should go tonight," Cheryl coaxed. "You should relax some more. You're going to burn yourself out."

"That's the same thing the psychiatrists told me," Mary thought about years gone by. She remembered back to her two nervous breakdowns, each of the doctors calling her a "type A manic-depressive." She hated being labeled by some jackass doctor, and she never went back to see either of them again.

"I relax enough as it is," Mary said, both to Cheryl and herself.

"Suit yourself," Cheryl replied, turning back to her work.

At that moment, the other office worker, Stella, came into the room with a bundle of letters. She handed a small stack to Cheryl and another to Mary.

"I was just downstairs when I saw the mailman arrive," Stella said, "so I thought I'd pick up your mail for you."

"I like that guy. What's his name?" Cheryl asked.

"Craig," Stella said.

"Yeah," Cheryl remembered. "Craig. I like him."

"Me too," Stella agreed.

"You know what he said he was doing tonight?" Stella continued.

"What?" Cheryl asked, hoping it was something exciting.

"He said he was going to church."

"What?" asked Mary, listening in to the conversation.

"Church," Cheryl said, listening avidly to Stella.

"I didn't know they still had those things," Mary said with a smile.

"Me either," Cheryl laughed.

"Do you go to church?" Stella asked.

"No," Mary confessed. "I don't go to church."

"I do every so often for confession," Cheryl said as though she was sharing a secret.

"I do at Christmas and Easter," Stella remarked. "I like the Christmas service especially, with the poinsettia decorations and the candlelight processions. It's so pretty."

"Anyway," Cheryl concluded. "I think he's cute."

"Who?"

"Craig, the postman," Cheryl said.

"Yeah, but you know how those government employees are," Stella said knowingly.

"What?" Mary asked.

"Boring," Stella added.

Mary thought about the government, and especially the IRS reviewing her income taxes. She lied about dependents, stating that she had two kids, even though it was her ex-husband who had them. After her first nervous break-down, she was denied custody when she was divorced by him. Still, she tried to visit them at least once a year. She loved her kids.

"Did you hear what happened in administration?" Cheryl uttered quietly with a smile.

"What?" Stella asked, anxious to hear some gossip.

"I heard Mr. Lynch got suspended until he went to a detoxification center to dry out."

"Alcohol?" Mary asked.

"Cocaine?" Stella asked.

"Uppers," Cheryl said. "He finally got so wound up that he was told to take care of things or be fired."

"Poor guy," Stella tsk-tsked.

"Yes, poor guy," Mary agreed.

"Say," Stella asked. "Do you know what I saw coming in today?"

"What?" asked Cheryl.

"There was an artist drawing the sculpture in front of the building?"

"You mean that one with the frizzy hair and the sweatshirt and jeans?" asked Cheryl, always noticing what any competition was wearing. "I saw her."

"What about her?" said Mary, sipping her coffee.

"She's real good," Stella told. "She does great work and her sketching is excellent. I asked her if she'd consider sketching me one day as a present for my boyfriend."

"And..." Cheryl begged.

"And she said she would," Stella added. "But, I remembered where I had seen her before."

"At the museum," Mary surmised.

"Nope. At the Cock & Bull restaurant. She's a waitress."

"Sounds strange for an artist," Mary said.

"Not really," Cheryl added. "Half of the actresses we represent started as waitresses. They had to do something until they got 'discovered' and into the business. It makes sense to me that she'd be waitressing to make a living."

"So, she said she'd do it."

"Did you get her card?" Cheryl asked.

"She didn't have one. She wrote her name and number on a piece of paper," Stella said, digging into her purse for it.

"Nice handwriting?" Cheryl asked, being an amateur handwriting analyst on the side.

"I don't think so. She writes like she's an epileptic and has arthritis to boot," Stella admitted. She picked the piece of paper out of her handbag and gave it to Cheryl.

"Sabrina?" Cheryl asked, looking at the paper.

"That's her," Stella said.

"Sounds artistic to me," Mary chimed in.

"Me too," Stella said. "And that's a good sign."

"Well, I have to get back to work," said Mary.

"Me too," Stella echoed sadly.

"I guess I have to do things, too," Cheryl said lamely, and started to shuffle papers about on her desk.

Mary started down her list and prioritized what she had to do. She thought about going to the party, but didn't know if she could. She decided to wait and see how she'd feel around five o'clock, which was when the antidepressant would be wearing off. If she still felt fine, maybe she'd go. If she felt a little low, she'd take another pill and then see how she felt a half hour later, just before quitting time. "Who knows," she mused. "Maybe I'm due for a change."

Then, with the Elavil starting to take effect, she began to work.

Chapter Nine

One week later
June 1, 2027

The Chaplain lasted another extra minute. But then again, they were thirty minutes late starting. Tom Baker, the practical joker of Congress, had arranged for every news and wire service in the nation to be crammed into the small conference room for a statement by Sam Bunker about what he had been doing lately. When Sam and the other three members of the committee went from their chambers to the conference room, they opened the doors to find the press waiting for them.

"Shit!" cried Sam Bunker, seeing microphones and flashing lights.

"Is that what you've been up to lately?" said a reporter from Nantucket.

"Is this a committee meeting?" asked another.

"Have you seen your wife lately?" asked a third.

"And when was the last time you were in your home state?" asked the one covering Sam's home town.

"Are you now, or have you ever been, a member of the Communist Party?" asked a reporter.

Recovering from the shock, Sam went to the telephone in the corner of the room, and spoke softly into it.

Five minutes later, twenty-five National Guardsmen entered the building. They had rifles in hand and were ready to shoot if necessary. The reporters looked on in shock.

"Get these assholes out of this closed meeting," Sam said to the leader of the National Guard unit. Sam smiled and nodded to the reporters as they were herded out into barred vans.

"How did they find out about the meeting?" Sam asked.

"They didn't," said Tom Baker, whose sides hurt from laughing, "I wanted to give this meeting a little lift. It sure depressed me last week." It took a full minute for Sam's scowl to lessen, but he too burst into laughter.

"Okay, you got me this time," Sam replied, but still made sure that the two armed guards were posted outside the committee chambers.

"Gentlemen, and lady," Sam Bunker said, as the Chaplain left, "Let's get going. Bob, do you have those import lists?"

Bob Emerson handed everyone a list with three columns. The first column had items that were imported, the second was a list of items produced in America, and the third column consisted of items only imported and not produced. They studied the lists silently. They were many pages long.

"Hell," Steve Harning cursed. "You mean that tennis racquets aren't made in the U.S.A. at all?"

"I had the list checked and double checked," Bob Emerson said flatly. "It's the gospel, believe me."

"I don't believe what I'm seeing," Tom Baker said, laughing at the insanity of it all.

"What's that?" Frederica Wright asked.

"American flags are no longer made in America," complained Tom.

"Neither are fireworks for the Fourth of July," replied Bob Emerson, "They're from China....Baseballs are made in Korea"

"This is an abomination," said Sam angrily, "and it's time it ended. I can't believe half of this list. And what's worse, have you seen what's on the list of things not made in America?"

"What?" asked Bob, thinking his staff had missed something. He knew he had given the whole staff the day off as a reward for coming up with that list on such short notice.

"Banjos," Sam wailed. "The American banjo is made in Korea. There are no more banjos made in the United States. We have gotten lazy," he said dismally, shaking his head.

"It's the same thing with harmonicas," Frederica whined bitterly.

"Well," asked Sam. "Are we all lazy? Steve, did you make up some bills for limiting imports as we discussed, and for some subsidies to have items produced in America?"

"I sure did," Steve said, remembering how exhausted his office staff was. His heart felt like it was bursting because of his efforts during the last few days. "I've penned a general Import Limitations Act, with specifics below that we can add. I've also set up an American Booster Subsidy Act, which is something we can give to American manufacturers. Although this seems general, I can guarantee that no one will find the smallest loophole. As Chairman of the Judiciary Committee, I know what can and can't be read between the lines."

"I appreciate that," Sam agreed gleefully, reviewing the first bill put in front of him. "Is there any problem with merging Steve's subsidy bill with the import list and having it execute immediately?"

"Yes," remarked Bob Emerson. "How can we support this subsidy stuff when we're trying to save the taxpayers money?"

"Well," Sam Bunker replied, after thinking for a few minutes, "initially, the increase in tariffs on imports should lessen the financial burden. Later on, when goods start being produced here, the cost will come back in taxes. Offhand, I'd say we can't lose.

"But then again," Sam Bunker continued in his most soothing voice, "when John Jones told me about this committee, he said everyone had agreed that we should go ahead and write laws. All we need for any bill to become law is the President's signature. Hell, with our power, we can add it to the Bill of Rights if we want. And John Jones said we'll have more than enough money to do it with."

"So let's do the merging of the imports and the subsidies," said Bob Emerson, solemnly. "What are we waiting for?"

Everyone nodded in agreement.

"The bill passes," Sam strongly stated. "Now hold onto your hats, folks, 'cause we're starting to roll. In months, this act will have its ramifications seen. Americans will be doing the producing, not some foreign group that uses American labor!" Sam read aloud from the stipulations in Steve's act and realized that the act was iron-clad. "God," he uttered in amazement, "we really are good!"

"How about the literacy bill?" Sam asked.

"I still think we should put it in with the drug bill," Tom Baker said.

"Anyone have problems with that?" Sam Bunker asked.

No one spoke up.

"Last chance to disagree," Sam looked up and said. Everyone looked at him and smiled. Sam knew that if they had reservations about anything, they'd speak up. John Jones really did his homework, he thought.

"Next is the arm-for-an-arm bill for violent acts," Sam said as he went down his list.

"I have no debate," Bob Emerson admitted.

"Neither do I," said Tom Baker and Steve Harning almost at the same time.

"I say do it," added Frederica Wright. "'Do unto others as they do unto you,' is soon going to be a law. It's about damned time," she said.

"I've talked to all the Federal court judges, and all the Supreme Court judges too," Steve Harning reported. "I'll bet my bottom dollar that no one will be able to get an injunction against this law. Not an individual, consumer concern group, or a civil rights group. Nobody."

"This may be tied in with the drug issue," Tom Baker noted. "Since we voted to legalize drugs, we have to increase the court and prison system to handle new people coming under the legal system."

"First," Sam Bunker asked, "Is there any problem with the arm-for-an-arm bill?"

No one spoke. Sam then nodded to Steve Harning, who wrote himself a note to pen a bill about personal rights and get it back to everyone. "This does negate a lot of the recent prison reform act by Emil Wardlaw," Steve concluded.

"That doesn't mean crap to me," said Frederica Wright. "I thought the prison reform act was junk in the first place."

Everyone nodded.

"Just to make sure," Sam told Steve, "write it so that it will be an amendment to the Bill of Rights in the Constitution. Call it the 'Personal Rights Act.'

"Moving on," Sam continued, "the next thing on the list is the drug issue. Tom, you've obviously given this some thought," he said wryly. "Tell us what you've come up with."

"Thanks, Sam," Tom said, taking the floor. "First, let me start with the kids. We have to have mandatory drug education starting in the second grade and on up."

"Second grade?" Bob Emerson interrupted. "Isn't that a mite early?"

"According to my sources," said Tom Baker bitterly, "pushers are initiating kids into drug rings by as early as eight. Anyway, we have to make this mandatory starting with seven-year-olds, and keep it compulsory up through high school. All kids have to know the inherent dangers of drugs. We're including education for alcohol and cigarettes for good measure. These classes are to begin immediately, whether it's summer or not. If kids don't want to attend, they will be forced to."

"Sorry," Sam added in, "but even we can't force kids to spend this or other seasonal time off stuck in school. It's inhumane. It's....un-American. I remember; I know. Is September okay?"

"It'll have to be," Tom concluded, who saw the others around the table nodding approval.

"Good," Sam said. "Now, how do we force them?"

"The same as my literacy idea," Tom Baker replied. "Put them in schools, or behind bars if needed until they learn what they have to."

"That makes it necessary to increase the prison system for juveniles," voiced Bob Emerson.

"Absolutely," said Tom Baker. "We'll need to hire tutors to teach the students, and police to enforce our policies."

"Well," Sam admitted. "That covers the kids. What about adults? Are you going to force them to go to your classes?"

"It can't be done," Tom threw up his hands. "It's like selecting jurors for a trial. No one with brains wants to serve time on a jury. I'm convinced that there is no way to force adult Americans to do anything they don't want to do."

"Then," asked Steve Harning, "what do you suggest we do? Nothing?"

"Not quite," Tom Baker said, with the slightest of smiles. "With all drugs legalized, there is an inherent danger to the American citizen. People might try to drive, sail, or fly under the influence of drugs. What I propose is a mandatory jail sentence of seven years, irrevocable, if a person is caught operating any vehicle under the influence of substances like alcohol or drugs."

"Sounds pretty tough," said Bob Emerson, eyes widening.

"It sounds like the only way to go," concluded Sam, after giving it some thought. "People have to realize they have the potential to cause injury to others. If they are inconsiderate to others, they have to pay, and pay dearly. Pure and simple.

"In addition," Sam continued, rolling with the idea, "there are blood tests now to detect all drugs produced. We should stipulate that no one would be allowed to refuse a blood test."

"You sure have been doing your homework," Frederica admired. "I never knew you to be so well informed on blood tests. It looks as though appeals would be virtually impossible with this law."

"Thank you," Sam said proudly.

"And what about pushers?" Frederica Wright asked Sam quietly.

"The mandatory, non-bailable, non-parolable sentence for the first offense would be twenty-five years."

"Twenty-five years?" Steve Harning cried, as though he hadn't heard what was said correctly.

"Without parole?" Bob said, smiling at the thought.

"I think it's appropriate," Sam Bunker grinned. He thought about how he should have told Emil Wardlaw about his twenty-five-year future commitment before giving him the chance to escape gracefully.

They each nodded. They felt it was high time a pusher's job became more hazardous.

"How about legitimate suppliers of drugs?" Tom asked.

Frederica spoke. "They all have to be under government control before we can go one step further. They'll be allowed to exist, but only if we have a say in it. We'll be in control of licensing drug manufacturers and they'll have to comply with a lot of legislation in order to survive," remarked Frederica Wright. She thought of the government policies and regulations that would be needed to assure quality control. Frederica was in her element now – government operations. "The drug agencies will complain about the government crackdown," Frederica surmised. "What we could do is add to the law a mandate that drug developers have thirty years of exclusive drug rights instead of the current eighteen-year rule before generics are allowed. That way, if someone produces a good drug, they'll have financial protection for a while."

"Sounds good, Frederica," Sam agreed. "Please work on it. Folks, I don't want just anyone to get drug licensing. They're going to have to pass the most stringent regulations," he said. "I don't want the underworld's hands on drugs any more!

"The easiest thing is marijuana," Sam continued. "Frederica, it'll be your job to select members from the American Tobacco Growers Association to grow marijuana. Do this while you help Steve write the legislation for the Drug Enforcement Act. Have the tobacco growers who want to participate grow their crops now, so that the supply will be there when marijuana is made legal. We must remember that we have to meet the public's demand for drugs."

"It's already been done," Frederica admitted. "The growing part, that is. The smart tobacco growers already have fields in Mexico and South America. Other tobacco growers have fields in America, like Marin County in California and other hippie-type areas. They've been waiting a long time for the legalization of drugs."

"We still want the folks at home to be growing most of the stuff," Sam Bunker admonished. "Remember, we're tired of importing everything."

"Done," Frederica agreed, making a memo to herself on what she was to do. She knew she was going to be a busy woman for the next few days.

"And what about the M.A.A.?" Sam Bunker asked the group.

"The Medical Association of America?" Bob Emerson said.

"They're not going to like this," Sam knew, "not a bit."

"Screw them," Frederica spoke again. "I've been thinking about this, being a M.D. myself, and I've figured out ways to..."

"You're a M.D.!" Bob blurted out unbelievingly, knowing Frederica hated doctors.

"Yeah," Frederica replied. "I'm not proud of it, though. I wanted to help people, so I became a doctor, but I never got used to the suffering and watching patients die. When a patient of mine died, I couldn't get over it. I transferred over to law and tried to forget my medical career. I buried it behind me, along with my less fortunate patients."

"I'm sorry," Tom quietly remarked. "It must be painful for you to talk about it."

"I'm okay, now," Frederica said without conviction, "and we need my insight into the medical world."

"Go on," encouraged Sam.

"Doctors don't know much about drugs," she said. "They know the areas of the body that the drugs act upon. They try to learn what a drug does but they don't know drugs per se. At least, most of them don't know as much as pharmacists. Pharmacists are able to compound drugs, achieve proper dosages, and more importantly, figure out how drugs interact with each other. Doctors, as a general rule, don't know how drugs interact with other drugs."

"Then how do doctors prescribe medication without this knowledge?" asked Bob Emerson.

"They use a big book, called the *Physician's Desk Reference*, or 'PDR.' This book lists all current drugs in use, dosages, and their side effects. This book is on the desk of most doctors, and you can even buy it in bookstores.

"What I propose to you, to control the M.A.A., is to give pharmacists the status of medical doctors. They deserve it, and they'll be able to treat and diagnose patients."

"How would we do that?" asked Sam.

"First, we subsidize insurance companies handling malpractice suits for the Pharmaceutical Association of America, then write a bill authorizing treatment nationwide by the P.A.A., and go from there. Pharmacists shouldn't be spending as many years in school as a medical doctor does just to count pills."

"So," Tom humorously quipped, "if I have this right, you're taking power away from the M.A.A., and giving it to the P.A.A."

"Exactly," said Frederica, smiling. "M.A.A. versus P.A.A. Maw versus Paw. I'll bet the newspapers will have a field day with that one."

"So how else can we give pharmacists power?" asked Sam.

"Easy," Frederica concluded. "We do it financially. If we make the minimum salary equal to that of the average M.D., they are equal."

"What if the large drugstore chains complain about paying salary increases?" asked Bob.

"They won't for long," Frederica stated. "When drugs become legalized, people will get them at the pharmacies. The pharmacies will have to stock more drugs, but they'll be making a lot more money. Things like marijuana cigarettes and stuff like that could be sold at liquor stores. Liquor stores could be licensed for marijuana. But other drugs would have to be purchased from pharmacies."

"I hope this information will be kept quiet until it breaks," Bob Emerson worried aloud. "If people found out now, there could be a lot of shady deals."

"No problem," Sam added in. "Congress is pretty safe these days. If we keep this on the hush until it becomes legal, no one gets rich quick.

"So," Sam concluded tiredly, taking a deep sigh, "Why don't I summarize what we already have and let's wind up for the day. We have the import act/subsidy act which will be the first bill passed by our committee. From here, the bill goes straight to the President. Once he signs it, it's law. Then there is the arm-for-an-arm bill for violent crimes, to be called the Personal Rights Act. Personal Rights Act sounds better than the Arm-for-an-arm Act, wouldn't you say? Steve, you said you'd write that since you have a special interest in it.

"We also have the Drug Education Act and Drug Enforcement Act, both of which need to be penned. Tom, I want you to figure out the Drug Education Act. Frederica, I want you to work on the Drug Enforcement Act and the Pharmacist Act. Bob and I will take on the Drug Legalization Act."

"However," Sam added as people wrote lists of things to do in the next week, "there are other things that must be done before these bills become law. We have to increase the police, the prisons, the courts, and hospitals. The police and courts we've already discussed, from apprehending the offenders to their parole. But, just to make sure nobody gets hurt, we have to increase hospitals at least two-fold. That way, the public is safer and our asses are covered."

"I'll write a bill for increasing police, courts, prisons, and hospitals," Bob said. "Then I'll run it by Steve to make it solid. Politically, if we introduce the bill for increasing courts, police, and the rest of the stuff prior to the Drug Legalization Act, the clergy would be happy and the streets would be better protected. The M.A.A. would be happy too. The public would also appreciate the fact that there would be more police to take care of things."

"I'm counting on it," Sam smiled, as though he had already thought about it. "By the way, folks, run everything you write past Steve for loopholes.

"I'd like the Personal Rights Act to become active at the same time as the Imports Act," Sam stated. "I want both of them to get to the President soon."

"Meeting adjourned," Sam ordered. "See you next week. Let's move."

The people left the conference room. They felt the weight of the nation on their shoulders, and each prayed the country would soon be able to stand on its own two feet.

Prescription for Mayhem

Chapter Ten

Sam Bunker was being talked about at that very instant in Miami, Chicago and New York. It was a conference call made by Julius "Julie" Giuliano in New York, titular head of the Mafia for the whole United States; trying to get all his friends and those who owed him favors to find out what was going on in Congress.

"Whaddya mean, there's nothing we can do about this?" Julie Giuliano shouted into the phone.

The phone was quiet at the other end. Even the phone scramblers didn't hiss as much as they usually did while trying to connect the call. No one answered Julie. They knew better.

Julie was a big man. He stood six-feet-six-inches tall, was bald, and had thick lips, a hook nose, and bushy eyebrows. His body had once been muscle, but was now covered with rolls of fat from long years of an easy life. He had killed his first man with a baseball bat at the age of ten. By the time he was twelve, he began using knives, then guns.

When Julie was upset, someone often died. Julie hated not knowing what was going on. He was glad his nephew, Emil Wardlaw, had passed the Prison Rights Act, making things easier for his relatives who were still in jail. Other bills making gambling legal made things cushy for everyone.

"Emil," Julie asked. "What are they cooking up in Congress?"

"I don't know, Uncle Julie," Emil Wardlaw softly replied calling from Miami. "But it can't be too much. The person who got me and the others out of Congress said that it was the Alonso guy who fingered us."

"Alonso again?!" Julie bellowed into the phone. Ever since Alonso defected, the contract on him had remained unfinished. The organization had been damaged because of his squealing. Julie thought for a second, then wrote a note tripling the contract fee for killing Alonso. One of the most trusted men in the family, and he had betrayed them all. A regular Judas. Someone had to find him soon.

"What about our lobbyists?" Julie asked Emil.

"They've also been asked to leave quietly. After the eight of us left, the lobbyists who hung around us were told that they had to leave the next day."

"Isn't there anyone left to protect our interests?" Julie asked.

"No, Uncle Giuliano," Emil said. "There isn't. We were caught with our pants down around our ankles. We had to get out."

"How'd they find out?" Julie asked.

"Some of the Congressmen noticed how we were voting on issues like prisoner's rights and gambling legislation, like you told us to, and they put two and two together. It took Alonso to nail me, and then they gave us enough rope to hang ourselves."

"Alonso," Julie thought. "The 'Dick' Alonso will soon have problems sleeping. His days are numbered." He asked, "What do we do now without lobbyists?"

"Nothing, Uncle Giuliano," said Emil diplomatically, "until we can get more people into Congress. The people who resigned had others appointed by presidential order. We can't do anything for two years in our home towns, unless we bribe someone in Congress."

"Do it," Julie commanded.

"Uncle Giuliano," reminded Emil, "we tried that in the past, remember? And it failed every time. Every time we try to buy someone in Congress, they've always changed sides. The last time it happened, we lost good people."

"The kid's right," Julie admitted to himself. "Still, we have to do something. If they tried, they could put us out of business."

"What chance do they have of getting to us?" Julie growled into the phone.

"Slim to none," Emil replied, choosing every word. "We got that prison rights act through years ago, and now it's law. We're doing well on the gambling and pornography rackets, but drugs are still our biggest money maker. Drugs are about ninety-five percent of our income to date. It's impossible for anyone to destroy the groundwork we laid."

"It better be," threatened Julie quietly into the phone, "or you might have to make up for the mistake." The other members of the family in Miami and Chicago said nothing. They knew Julie could make his own family members comply.

Emil thought about how he should have gone to Atlantic City or Las Vegas with other members of his family and gotten into gambling instead of politics. Now his political career was washed up. He knew the family would take care of their own, one way or another.

"Think about our problem," Julie commanded, and then hung up the phone.

Two weeks later the ends of Craig's fingers hurt. He had stuffed political pamphlets into every mailbox on his route. Congress had sent the nation valuable information on the Import Act and the Personal Rights Act. Craig opened up his pamphlet the day he got it at work. What Congress had done with the approval of the President was to declare a state of emergency regarding all imports. There were severe restrictions limiting what could be brought into the United States. Another approved law gave subsidies to American businesses already named, to encourage Americans to produce materials that were usually imported.

The press found out about the new laws at the same time everyone else got the pamphlets in the mail. Reporters were busy interviewing Asian consulates, talking to people on the street, and asking anyone else who might have an opinion about about the new acts. There were arguments about the Imports Act, but people were unprepared and shocked by the Personal Rights Act. No one could take it calmly. The victims of abusive crimes could now demand reciprocity. Those people who were raped could demand that the rapist be castrated. Thieves could now find themselves missing fingers, hands, or anything else. Civil Rights groups began to talk of challenging the law, stating that the loss of body parts was cruel and inhuman punishment. No federal court judge was ready to grant an injunction. The judges responded with the undisputed fact that the Personal Rights Act was a right of the individual, now a part of the Constitution's Bill of Rights, and that civil rights groups had no jurisdiction to challenge an act that would vary from one individual case to another.

The pamphlet did say that more laws were coming to increase the police, courts, prisons, schools and hospitals, and would be announced in the next few weeks.

Aside from the initial shock, most people took it pretty well. The *Christian Science Monitor* was the first to report that crime took a huge nosedive within the first few days after the law was announced. Abusive crimes dropped as well. People were safer on the streets than they had been just the week before. The church, initially against the removal of body parts, did grudgingly admit that things had quieted down.

Julie Giuliano was not taking the Personal Rights Act well. He knew if one of his people murdered someone, they were apt to be sent to death row. His people would have to be a little more careful about "leaning" on others. After thinking about it, and phrasing a few bad words about his nephew, Emil, he told himself that it wouldn't be so bad. He just had to be a little more careful.

Don Browning, M.D., hardly noticed any difference in the emergency room where he worked part time at the city hospital. Don, a five-feet- nine-inch curly-haired resident in family practice, felt that patients didn't give him the respect he deserved. Because of his freckles and boyish face, Don had worked hard to get where he was. Although in a family practice residency, he knew that he was on the road to success. He made enough money to live on by doing extra work in the emergency room. He liked the drama and the life-and-death decisions he had to make.

Doc Browning also liked to feel important. He lived for his work, and had little time for anything else other than an occasional basketball game with the guys, or watching something on TV. Doc Browning noticed that the knifings and abusive crimes took a sharp decrease after the Personal Rights Act started, but driving accidents and heart attacks made up for it. All it meant to him was that the people he would be treating wouldn't be handcuffed, and that made him a little more comfortable.

"Get a 'D and W' in this guy, stat!" he shouted to a nurse. He tried to stop the bleeding from the brachial artery on a man's arm.

"Call for a blood typing, stat!" He knew that they were going to replace a lot of blood into the man.

"Make sure he's insured when you have the chance," shouted the ward clerk, peeking into the room.

"He's unconscious," noticed the orderly.

"His buddy said that he was doing PCP when he walked into traffic. He was crossing the street for a beer!"

"Let's hope he stays unconscious," Doc Browning prayed. The last thing he needed was some zombied PCP freak who would need twelve people to hold him down. PCP always gave people unnatural strength. Doc Browning was sweating. He had the nurse wipe his brow as he tried to stop the bleeding.

"Cautery?" asked the nurse.

"Not yet," grunted Browning, "and stop telling me how to practice medicine!"

"Cautery," he stated moments later, after he closed the artery.

"Yes, doctor," remarked the nurse practitioner with a yawn.

The nurse practitioner looked bored. She had seen the same thing unfold hundreds of times in the past. It was always the same. She would triage the patient, call the doctor, who would invariably ask for X-rays, or a CT scan if the patient was unconscious.

Doc Browning was more taken aback by the Import Act than anything else. He wanted a new sports car, and now that prices had skyrocketed he felt he'd have to settle for a Corvette instead of the Ferrari he'd been eyeing. He sighed as he left the bleeder to the nurse practitioner to bandage and went on to the next patient.

The next patient had probably broken his arm falling off a ladder, Doc Browning thought as he reviewed the X-rays. He didn't see any fractures. Fortunately, all of the X-rays were reviewed the next day by a radiologist.

"Doc," said the ward clerk, "you better finish up with everyone, tout suite. I heard over the radio that three ambulances are coming in with some kids shot or knifed in a gang war. I hope your Spanish is good. You may need it."

"Life is tough," Doc Browning said, as he listened to the sound of the approaching sirens.

"Life is tough all over," said Elaine Russell to herself. She heard the ambulances drive by and the sirens woke her from a nap. She lived in a bungalow and had never worked at a real job before. Elaine had graduated from high school then taken over managing the bungalows for her sick mother. When her mother moved to Las Vegas for health reasons, Elaine kept the managerial job.

Elaine was tall for a woman. She was five-feet-eleven-inches tall, had sandy blond hair and a good body. She was chronically sick and always had problems sleeping. It drove her crazy. It was the sleeping that gave her the most difficulty of the two. If she got two or three hours of continuous sleep a night, it was wonderful. Most of the time, the only way she could sleep was to take some sleeping pills or have some drinks. One of her latest boyfriends said that she had a phenomenal threshold. She remembered talking to him earlier that morning in bed.

"You don't love me," Elaine said.

"It's not that," he said sleepily, "but I tend to fade out. I'm usually asleep before four or five in the morning. I just can't go on like you do."

"Could we go out for some drinks?"

"No, we can't. The liquor stores closed an hour ago."

"How about TV?"

"I'm tired of TV. You always keep that sucker on. You even fall asleep to it. Yesterday morning, I woke up singing TV commercial jingles."

"Well," Elaine throatily whispered, tossing her hair a bit and lowering her eyes, "we can make love."

"No we can't," he groaned. "I'm too damn tired. I need to get some sleep. Why don't you wake me up in the morning, early, and we'll do it."

"I don't know if I'll be in the mood later."

"Look," he complained. "I got you all the drugs you wanted, didn't I? Why don't you take one to put you asleep and give me some peace?"

"Baby," Elaine moaned, "I've been sick."

Her boyfriend thought how true her words were. She had been in bed most of the five weeks that he had known her and it seemed hard for him to distinguish whether she was sick or healthy. She was always taking pills and at times, he didn't know what was bothering her. Nor did she.

He knew that she couldn't hold a job. When he had met her at a bar, she was single. Her last boyfriend, the italian motorcycle mechanic, had beaten her up and sent her to the hospital. The only thing they had in common was that they both liked to ride motorcycles. He knew she found italian motorcycles, Ducati's, exciting. At times, he didn't know why he stayed with her.

Then again, he did. With the right pills in her, she was phenomenal in bed. She would make love like a crazy woman. She would respond like no one he had ever known before. But, the times she was wonderful were balanced by the times she was bitchy. He remembered the times he wanted to have sex and she didn't. When she was in the mood, she would tease and coax him, dancing with him close and sometimes naked. When she was bitchy, she would leave him with a painful erection, his mind thinking only of throwing her on the floor and making love to her. She was very innovative in lovemaking. She made love softly at times and sometimes wanted it rough.

"Baby," she whispered, softly breaking him out of his introspective mood.

"What?" he responded tiredly, eyes starting to close. He didn't care about anything anymore. He just wanted to sleep.

"Why don't I give you something to keep you awake for a while," she suggested. "That way, you'll be awake and able to deal with whatever comes up." She smiled and gave him a look that told him exactly what was going to be coming up.

She put a green pill in his hands and tried to keep him awake while waiting for the drugs to take effect.

He took the pill, swallowed it, and then sat back while he concentrated on any feeling hardening between his legs. He just hoped that the pill she gave him was one that would allow him to remember this evening for years to come.

"It's showtime," he surmised twenty minutes later, bored with trying to stay awake watching television, as the drug started waking his body. He reached for her.

Elaine then stretched her body, yawned as the sirens faded in the distance, and changed channels on the TV to see what was on.

Prescription for Mayhem

Chapter Eleven

Four weeks later
June 29, 2027

Sabrina woke up and went to the kitchenette. She put the coffee pot on and took a shower.

She didn't know how long she had slept. She stared at the canvas sitting on the edge of her bed. Although she had only planned to paint for a short while, she had worked late into the night. Today, she might check out the new exhibit at the art museum and sketch something worthwhile, then go to wait on tables at the Cock & Bull restaurant.

Her hair was frizzy. She usually tied it back in a ponytail. She picked up yesterday's mail from the table in the kitchenette and opened the envelopes.

The item that caught her attention was a flier from Congress. It looked similar to the one that came in the mail two weeks ago. In it was a notice that Congress had passed a bill to increase prisons, courts, police departments, and hospitals. Hospitals were a good idea, but she wasn't too sure about the rest. America was becoming more of a police state, with new rules daily telling people how to live. She wanted to live her own life, make her own mistakes and her own statements. Kind of like the way she felt about art. Art had to be spontaneous and free flowing, like her soul.

She read the Drug Education Act that stated it was mandatory for school kids to learn about drugs. It seemed sensible, and she felt it was about time to make drug education compulsory.

Then she noticed the Drug Enforcement Act. Sabrina knew that most of her friends did drugs. She even had some friends who were in jail on drug charges. She visited them occasionally and attended demonstrations to get the laws changed.

The summary of the bill was short. It was illegal to push drugs. The pushers would be punished for any offense by a twenty-five year sentence without any bail. Once convicted, if an appeal failed, there would be no further appeals. She read on. It said nothing about the drug users, only the people selling the drugs to others. She felt it strange that they would neglect to punish the person taking the drugs. "They must be taking things in steps," she thought aloud, making the laws change a little at a time. She didn't take drugs nor did she feel them to be necessary. Drugs were for a personal escape. She had her escape in art.

She could sketch and paint with a firm, strong line, and her teachers and friends had encouraged her to take further steps. One teacher said that she had great potential as a commercial or graphic artist, but felt that she lacked the talent needed in the world of fine art.

"You need character," said the instructor, a well-known, respected artist. "To be a Picasso, Van Gogh, or Monet, takes character. To suffer, to experiment without worrying about what will please or displease the viewer is necessary. You must live only for your art. And once you find your style," added the instructor, "you will be the success you dream of being."

Sabrina had graduated the Art Institute and gone out on her own. She painted what she saw, searching for the elusive truth on her canvases – character. Much of her work was of beauty in the world. But it was the beauty of observation, not of creativity, that she captured. She desired a beauty of imagination, not as genuine as a beauty of truth, for only imagination would make a viewer think it was real, or beautiful. But she also knew that as long as she kept looking, one day she would change. She would find the character that she knew was inside her, and that would naturally flow onto the canvas.

Kevin Manila woke up after tossing and turning. He checked under his pillow for his gun, and put the safety back on. He had been a cop for only three years but he could not forget his routines. He had worked on vice detail for two months and with the Drug Enforcement Agency for a year. Now he was having a great time as a motorcycle policeman. The pay was good and the benefits were great. Every so often he had to get rough with smartasses, but he was thankful that it didn't happen much.

Kevin's buddies had been happy since they got the note from Congress approving the Drug Enforcement bill. Now, if slimeballs were convicted of pushing drugs, they'd get a twenty-five year sentence. With Congress increasing the number of policemen, prisons, and courts, there were chances that Kevin would be promoted soon. It was almost enough to renew Kevin's faith in America.

Kevin had jet black hair, as did most Filipinos. Although a good boy in school, he had fought for things he believed in. His principal told him he should use that energy to enforce the law. In time, he decided that maybe he should be a cop.

It was quiet on the force these last few days. There hadn't been many calls to stop family squabbles. Not so many people seemed to be gunning for each other. "That Personal Rights Act is a good thing," he thought. "Now, if only something could be done about gangs."

He knew gangs hadn't changed much. With juveniles, the law wasn't applicable. His police station was changing their emphasis on drugs. There was a big push coming down from the national government to the state government. All the police stations in his district were to crack down on drug pushers. Now, it seemed that there was enough federal money to deal with it right. "Maybe this might make a dent in the drug subculture, but maybe not," he thought. "It seems for every one who gets caught, five more take their place. Just like cockroaches."

He read in the paper that the government was planning to use the pushers and others in jobs like accounting and secretarial positions for prison reform. The government felt that as long as they had to feed the prisoners, they should get some free work out of them. "Good luck trying to get some work out of them," he said to the newspaper.

Kevin wondered about the court system increasing. Although no new federal court judges had been appointed yet, new ones were to be appointed to ease the burden on the court system. The court system would be increased at least two to threefold. Waiting five years to get to trial would be a thing of the past. He read that cases would be tried within three months. This meant that lawyers were going to be kept pretty busy. That thought alone made him smile.

Craig was up at dawn to sort the mail. He delivered the mail from nine-thirty until three o'clock. Then he needed to deliver a large certified package for a man named Poindexter over at Thalberg, Chaney, and Fairbanks.

It meant a special trip back to the post office to pick up the parcel, deliver it, and have someone sign for it.

It had been a long day and Craig was tired. Craig took the parcel to the office of Thalberg, Chaney, and Fairbanks. The male receptionist wouldn't sign for it and told him to go to the Public Relations Office.

Craig took the heavy parcel down the hall to the Public Relations Office. He heard someone typing and swearing at the same time. A woman, about thirty or so, was sitting at her keyboard. She was looking at a computer screen and cursing at the mistakes the computer's spelling program found. She didn't like being corrected. Her longish hair lay on thin shoulders. Her breasts were well-defined but her body was abnormally thin. She would have had beautiful eyes, were they not overly made up.

"You goddamn computer," she swore to the screen. "How do I know you can spell pontificate? You didn't go to high school! If you think I'm going to let you approve this, sign my name to it, and send it to the major newspapers across the nation, you're crazy."

She found a small pocket dictionary to check the spelling of the word "pontificate." The small dictionary didn't have it listed.

"Uh, Miss," said Craig, resting the parcel down on the desk in front of her.

"How do you spell 'pontificate?'" she asked, looking at the terminal screen.

"P-O-N-T-I-F-I-C-A-T-E."

She checked the computer screen again. "The goddamned thing's right," she said, and saved the program.

"Well," she said, and looked at Craig. His thinning hair was ruffled from carting the package to the office. His glasses steamed from his efforts. He had a cute face, a nice smile, and seemed genuine.

"Who are you?" she asked.

"I'm Craig, the mail carrier for this building."

"I'm Mary Lane," she answered back.

"Pretty name, Mary," he smiled.

"Actually," she replied, "my father wanted to name his first child Jesus, and it took a lot from my mother to convince him to name me Mary. It's not exactly Jesus, but it's close."

Craig laughed.

"My father also made sure he kept my mother in line. She wanted to spell Mary with two R's, to make sure that my goal in life would be as plain as my name, Mary Lane."

"Nice name."

"Let me guess why you're here. Is it a postage due letter?"

"Not exactly," Craig smiled, pointing to the box next to the desk.

"Is that for me?" she asked, batting her lashes at him.

He laughed. "Only if your name is Poindexter. And, you don't even look like a Felix to me."

"Don't be catty," Mary jokingly said. "Poindexter is one of my bosses."

"Good," Craig replied. "Because this package feels like dumbbells."

"They could be," Mary thoughtfully said. "It's probably for one of our clients who doesn't want to be seen in a gym."

"It must be exciting being in the entertainment industry," Craig said, remembering the one time he saw some TV stars when he was delivering mail.

"Not really," Mary flatly replied, a bit tiredly. "It's kind of like making mountains out of molehills."

"Wouldn't you want to be a star?" asked Craig. "I don't have the looks, but I think it would be fun to be in front of cameras."

"Not me, mister. I'm happy doing what I'm doing, and when I'm in the mood, I can see any star I want to."

Craig handed her the notice to sign that the parcel was delivered in good condition. Mary checked out the parcel, noted its condition and gave the card a quick swipe of a signature.

"Thanks," Craig smiled. "I've got to get back to work. It was nice meeting you, Mary."

"Nice meeting you, Craig."

Craig then left the office, closing the door on the way out. Mary looked at the box in front of her desk and realized that it was too heavy to move. She should have had Craig move it for her. She smiled, thinking that Craig seemed to be a nice guy.

"Imagine giving someone like him cocaine and watching him fly to the ceiling," she thought. She smiled again, thinking that Craig was probably the kind of guy who never did that sort of thing. She remembered spiking a guy's drink once with a downer, and then dragging him off to bed. It was one of the craziest things she'd ever done, and it still made her nerves tingle to think about it.

She then realized it was time for her mid-afternoon joint and a cup of coffee. She grabbed her purse and walked to the elevator, planning to go up to the roof for a smoke.

Prescription for Mayhem

Chapter Twelve

"Whaddya mean, you can't do anything!" shouted Julie Giuliano into Emil Wardlaw's face.

"I can't, Uncle Giuliano," Emil whispered, slowly looking down at the floor. "I'm not a member of Congress anymore. I was told that if I returned, they'd expose me...uh, us. I was fingered by Peter Alonso."

"The 'Dick' Alonso," Julie growled slowly, pacing back and forth in his huge living room. The room had marble floors and silk covered walls. The corner moldings were covered in gold leaf details. The house had been in Julie's family since his great-great-great-grandfather's days, during the roaring twenties, when the families moved booze and backed speakeasys. The walls were covered in blood on occasion, but redecorating eliminated any signs of violence.

Julie swore vengeance on Peter 'Dick' Alonso. If given the chance, he would strangle him.

"So, what can we do?" Julie shouted.

"I made a few calls to some of my ex-colleagues on Capitol Hill," Emil replied.

"And?"

"And they said that they didn't have anything to do with the Drug Enforcement Act, although everyone I talked to was for it."

"The vipers," Julie shot back. "They're trying to put us honest businessmen out of business."

"It seems the act came out of the new *Guidance and Direction Committee*, with the full backing of the President and Congress."

"I don't remember hearing about this group," Julie said, thinking back for some mention of the committee.

"They were just formed to guide America out of its slump," Emil said. "They were given power by a unanimous vote of Congress, and they have the President behind them all the way."

"And the first thing they did was this Personal Rights Act?" Julie asked.

"Yes, Uncle Giuliano."

"That means if we lean too hard on a guy and muss him up, he could do the same thing to us, right?"

"Yes, Uncle Giuliano."

"So, we've been cutting down on the leaning. All it means is we have to think more before we get tough, and not get caught."

"Yes, Uncle Giuliano," agreed Emil, knowing that his uncle was a man of action and not words.

"But this Drug Enforcement Act is something else," Julie bellowed.

"Yes, Uncle Giuliano."

"If they put one of our boys away, they do it for twenty-five years, right?"

"Yes, Uncle Giuliano."

"No bail, right?"

"Yes, Uncle Giuliano."

"We're in deep shit," he said, eyebrows furrowing in thought. "If any of our boys are caught, they'd have to spend twenty-five years in the slammer without bail? People would be crazy to do that!"

"Maybe, Uncle Giuliano," Emil said very softly.

"If they were caught and given the choice of spilling their guts, or working on a rock pile for twenty-five years, they'd spill their guts, right?"

"Maybe, Uncle Giuliano," Emil whispered.

"We're in deep shit," he repeated. "Can you buy anyone in Congress?"

"No, Uncle Giuliano," Emil said weakly.

"No one?"

"No one, Uncle Giuliano."

"How about federal court judges?"

"I tried, but no one will give us an injunction. There are over three hundred federal court judges, but no one in our pocket right now. If you think about it, who would issue an injunction against a law punishing those who 'addict and use children?'"

"Children? Do we use children?" Julie asked, looking at the Mafia accountant, a small man quietly sitting in a corner of the room.

"Five percent are under ten years old, sir," said the accountant.

"They're not members of the family, are they?" Julie asked. reassuringly. He then looked to Emil, watching his face, and said, "Is there any way we can get through to the committee?"

"I don't think so," Emil replied honestly.

Emil remembered bitterly his last visit from Sam Bunker. "That old man had me between a rock and a hard place then stood back to watch me kill myself. Cagey old bastard," he thought.

"So what can we do?" Julie asked. "The increase in the police force is just starting up. These guys are going to be on our asses to nail us! We have to do something! How much is the police force increasing?"

"At least two hundred percent, according to the *Congressional Record*," said Emil.

"Well, said Julie, slowly turning to the accountant, "we just have to cut back. Let our boys know supplies will be slowing down while we cover our tracks. Tell the pushers that they are not to talk if caught. If they do talk, let them know that our boys in the slammer will kill them. We'll protect their interests while they're in the slammer if they're good to us."

"Yes sir," the accountant replied, writing down notes. "But this will decrease our revenues and protection business because of these people who will be in the slammer for twenty-five years."

"I know," Julie agreed matter-of-factly.

"In addition, sir," the accountant continued, "we have the problem of a big increase in the police. We'll have consider buying off more police."

"I know," Julie nodded.

"However, I'm not sure the police payoff expenditure is warranted," the accountant said. "If we're going into hibernation, so to speak, from a dollar and cents figure, we should save our money."

"I don't think it's warranted either," said Emil, standing next to the accountant.

"Okay," Julie agreed. "We cut our losses by not bribing the new cops who hit the streets."

"Yes, Uncle Giuliano," said Emil.

"Let's just hope that the new cops are as stupid as the old ones," Julie said, as he bit off a piece of cigar and spat it toward the marble fireplace.

"I'm sure it'll be," Emil said confidently. "What's out there that'll make things change?"

"Jeezus H. Christ, these people look stupid!" Kevin Manila said to himself as he entered the morning briefing. More than half of them were people he'd never seen before in police uniform. They looked untrained and out of place. Kevin was proud of his advancement to sergeant. He felt he didn't deserve it, but he still accepted it. The increase in salary sure would come in handy.

"So," concluded the lieutenant, "that's it for today. Any questions?"

"You mean, sir," asked a rookie, "if we see anyone or suspect anyone of selling drugs, we halt and detain them?"

"Right," the lieutenant said. "You are not to arrest users. We are not after the users, officers, we are after the pushers."

"I think we should jail all those miserable bastards," a new recruit spat out.

"Rand," the lieutenant spoke down to her, "I admire your character, but we have to do things by the book. It's time we showed them we mean business."

"Yes sir," growled the new recruits, anxious to get to work.

Kevin made his way to the coffee machine. As he sipped from the plastic cup he told himself that he was glad there were more police, but he hoped that they would be better trained. Ninety percent of being a cop is something he learned on the streets. Unfortunately, most rookies didn't realize that until it was too late.

Still, it was better being on motorcycle detail than on vice. Kevin was glad that he didn't opt for border patrol, even though the pay was great. The new government policy was to capture all "wetbacks." Their punishment would be six months hard labor and deportation back to Mexico, or wherever they came from. For the second offense, they would be sentenced, without trial, for up to five years at hard labor, then deported. When there were families, both parents would be sentenced to jail. The children would be taken to the appropriate Consulate with the directive that the child was "undesirable" and must be deported within twelve hours.

After this information hit the world, immigration to the United States dropped dramatically. It was a tough policy and a lot of people didn't like it.

Doc Browning looked around the nearly finished emergency room complex in the new county hospital. Crews were working around the clock to meet the deadline. "There are so many hospitals being built," Browning thought. He had been asked to head up the new emergency facility on evenings when he wasn't in his family practice residency. The new opportunity meant more money but also greater responsibility.

The new emergency room had much more equipment than he'd ever seen. There was a comprehensive cardiology bed. There were three beds for burn and shock victims. There were twelve more beds designated for people suffering from overdoses. He didn't know why there were so many beds reserved for overdose and shock victims. He felt that the beds could be moved around depending upon the need. Although there were fifteen beds for laceration victims and amputation procedures, the administrator had said that they would double the number of beds by the end of the year. There was a first of the year deadline for twenty-five new emergency rooms to be operational in the Los Angeles area. Even if things were behind schedule, there would be enough money from the government to cover everything in order to meet the deadline.

He was not pleased that nurse practitioners, pharmacists, and other ancillary personnel were going to be doing most of the work, with the diagnoses left to the doctors. Nurses would triage the patients, decide what was needed, and whether the doctor should see them. The doctors would be busy with laceration repairs, X-ray interpretations (following the X-ray tech's initial screening), and diagnoses. Once the diagnosis was made, it was up to the pharmacist to provide the drugs to be dispensed to patients. The reasoning, Doc Browning was told, was that all of the malpractice insurance would be provided by the government. It would be like working in an army base. No one could ever sue an army doctor for anything but gross negligence.

"It bothers me," Doc Browning muttered to himself, "but I'll have to accept it." He was guaranteed that if he and the other four doctors under him on his shift got too swamped, more would be hired.

Doc Browning resented giving the ancillary help too much power. It would allow them to make decisions that should be left to him. He did feel that pharmacists knew more about medications than he did, but he wasn't sure about the nurse practitioners or X-ray technicians.

"Maybe I'll be able to get that Ferrari after all," he thought, as he reviewed his salary for the next few months. Even with the import tax bumping up the price of his car $20,000, he still might be able to afford the downpayment for it. From now on that meant working for the government, and with that, the usual governmental regulations and red tape. He hoped it wouldn't be anything like the rotation he did at the San Francisco Presidio army base while he was a med student. The army regulations made him spend more time filling out forms than he did practicing medicine.

He remembered thinking at the start of medical school that he'd be able to spend all his time helping patients. He estimated that over sixty percent of his time was filling out forms or writing in charts.

Elaine Russell sat by her television in her bedroom. She had a sore throat and decided to stay home. Elaine took some antibiotics and watched Jeopardy, waiting for the medication to take effect. She kept looking out of her window toward the grounds of the new hospital. There was a lot of noise. It felt good to know that she would be within a few minutes of a hospital. Having overdosed once before, she liked the security of having a hospital nearby.

She knew that she didn't have much resistance to viruses and was sick a lot of the time. If it wasn't the change in the weather, it was a bacteria or a fungus that would bother her. Elaine always took pills for whatever ailed her. She had everything she needed at her bedside. The television was there, on all the time. And she could stay in bed and manage her mother's bungalows. There were her two cats sleeping on the blanket, and an occasional boyfriend a phone call away to keep her satisfied when she felt like having sex.

Elaine felt better now that the hospitals and police force were being increased, even though she didn't want the police to know about her drugs. Although one or two of her male friends were doctors and wrote her legitimate prescriptions, she was still concerned. When she needed the pills and couldn't afford to buy them legally, she often took a pharmacist she knew to bed. Pills were too damn expensive! The only cheap pills were aspirins, which didn't do much for her. Her resistance to medications was strong.

She still had a good supply of pills and would be feeling better if it weren't for her recent cold. She then has a series of sneezes, and reached for some Kleenex.

Chapter Thirteen

One month later
October 28, 2027

"Let Satan challenge us, as he did to Job so long ago. And, let our efforts be a fragrance of Christ to you, for we are vapor, nothing more. We will persevere in our trials, and conquer them, for we have your strength, and know that you will never give us more than we can handle. With you by our side, nothing is impossible. For you are holy, Lord. And worthy.

"In the name of your precious son, Jesus, who showed us how to act, to breathe, to live, think, and die, we pray. Amen."

"One minute and twenty seconds," thought Sam Bunker. "We've done the impossible in lawmaking, and now here is a sermon in less time than was allotted. Maybe we *can* do miracles," he thought.

The Chaplain left the chambers. The militia outside stood on each side of the closed committee doors.

"Well?" Sam said.

"So far, so good," said Tom Baker. "It's been pretty hectic these last few months, to say the least."

"No fooling!" wailed Bob Emerson.

"I think I may be ready for another bypass soon, the way we're going," surmised Steve Harning.

"My eye hurts from everything I've been writing," Frederica Wright said, wishing she'd never had cataract surgery. Her one good eye worked as hard as two. She had a pain in her eye all the time. She even felt a phantom pain in the socket where her other eye was removed.

"My congratulations to you all on the Import Act," Sam Bunker spoke. "We're getting some flak from overseas producers, and they've got their lobbying machines going. They're mad! They can't get any production facilities going in this country now so they're doubly mad. Then again, have you seen what happened to the stock market? Analysts have never seen America looking this strong since the end of the Korean War. We're off to a good start.

"The Drug Enforcement Act has the approval of the American people, even though the cost of increasing the courts, police, and prisons has been sizable, especially since we want it done as soon as possible. It has meant revamping existing facilities, buying and converting other buildings, and building new courts and prisons wherever possible. We have a deadline, and we'll meet it.

"The increase in the police has been noted by the public, and they appreciate it. Our constituents can walk the streets safely with the police visible. The Personal Rights Act has caused a decrease of eighty percent in violent crimes over that of previous years. People are more careful about violent crimes. They know that what goes around, comes around to them.

"I was given the duty to increase hospitals," Sam continued, looking down at his notes. "Emergency facilities across the country are being increased by ten to fifteen times the previous number. Some people say that we're preparing for destruction. Yes, I'll give them that," he said thoughtfully. "It's a war we're fighting. And this is a war we have to win!"

"Okay, Sam," remarked Tom Baker. "Get down from your soap box. You've got my vote," he said as he laughed.

"I do get carried away at times," Sam admitted, turning a bit red in the face. "We have to make sure that everything is ready for April 26th, when the President will address the country."

"What's the significance of April 26, 2028?" asked Tom. "That's almost six months away. Does it have something to do with us?"

"This is for the Drug Legislation Act, isn't it?" questioned Frederica.

Sam nodded his head. "If we approve the final bill today. How is the progress going on that?" he asked.

"Well," Tom Baker said. "In one month, we've covered the equivalent of one year of drug education for every kid in school from age eight on up. Most kids have been studying this two periods a day for the last month. They know what they're getting into. Even the truant children have been caught and personally tutored."

"By April, they should be experts on the subject," Sam hoped.

"I sure pray they will," replied Tom.

"How about the tobacco industry?" Sam asked.

"We've had the major tobacco growers in the country allocate and grow fifty percent of their crops as marijuana for 'research,' keeping it secret from other growers," said Frederica. "And, with our subsidies to the drug industry, pill production is at a record high, so to speak," she quipped then smiled as she said "high."

"Cute pun," said Bob.

"Is there a chance of payoffs?" asked Steve Harning.

"Not the way we're doing it," Sam knowingly said.

Frederica nodded her head. "With the slightest notice, the growers could inundate the nation with enough marijuana to provide each person with more cartons of cigarettes than they could ever smoke, and they're ready," she said with emphasis.

"Another action item you gave me," added Frederica, "was to write a Pharmacy bill giving them the status of M.D.'s. I have done that. It's short, iron-clad, and rings true. I ran it by Steve to make sure of that."

"Frederica's bill is going along as a rider with the drug legislation pending," said Sam.

"And," Sam began, "I've penned the Drug Legislation Act. It's probably the most comprehensive and powerful act in America since the writing of the Constitution itself. It too is iron-clad and far-reaching in scope. It could blow someone's mind."

"Bad pun," Tom Baker frowned sarcastically.

"Thank you," Sam said dryly.

"Give me some credit in this," cried Bob. "I did most of the writing, if you remember, Sam."

Steve thought back how he was molested by alcohol-soaked adults when he was nine years old and shivered slightly. He hoped the group knew what they were doing.

"Gentlemen, and lady," Sam said, in his deepest, most professional voice, "I want you to review this with me, if you would, please."

Everyone got a copy of the bill from Sam. They spent half an hour reading it.

"First," said Sam, after everyone finished reviewing it, "this bill permits those over the age of eighteen to buy any and all drugs they want, regardless of the drug's effect. If they want to buy five pounds of cocaine, they may. If they want to purchase heroin, they may. No drug is excluded. Psychedelics, uppers, downers, diuretics; there are no exclusions. All they have to do is go to a pharmacy, make their request and pay for it. No prescription is needed!

"Second, there are no 'dry states' with regard to drugs or alcohol. This law supersedes all local and state jurisdiction. Anyone who wants booze or any drug, will, by first amendment right for pursuit of life, liberty, and happiness, be allowed to get it."

"Can we do that?" asked Bob Emerson, thinking of the times he had secretly bought and stocked booze. "Won't the states object?"

"Probably," replied Steve. "But there is no way to get an injunction against this unless they can get a group of federal circuit court judges to go along with them. And they won't be able to. That is something I've taken care of. All the court judges know what we're trying to do, although they don't know the specific details. They also know that there are congressional bills with the presidential seal on them that will remove the judges from office if they try. Besides, this is an amendment to the Constitution we're discussing; not an easy thing to overturn."

"Sounds like quite a story, and good bluffing," Sam agreed.

"Oh, it's no bluff," Steve Harning said quietly. "Each federal court judge has been personally shown a document with his or her name written on it, stating the backing of Congress and full presidential approval. They will be removed from the bench if they step in front of us."

"What if they can be bought?" asked Bob Emerson, thinking of the many times in the past he'd heard of political corruption.

"Let me put it this way," Steve replied. "They could be offered the moon, but if they sign their names to anything against us, they will be taken out of office, tried, and convicted. I never lose a case," Steve voiced dryly, knowing full well what the Judiciary Committee could do.

"I don't either," chimed in Frederica Wright of Government Operations, smiling like it was the truth. And it was.

"What do you arrest them for?" Sam asked.

"Treason. They are tried for treason against the United States," Steve answered. "And if you know your law, the current penalty for treason is life imprisonment without bail or immediate execution by hanging. In this case, I'd push for immediate execution. They know we mean what we say. I've found it rare for someone to see a court order removing them from office, signed by the President with the seal of Congress on it, to be courageous. Hanging is such a long and messy way to die."

Sam sat quietly. He hoped that things wouldn't get out of hand. It began to sound like America was turning into a dictatorship, but he also knew that desperate people use desperate measures.

Every time Sam said "legalizing drugs" to himself, he envisioned people killing themselves. By legalizing drugs, he felt as if he was giving a loaded rifle to children without the knowledge of how to use it. His dreams involved pictures of children tying rubber straps around their arms and shooting up. He thought of his grandchildren and great-grandchildren, and told himself that he was doing what needed to be done, even though he wasn't sure of the outcome. He was scared. Scared for himself and scared for the nation. He wished he were plastered, but watching Bob Emerson struggling day to day against taking a drink put off Sam's desire to drink more.

"What about people found driving under the influence?" Tom asked.

"A mandatory sentence of seven years in jail with no parole," Steve stated. "It's a felony."

"Felony?" questioned Bob.

"Felony!" Steve thundered.

"How about people trying to get into the drug business once this starts?" Sam said, remembering the stories of the rush to California in the 1930's, and how everyone tried to make bathtub gin during prohibition.

"No problem," Frederica offered sensually, smiling with her best Government Operations smile. "We have it so there is no way drug manufacturers can expand pill production unless we give them approval. We'll keep out any newcomers, and I'm sure no drug manufacturer will want to quit the business after we make production legal. Business will be too good. We are controlling them with our limitations on how they do business. Once everything becomes legal, we'll be holding them back from saturating the public markets."

"Say," wondered Tom, "when does this all happen?"

"Once we approve it. Today if possible. The President will be giving a speech nationwide on the 26th of April," Sam said.

"Why the 26th of April?" Steve said. "You never did give us a reason for it."

"That'll give us time to make sure everything is ready," Sam told. "That date was picked randomly by the President. Beside the fact that an old girlfriend of mine had her birthday on that date, there's no reason I can think of."

"Who cares," snapped Frederica. "If you want to make sure our preparations are thorough, I understand. The sooner the better for me," she added.

"Me too," agreed Steve.

"I still have my reservations," Bob spoke up.

"I personally feel we're stepping into the biggest pile of manure we've ever imagined," worried Tom. "The smell's going to be around for a long time."

"I think so, too," spoke Sam thoughtfully.

"I so move that we pass this bill," said Frederica strongly.

"Seconded," said Steve.

"Ayes?" asked Sam by reflex.

Everyone was for it.

"Nays, for the record," Sam asked.

No sound was heard in the chamber.

"The motion passes," Sam said, slightly amazed.

"Sam, why don't you be the first one to sign it?"

Sam took the pen and wrote his name across the whole page in a beautiful script. He then handed the paper to Steve.

"I want to make sure that everyone knows I'm as much to blame as anyone else for this," Sam smiled.

Steve just grinned, signed his name with a flourish, and handed the pen to Bob, not saying a word, but with a look on his face that said that he was at peace with himself.

"I don't think John Hancock could have written a larger signature," Bob Emerson said to Sam as he wrote his signature, doing his part to sign the Drug Legislation Act into being.

"That's just 'cause Sam wants the pleasure of reading it without his glasses," Tom joked without conviction, signing with shaking hands. "He's really vain under all of his so-called midwestern humility."

"And this makes it official," Frederica concluded, as she signed her name to the bill last.

"Folks," Sam said, "we have just committed three hundred million Americans down a path that will not be forgotten. We have forced them to accept an act legalizing something many of them don't want."

"I know this is sillier than any reason for making the date the 26th of April," Tom asked, "but I'd feel better if we pray about this. As of now, it's out of our hands."

"I agree," said Bob Emerson.

Frederica held her hands out to the left and right of her. Hands were grasped and the circle was completed.

"Sam," Tom said. "You're chairman of this cockamamie group. Why don't you lead us?"

"I haven't prayed formally since I was sixteen, when I prayed that my girlfriend wasn't pregnant," Sam Bunker reminisced. "What do I say? How can I pray to someone that I haven't talked to for years?" Sam was silent for a moment they held hands; everyone lost in thought.

After a short while, Sam's eyes closed and his mouth opened to speak: "Make it work. Please, make it work!"

"Amen," said Tom.

"Amen," said the rest.

"You know, Sam," Tom spoke with amazement, "that's the first time I ever heard you say anything in less than five minutes. Maybe we have a trend starting."

"Go to hell," Sam snarled.

"See, folks," said Tom, "he's doing it again."

Everyone laughed, but as Sam left holding the signed bill, his pounding heart echoed his prayer through his head. He walked slowly, taking the long way from Capitol Hill to the White House; the military guard flanking him as a precaution. "Make it work. Please, make it work!"

Prescription for Mayhem

Chapter Fourteen

Six months later
April 26, 2028

"Nine o'clock on the west coast and midnight on the east coast. This is not exactly the best time for a live statement from the White House," thought the President. But then again, the current President was known for being a little more imaginative than the Democratic Party felt was good. After reinstating the lunch program for school age children, insuring they would have at least one good meal a day, he had done much in his power to show Americans that he cared. Although few said it, the President was a man for the people and their rights.

"Ladies and gentlemen," came an off-camera voice, "the President of the United States of America."

"My friends," the President began, as he looked straight into the camera. "You re-elected me a little more than two years ago. My campaign promise was to do something about the moral decline of America, especially regarding the areas of violent crime, drug use, illiteracy and unemployment, all without raising taxes.

"I recently signed into law the Personal Rights Act, making the punishment equal to the crime. This has decreased violent crimes dramatically. Consideration of the individual is now as important as freedom is to this nation of ours. The bill was long in coming, but it was with pride that I signed it into law.

"Secondly, I wish to address the Import Act. America has grown soft and it is easier to sell something as a middleman than produce it. If we don't produce goods, we are nothing but a nation of shopkeepers. To keep the nation strong, we have to show that we can make things from scratch. Some of you aren't happy with that, but, my friends, it is no longer a bargain to have goods produced elsewhere. We must make goods here at home.

"Thirdly, I would like to address the Drug Education Act. This act was designed to give children the knowledge of what drugs can do to them, from the most harmless of drugs to the most addicting. All children still in school have been educated in drug awareness. Even truants have been lassoed and taught about drugs. I am proud to say that in the last few months the children of America now know what they are doing. If people know what they are doing, they then have the power to make choices and live their lives any way they wish.

"Fourth, I would like to address the Drug Enforcement Act. This act is meant to punish those who would enslave our children and citizens without their knowledge. It has been one of the finest documents I've ever had the privilege to sign. Anyone pushing drugs illegally is subjected to a twenty-five year jail sentence without any hope of parole. We are increasing the courts, prisons, and police forces throughout this glorious country of ours to make this a reality in days to come.

"While on the subject of drugs, I'd like to review the findings of the *Guidance and Direction Committee* formed under my administration. They have worked to contain and finally control the drug problems our nation faces. It has cost billions of dollars a year to fight drugs in terms of loss of manpower hours, harm to the individual, and going after the pushers. The estimate by the committee is that the drug cost is at least one-third the defense budget cost, possibly more. We can't afford that abuse any longer, hence the introduction of a new bill.

"What was given to me was a proposal to stop the drug problem forever! I spent a great deal of time deliberating about this and am convinced that it is a sound proposal. It is time to stop going in circles, and time to rectify errors."

"The errors, you ask? Let me refresh your memory. During the bustling 1920's, Congress prohibited the sale and manufacturing of alcohol although the people wanted it. The criminals provided the alcohol the public wanted even though it was illegal. Criminal elements grew like weeds and are still here today. But criminals didn't stop there. Gambling, prostitution, pornography, and anything else that brought in money was provided by the criminal element.

"Due to public pressure, Congress changed its mind and made alcohol legal again. The criminal element submerged but did not disappear. That criminal element is still with us today. But only for today."

"Tomorrow is a new day, and a new start for America. In the past, the government felt that it was its job to protect you from unsavory elements and limit your freedom of choice. We will no longer limit you. For the fifth item I have just signed into being is an act that ensures you the right to make your own choices. It is the Drug Legislation Act. I am convinced that it is vital to our nation's welfare. Let me tell you the particulars.

"Starting at twelve midnight, Pacific Standard Time, anyone over the age of eighteen may purchase drugs from any licensed pharmacy or drug outlet. Whether it be methadone, heroin, or cocaine, it will be available starting tomorrow. You will no longer need a prescription from a doctor to obtain medication. This is a grave responsibility and is now the law of the land. We have handed the freedom to control your own lives back to you. You can end your life or begin it. It is, my friends, your choice.

"There are no restrictions nor limitations on what drugs you may buy, as long as you do so through legally licensed pharmacies or other outlets licensed by Congress. However, there are some considerations you need to know.

"One. It is now law that if you are found operating a vehicle of any type and you are under the influence of drugs or alcohol, you will be subjected to a blood test. You cannot refuse the blood test. The imprisonment for this offense is seven years with no possibility for parole. You earn seven years in jail without parole for subjecting the public to possible danger. It is a mandatory jail sentence and a felony. Mandatory. Simply stated, you cannot drive if there is a chance that you might harm your fellow man. Life is sacred, and consideration for the life of others is equivalent to life itself.

"Two. As a reminder, the penalty for selling drugs through non- licensed outlets carries the penalty of a twenty-five year prison sentence, without the possibility of parole.

"Three. This law supersedes state jurisdiction, unless they have an election and obtain a seventy-five percent vote for drug abstinence. This is a seventy-five percent vote from *all* of the adults in the state, not only registered voters. The important part of the Drug Legislation Act is that you now have the power once taken from you returned. Use this power wisely.

"The sixth item I have signed into law is an act authorizing pharmacists nationwide to dispense any and all drugs, and to treat and diagnose problems. If you have questions about drugs, pharmacists have been further educated in the actions, interactions, and precautions of all drugs produced. They can treat all diseases from colds to bacterial infections. They will help guide you on the road to understanding your body and yourselves. Copies of the acts are available to all of the media following my speech. That is all for this evening. Good night. And may God bless you."

"This has been a speech by the President of the United States," said the off-camera announcer. "Please stay tuned to this channel as our analysts dissect and discuss the President's address to the nation."

Sam Bunker sat in his library at his Georgetown home and turned off the television with his remote control. It was quiet. His wife was visiting relatives in Ireland and the servants were off for the night. He sipped a Scotch and soda, reclining comfortably in his favorite chair.

"The press will have a field day with this one," he said to the empty room. The newspapers would probably be putting out an extra edition. Television shows would be interrupted, and in the morning, all hell could break loose. Pharmacies were going to be inundated by requests for drugs. He hoped that his group had made sure the supply would exceed the demand. Marijuana cigarettes were going to be on the streets in one or two days. "Hell," he said aloud, "even the most conservative polls say that forty percent of the people over forty years old have tried drugs at least once and support drug legislation for legalization."

He knew there must be some celebrating in the streets, but he hoped it wouldn't get out of hand. "The President did a good job of presenting the act to the nation," he mused as he took another sip of his drink. He had some grave apprehensions about the response to the act. It wasn't the people who were for the act, but those against the act that worried him. The nation was going to be caught in a crossfire between the M.A.A., P.A.A., those taking drugs, and those not taking drugs. He sipped his drink and prayed that such a conflict wouldn't happen.

Sam smiled as he thought about his half-assed prayer in committee almost six months ago. He stuttered like a school kid and sounded about as coherent. His smile vanished as he realized that the church was definitely going to be against the act. "The Catholics, Baptists, Presbyterians, Lutherans, Methodists, Congregationalists, Jews, Mormons and every other church group will probably be out for our blood," he surmised. He knew that what he was doing was right, and he wasn't afraid of problems, nor of death. He had lived his life to the fullest, and there were parts that made him sad when he thought of them. For a moment, he remembered his first wife, twirling the swizzle stick in his drink.

He was a little concerned about the civil rights activists. "Those jerks think they have the power to protect the people, instead of letting us live our own lives," he growled into his drink. "This'll show them."

The phone rang. Sam leaned over to the phone on the end table next to the lounge chair and answered it.

"Sam Bunker?" said the voice, "This is Pat Heeley at the Times. Do you have any comments on..."

Sam slammed the phone on the cradle. The press was caught with its eyes closed and napping, as was everyone else. He hoped that the Mafia was caught short as well. He swirled his drink as he thought about Emil Wardlaw and the other eight members of Congress whom he'd forced to leave. "Mafia, all Mafia," he said softly. He hoped that none of his so-called ex-Congress Mafia 'friends' would be able to enter the legal drug business. With drug licenses being controlled by Congress and a court order preventing a pharmaceutical house or outlet from selling common stock or selling the business without Congressional approval, it might work.

Sam got up and went to mix another drink. He prayed that he and his committee covered their asses and loopholes, as they were moving forward quickly. He was pouring his drink just as he heard a siren. He made the drink strong and hoped the sirens wouldn't become commonplace in the days to come. He drank the drink quickly, belched, put the glass on the table and went upstairs to bed.

Tomorrow, the sun was going to be rising over a new country.

Prescription for Mayhem

Chapter Fifteen

Jim woke around eight, happy that he had another day off. He was sore from digging a drain pipe for the plumbing in the new building his firm had contracted to handle. He turned on the television to help him wake up.

"Dr. Jones, as head of the Medical Association of America," said the commentator, "what do you think of the new act the Congress passed yesterday?"

Jim's eyes focused on three people before the TV cameras.

"I think that the President was totally wrong in approving this amendment to the Bill of Rights," Dr. Jones said. "People aren't ready to have drugs legalized. They might do damage to themselves. We have to protect them."

"What about the law making all pharmacists able to diagnose and treat any disease?"

"Pharmacists know pharmaceuticals, but they still don't know the best way to treat disease," said Dr. Jones. "They may not know what each drug is good for, even though they know how to compound them."

"I disagree," voiced Dr. Freudiger, head of the Pharmaceutical Association of America, who was sitting next to Dr. Jones. "Pharmacists understand the nature, effects, and side effects of drugs much more than the average medical doctor."

"This is different," retorted Dr. Jones, "from just prescribing Inderal for heart problems."

"Inderal," said Dr. Jones to the moderator for the benefit of the laymen listening in, "is the most prescribed drug in America for heart problems and blood pressure problems, aside from water pills, that is."

"I challenge you," spoke Dr. Freudiger, rubbing his head a bit, "to tell me what the side effects, contradictions, and precautions for Inderal are. Here and now."

"This is absurd," shouted Dr. Jones.

"Liar," Dr. Freudiger said succinctly so that the sound of the word could be heard throughout the sound stage. "You don't know them. You might be able to derive one or two, but you don't know the rest without a PDR book in front of you. You are a fraud!"

"This is libel," Dr. Jones warned.

"Not libel, you pathetic fool," Dr. Freudiger stated quietly, but firmly to the camera. "If you take me up on this challenge for what you say is 'the most prescribed drug in America,' I will gladly show you how little you and the rest of the physicians in America know about pharmacology. Remember who taught you pharmacology in medical school? Never mind, I'll tell you. The pharmacology courses for medical students were and are taught by pharmacists."

Dr. Jones sat quietly, thinking of a reply.

"The fraud is over," Dr. Freudiger told him grimly.

Jim changed channels, confused a bit by what he heard. After a few minutes he heard a summary of the President's speech, legalizing drugs nationwide. He went downstairs for the morning paper and saw the headline, "Drugs Legal." Just for good measure, he checked the date, noted that it was April 27th, and not April Fools' day. He went upstairs and sat at the living room table with the paper in his lap, trying to absorb what had just happened. "Drugs are legal?" he wondered. He went to the phone book to call up the nearest all-night pharmacy.

"Hi," he said in a disguised voice to the person who came on the line. "Can you connect me with the pharmacist, please?"

"Pharmacy," answered another voice, "may I help you?"

"Yes, I was wondering how much a gram of cocaine is selling for."

"One minute please," the voice replied. "I'll check on it and get right back to you."

After a pause, the voice came back on the line.

"I'm sorry sir, we don't have grams of cocaine for sale."

"I was right," Jim uttered, pleased with himself for his ingenuity. "This must be total bullshit."

"The smallest size we have is a two hundred fifty gram bottle. The price of it is six dollars and seventy-nine cents. Would you like me to hold it for you until later?"

"No, thanks," Jim mumbled, dazedly, as he hung up the phone.

He sat there dumbfounded. Just a month ago he was paying one hundred fifty to two hundred bucks for a gram of cocaine. Now it was selling for seven bucks for two hundred fifty grams. Two weeks ago that would have cost him over fifty thousand bucks. Now it's less than seven bucks. Jim started to laugh. "It's crazy," he cried, "the world has gone crazy."

"It's insane!" screamed Julie Giuliano. "The world has gone nuts! What do we do? I shelled out billions of dollars over the last two weeks for drugs to cover the the next fiscal year. It was going to be our best year ever. Cocaine, heroin, speed, and all the rest of next year's drug crop have our lives tied up with them. We have only a small amount of capital left for operating expenses. What do we do?"

"Don't pay," stated the family accountant in Julie's ear.

"Too late," he said. "It's paid for."

"Then sell it and recoup your losses."

"If we try to move that much stuff, the feds will catch someone down the line, and the dominoes will fall."

"Can we move the stuff we have now?" the accountant asked.

"We can't compete," Julie bitterly said. "We don't have a license. Besides, why would anyone pay a thousand dollars for heroin when they can now get it for three and a half bucks from Thrifty's drugstore? What do we do?"

Julie stood, getting angrier by the minute. He was the tenth head of the family. He had a heritage to live up to. Tens of thousands of family members depended on him for their livelihood. Now he felt that they might be filing for welfare benefits if he didn't do something.

"Tell me," Julie asked the sky, "How can we change this? Who do we kill?"

"I don't know," spoke the accountant thoughtfully. "You have to talk to your nephew, Emil Wardlaw, about that. It's a congressional act that did it."

"Get Emil in here now," Julie ordered, then got a drink to help him forget the throbbing hangover he had.

An hour later, the former head of the Appropriations Committee for the House of Representatives, Emil Wardlaw, stood shaking before his uncle. Julie Giuliano was taking deep breaths, and exhaling through his nose. His teeth were clenched and his eyes bloodshot.

"Emil," he asked softly, "Do you remember telling me that we didn't have anything to fear from Congress?"

The accountant stepped back near the door. The last time Julie Giuliano used that quiet voice was the time he gave the kill command to burn an apartment house to the ground, killing seventy-five people in it.

"Yes, Uncle Giuliano," he answered with fear in his eyes.

"Well?"

"I don't know what happened," he answered truthfully.

"You don't know what happened?" Julie bellowed as he clenched his hands around Emil's neck, lifting him off the ground. Emil started to choke.

"Tell me, you snotty little brat, what do we do?"

Emil made choking sounds.

"Well, you little shit, you've harmed the family more than anyone ever has! What do we do?"

Emil was turning blue.

"Well?!?"

"He's suffocating," the accountant noticed. "He can't answer you while you're choking him."

At that moment Emil's eyes rolled up in his head as he collapsed in Julie's arms. Julie dropped Emil and splashed some vodka on Emil's face. He knew that Emil would be coming around in seconds.

Emil woke and realized where he was and what his life was worth. He was in hell and his life wasn't worth anything.

"Emil," Julie asked, angrily. "How do we get out of this mess?"

"I can see about getting us a license to distribute and produce drugs," Emil quickly replied, pondering every word because his life depended on it. "That way, we can become legitimate businessmen and still turn some profit."

"That's a start," agreed Julie, calming down a bit, thinking that he had enough capital to float his organization for a year or two if necessary.

"I'll try to figure out who the guys are behind this," Emil replied thoughtfully. "...And I think I have a good idea."

"You better get back to me as soon as you can," warned Julie Giuliano, "...And I mean soon." He nodded his head toward Emil, dismissing him. Emil left, thanking his uncle with every step he took toward the door.

Elaine woke up, still amazed at what she had seen on TV the night before. News flashes on all the channels announced that all drugs were now legal. She knew that her life was going to be changed. She no longer would have to depend on friends for pharmaceuticals. All she had to do was walk to a drugstore and request whatever she wanted. Elaine knew she had enough of a stash to get her through the days to come pretty comfortably and there was no real need to test the system. She hoped it wasn't something the government would give and then take away because of public protest. She hoped the change was here to stay.

She decided that she would stay home, take some of the LSD she was saving for a special occasion, call a friend to come over and ask him to bring some food. If she felt in the mood, she might take the guy to bed. She loved the feeling of psychedelics. They made her feel free to soar and leave the world behind.

During the coffee break, Mary talked with the girls in the office about the changes in the law. They were all happy about it, but no one could figure out why Congress would ever do a crazy thing like that. Mary was especially happy. Now she could get any drug she ever wanted at bargain prices. She could get high if she wanted. Grass would be available and so would Valium and other downers to keep her a little quieter. And, at long last, she could give Carl Friedman the brush-off. She no longer needed him to get drugs for her. Besides, he scared her. There was something about him that impressed her as evil. She went back to her work to get it halfway done by lunch time.

Sabrina was happy about the news. Although she had never taken drugs, she was glad that now she had a choice. It bothered her when the government stifled people and she was pleased that it was now a thing of the past. Her friends who were caught pushing drugs were still in jail. Now that the Drug Enforcement Act came into effect, all existing prison sentences were retroactive. So they were going to be in jail for a long time. Surprisingly, it was also announced that persons caught on possession charges would be granted amnesty if their jail sentence was longer than seven years. Those in prison with less than seven years of service would still be incarcerated.

Kevin was tired. He had worked in a squad car half the night, running down accidents and trying to keep party-goers celebrating the Drug Legislation Act off the streets. There were more accidents than there should have been for a weekday but most of the offenders were stoned. He didn't know what to make of it as they took drivers downtown, got blood samples and put them in jail until the results of their blood tests came out. The new antibody tests for barbiturates, THC, uppers, and everything else made it easier to convict a person of driving under the influence. If they were convicted, it was a seven-year sentence.

"The stupid fools," he said, as he thought that a seven-year jail sentence would deter most people. "Some people just have to test the limits of the law. Their mistake," he shook his head, wishing them out of his mind.

It made Kevin feel good, knowing that the pushers would get punished. The users, he felt, just wanted to be happy. He believed that using drugs meant a loss of self-control, and he was still against it. He was worried about the American public mishandling this new freedom.

The phone rang. Kevin feared it was his watch commander, telling him that he "volunteered" himself for a double shift that night. Kevin really wanted the day to rest up and he had planned to relax that evening. The police were afraid that people would start celebrating tonight. Grumbling, he lifted the receiver.

"Hello? Yeah, it's me. Do a double shift tonight? I guess so. No, I didn't have anything planned. Okay. Bye."

Chapter Sixteen

Later that afternoon

Doc Browning was pissed. He was really upset about the Drug Legislation Act. He was amazed that such a bill passed through Congress. All these laws; the Drug Enforcement Act, the Drug Legislation Act, the Import Act, and Personal Rights Act were all amendments to the Bill of Rights. He couldn't figure out what the lobbyists for the M.A.A. in Washington were doing. Where were his dues going, if not to keep his profession intact? Why didn't they stop it earlier or get an injunction?

He was sure his salary would be cut soon, especially with the increase in salary to pharmacists. That was insult enough, he thought. With all the student loans for his undergraduate education, four more years of medical education and the family practice residency, he wasn't sure when he would be paying anyone back.

His answering machine recorded an urgent notice from the local medical society. There would be an emergency meeting regarding the new laws, but he couldn't go. He had to change and get to work in the emergency room, where the evening shift was soon getting underway. He expected everything to hit the fan with drugs on the loose.

On the way to work, he heard a radio announcement by a cigarette company about a smooth marijuana cigarette that was supposed to be "mellower" than the rest. "Only in California," he said. He then realized that the same thing was probably happening nationwide. The drug industry would soon pick up the pace, he thought. He could envision it now, "Seeing the world alive, vibrant, and joyful once more. Mellaril; a cut above all the other antidepressants. Not to be taken with alcohol and not for pregnant women. See your druggist for details."

He cringed at the possible damage the drug industry could inflict. In prior days, their job was to produce new drugs and get the medical world's approval through experience and clinical trials. Now, the physician was no longer a middleman. The manufacturers could take their products directly to the public. "All hell is breaking loose," he muttered as he arrived at the emergency room.

He was also upset that his current car, a Fiat, sounded like it was near death. He had to get a new car. Just had to. He was holding out for that Ferrari he wanted. He was getting closer every day to making the down payment for it.

"Thank God you're here early, doctor," uttered the ward clerk, taking his coat and briefcase. The clerk handed him a medium set of greens. He changed his clothes and walked into the emergency room.

"All hell's breaking loose," screamed the nurse practitioner. They had seven orderlies holding down a dainty twelve-year-old girl. The child struggled against the people and when she gripped the bed rails with her petite hands, the railing bent under the force of her exertions.

"Holy Christ!" exlaimed one of the orderlies, hoping the girl wouldn't get a good grip on him.

"PCP," Doc Browning cried aloud, and then ordered for them to pump her stomach. The little girl struggled as a tube was shoved up her nose to turn and end up in the stomach. The vacuum came on, but nothing came out once the tube was in place.

"Shit," he groaned as he started looking for puncture marks. He found one tiny mark near her thighs, just over a superficial vein.

"Probably a hallucinogen," he thought. "But it could be something stronger." He wasn't sure.

"We have to draw some blood for an antibody assay."

He went in close with a needle and signaled everyone to hold the girl steady, so that he wouldn't sever the vein.

When the needle was in her arm, after a few moments he attached the first and then second of two glass vials. She squirmed as in agony and broke loose from the grip they had on her. Her arm with the needle swung against the bedpost, breaking the second vial and causing the needle to rip clean through the vein. Blood poured out all over the emergency room.

"God!" he shouted. "I've got to stop that blood."

"Get that first sample to the lab, stat!" he ordered.

The nurse handed the sample to an orderly.

"I can't get her to stay still," cried one of the orderlies.

"The hell with it," said Doc Browning. "Get the gas."

A nurse took the anesthesia gas and held it over the young girl's nose and mouth. It took a minute for the child to calm down.

"I don't know what's in her," Doc Browning said tiredly. "Keep her under lightly, if you can. It's possible that her heart may stop, so hook up an EKG while we wait for the sample to come back from the lab. I'll start getting the glass particles out from her arm and suture the wound."

After the particles were out, Doc Browning rubbed his elbow. The girl had bruised it during the struggle. He kept massaging it as he walked back to the waiting room. An older man approached him.

"Doctor," he said.

"Yes," Doc Browning replied, reaching for a paper cup at the water fountain.

"I'm the father of the young girl you're treating," he said, watching the far wall.

Doc Browning nodded, wondering what kind of father would allow a twelve-year-old daughter to overdose on drugs.

"It's a terrible thing that's happened," the father spoke, looking at the floor.

Doc Browning nodded.

"Will she be fine?" he asked.

"She's stable for the moment, but we're waiting for the lab results."

"Thank you, doctor," he said, breathing easier.

"How did this happen?" Doc Browning asked.

"Her older cousin, Arnold, eighteen last month, showed up at my house, and forced my little baby to take the drug or he was going to hit her. Arnold has always been sweet on her, and a friend told Arnold that the drug was supposed to make the person love the world."

"Do you know the name of the drug?" asked Doc Browning.

"No, and Arnold wouldn't tell us. And now, he can't tell us."

"Why is that?" questioned Doc Browning.

"He's in prison. As God is my witness, I swear I'll make him pay for what he did to my little girl."

Doc Browning was called to the desk and got the results from the lab tests. He felt that she was going to be all right, but he wanted to consult the *Physician's*

Desk Reference for the drug dosage he was going to give the girl, just to be sure. Another ambulance arrived at the emergency room entrance.

"What's up?" asked the ward clerk.

"Some geek on downers fell asleep on the freeway and ran into a tanker full of acetylene. Twenty-one are dead, and the other thirty-five injured are being transported to this emergency room and five others," spoke the ambulance driver hurriedly.

"The driver should be glad he didn't survive," Doc Browning said, thinking about the lawsuits.

"Oh, no," said the ambulance driver in a hurry to answer another call. "He did. But, after the Personal Rights Act is done with him, he'll wish he hadn't."

Craig arrived at church for the meeting. He liked to be early, but traffic was awful. Drug-related accidents were everywhere, and the sounds of ambulances filled the night. The freeways were clogged and it looked like the traditional weekend traffic jam might extend into tomorrow morning. Craig's church was in Hollywood, as was his route, three blocks east of Hollywood and Vine. They had a midweek prayer meeting on Wednesday, but he was called at home by the church for an emergency meeting that night. He didn't mind. He liked to pray, and he hoped for some insight into God and the drug situation through this emergency meeting. It felt good to be needed, even if only for prayer power. Craig seldom felt needed.

"Lord, we are lost like lambs, and each has turned to their own way. Our brains are befuddled. Our goal is unclear. Please guide us and direct us. Put your mighty hands on this problem and solve it, we pray. For this problem is too big for us to handle. We're scared of drugs. For you are the vine, and we are the branches, and without you, we can't support ourselves. In the name of your precious son, Jesus, who died for each and every one of us, we pray. Amen."

With that opening prayer, the pastor of the church explained to the congregation how the Drug Legislation Act worked.

"It's a temptation," cried one elderly woman, as the pastor finished talking.

"Amen," agreed another.

"It's the Devil," offered a former bootlegger.

"But who can resist?" asked another. "There is none holy, no not one," quoting the Bible, but forgetting the verse.

"Hold on here," spoke Elder Perkins, a retired lawyer and member of the church since his mother brought him to Sunday school over eighty years ago. "You all know me?"

"We do," shouted members of the congregation.

"It sounds like a speech coming," the pastor said to himself, prophetically.

"I'm a recovered alcoholic," admitted Elder Perkins.

"Amen," said a few church members.

"When I used to drink, I consulted the Bible concerning alcohol and things like that."

"And...?" said a voice in the back softly.

"And, God does not state that you specifically should 'force' your brethren to do whatever you want them to. That means force them not to take drugs or drink. The Bible does say that neither a drunkard, nor reveler, nor person poor in character will enter the rest of Christ. Even Saint Paul wrote in the book of Timothy that a little wine is okay from time to time. You have to depend on the power of God to keep you away from temptations."

"It's the Devil speaking," screamed one person, who saw the Devil more than she ever saw God.

"Amen," another habitually voiced.

"Let me ask you all," said a woman, "Is it not true that some of the most powerful witnesses for Christ are those who escaped the snare and lure of drugs, thanks to the power of God?"

"Amen," a group of reformed addicts said with conviction in the back of the sanctuary.

"What do we do?" asked a retired schoolteacher.

"Think of it as being similar to alcohol," replied the pastor, taking the lectern again. "And fight against it, in the home and on the streets. Don't take the drugs! Resist temptations daily! And help the others who succumb to drugs. I'm not sure we can make the laws go away. But there is one thing we can do; pray. Please close your eyes, and let us commune with the God the Father of Abraham, Jacob, Isaac, our Lord Jesus, and you and me. For He is worthy, and willing, and He is able, Lord, He is able."

Members of the congregation closed their eyes and began to pray. Craig didn't claim to know everything, but he knew that Christ was the center of his life. It was Christ who gave meaning to his existence. Christ showed him how to live and Christ said that He would live with and teach anyone who believed in Him. Craig quietly asked Christ to show him the way.

Craig knew that with the new law, it was easier to lose God in the shuffle and join the Devil's army. Drugs were to him just another way for people to forget their brothers and sisters.

After the meeting ended, Craig went home and did his usual night Bible study and went to bed. He tossed and turned, with a nightmare of how someone spiked the punch at an office party. Craig was so drugged he couldn't sort the mail into the proper bins. This nightmare scared him so much that he woke up in a sweat.

Chapter Seventeen

The Next Day
April 27, 2028

Jim felt like crap. Ambulance sirens had wailed all night. And once the sirens started, all of the neighborhood dogs had to join in, howling.

He had slept fitfully, and it felt like it was going to be a long day. A sewer line had to be dug in West Hollywood. He jumped into the shower, then put some tapes on the stereo. He took his cup of coffee and wake-up joint out on the balcony with his morning paper and watched the traffic below.

He was upset. He'd gotten a call about his friend who used to sell him drugs. His friend had been caught by the police, and his wife was trying to raise a half million dollar bail bond for him. She was calling everyone in his black book for help. If he didn't donate money, she might snitch to the cops. But it didn't matter to him because drugs were now legal. If she said that he pushed drugs, that was another matter. He had always paid cash; so there was no way to trace anything to him. He had apologized to her for not having money to loan and she had said she understood.

Jim went to his stash and threw out all the illegal drugs. He wrote himself a note to go to a pharmacy after work for drugs with a legitimate pharmacy's name on it. That way he wouldn't have to worry about the twenty-five-year jail sentence if he were caught. He imagined all the pushers were going crazy. All the farmers in the mountains growing marijuana must be experiencing the same panic. It would be hard for them to go back to farming tomatoes and cabbage after the good life. "Yes sir," Jim thought, "illegal drug manufacturers and pushers are sure going to be unhappy."

Emil Wardlaw went to the phone booth, put in enough money for a three-minute call and waited with a piece of paper in his hand. The phone rang twice and Uncle Giuliano answered.

"The people responsible are the *Guidance and Direction Committee*. All laws originated through them," said Emil.

"Who?" said Julie softly, taking a pencil and paper in hand.

"Bob Emerson, E-M-E-R-S-O-N, Tom Baker, B-A-K-E-R, Steve Harning, H-A-R-N-I-N-G, Frederica Wright, W-R-I-G-H-T, and Sam Bunker, B-U-N-K-E-R. Five in all."

"Sam Bunker is the head of the committee," Emil said, remembering what Sam had done to him.

Julie put a check mark next to Bunker's name.

"Got it," said Julie. He hung up the phone for a split second, and then dialed a telephone number he knew by heart.

Julie's accountant was more worried about the gardeners than anybody else around him. The government literacy law subpoenaed everyone who wasn't literate in English, according to the time they'd been in America. Deportations were happening all over. Everyone except the native-born Americans had to take a literacy test. The accountant knew that most good gardeners they'd hired were cheap and didn't speak English.

Jim thumbed through the evening paper he bought at a liquor store. An article described ten churches in the area that had set up twenty-four hour telephone hotlines and prayer vigils in response to the new drug laws. The article included a long list of churches and synagogues for prayer groups and information centers.

"Just like the church to capitalize on people who can't hold their liquor and other things," Jim muttered.

After work, Jim went to the pharmacy. He was amused that his shopping list of drugs was such a bargain. "Gimme a hundred Quaaludes, no, make that two hundred Quaaludes, fifty Biphedamines number twenty, the black ones, a quarter key of cocaine, some speed, make it fifty, and a key of grass," Jim ordered.

"We have everything but the marijuana, sir," said the pharmacy's technician. "The only marijuana we have is in cigarette form at the front counters.

I'm afraid we don't sell it loose. If you'd like a special request, we can always special order it through the main office."

"Nah, that's okay," said Jim, taking the drugs and the bill. He stopped by the cigarette and tobacco area. All the major companies had added a line of marijuana cigarettes.

"This is great," he thought. "Now it's legal to smoke. And they're pre-rolled and filtered. Life is wonderful!"

He gave the cashier a twenty and a five and pocketed the change. On the way out, Jim read a prominent sign in front of the door, reminding patrons that it was a felony to operate any vehicle under the influence of alcohol or drugs, and that the penalty would be seven years in jail without parole.

He got to his car, put the carton of marijuana cigarettes and drugs on the front seat and opened up a pack. He lit up a joint and sat in the car for a few seconds. He wanted a beer and considered going to a bar to drink one, but his dress shirts were trashed and he needed new ones.

He started the car and drove toward the mall for a new shirt, when he heard a siren and saw flashing lights coming from a motorcycle behind him.

"Holy shit," he cried. "The cops!"

He drove the car to the curb and threw the drugs under the side seat. He tried to push the carton of marijuana cigarettes under the seat, but they wouldn't fit.

"Sir," said the policeman, Kevin Manila, approaching the driver's side window, "please step out of the car."

Jim slowly stepped out. He was scared and remembered the penalty for driving under the influence of drugs was a sentence of seven years with no parole.

Kevin Manila looked at Jim Auchstetter. He noted that Jim had long hair and was fairly short, even with his boots on. The policeman asked for Jim's license and looked at it.

"You made an illegal turn on that last signal you passed," Kevin said, taking off his motorcycle gloves. "The signs say that no turns are allowed from three o'clock until seven o'clock. I'm afraid I'm going to have to write you up on it. It's just barely six forty-five now."

"He's not going to nail me for drugs," Jim thought exuberantly. "This is great."

He watched the officer, getting his ticket book from the saddlebags on his motorcycle.

"I'm sorry, sir," Jim said, trying to get out of the ticket, "but I don't know this neighborhood. I just stopped to get something from the market. I'm sorry."

Kevin look at Jim, then smelled the grass. He figured that Jim was just celebrating the end of the day, probably on his way home for some beers.

"Sir," Kevin asked, "how many joints have you had this evening?"

"Joints," lied Jim, trying his best to figure out how to evade the question. "Joints? What joints?"

"Sir," Kevin stated. "I can smell them. Would you like to give me everything from your car willingly, or do I have to radio for assistance?"

"Look, I've only had part of one little cigarette! Here's the pack," he showed, handing it to the officer.

Kevin looked at the pack of cigarettes. There was only one cigarette missing. He thought that Jim didn't appear to be under the influence. Jim looked more embarrassed than anything else.

"Have you had anything else?" Kevin asked, looking at Jim's face. "No sir," Jim spoke honestly, realizing that he had a bag containing all sorts of drugs under his seat.

"I'd like to look in your car, if it's okay," Kevin told, calling for a backup from the motorcycle radio.

"Please," pleaded Jim. "I didn't do anything. I just made a turn fifteen minutes early. I'm not even from around here. You have my license. You can see I'm not stoned."

"Yes sir," Kevin said without thinking, seeing that his backup had arrived. He informed the other policeman of his plans and started to search the car. He found the carton of marijuana cigarettes and the bag of drugs. He looked inside the bag and found cocaine, quaaludes, downers, and uppers. "This guy must be having a hell of a party," he thought, making sure there was a legitimate receipt from a drugstore and that there were pharmacy labels on the bottles.

The other motorcycle cop talked to Kevin for a moment, and then took off.

"Sir," Kevin told, "I'm letting you off with a warning this time about turning left on a no-turn posted sign. Please watch the time if you do this again or you may possibly do some harm. And just as a reminder, should I have justifiable cause, or think you're under the influence, I could take you downtown and book you. You could serve a seven-year stretch if the blood test is against you, so please try to watch what you take."

"I'm free?" asked Jim dumbfounded.

"Yes, sir," said Kevin, returning the drugs to Jim. "You're free."

"Thank you, sir," Jim took a deep breath of relief.

"Be careful, sir," Kevin warned, moving toward his motorcycle.

"I sure will," Jim promised, getting back into his car. "And thank you for the warning. It'll never happen again."

Kevin went back on his motorcycle and returned to patrolling his area. He was glad that he could give someone a warning who would be better for it. He liked to avoid tickets whenever possible. He thought Jim seemed like a nice enough guy.

Jim signaled, and slowly pulled back into traffic.

"Asshole," he told himself, thinking about the cop.

It took a long time to get to the mall. Traffic was heavy and there were several accidents. At a stoplight, he saw a girl he had seen before in his neighborhood. He thought her name was Sabrina. She was carrying a huge art portfolio and was walking towards an art gallery.

Her hair was tied back in a barrette. The dress she wore looked all wrong on her. Her dress was too tight and her shoulders looked hunched. Her shoes had low heels, not more than an inch off the ground. Her hands looked strong.

When Jim got to the mall, he had to maneuver past an accident right in the middle of the parking lot. A crowd had gathered to look at an accident. Some man who had taken too many drugs thought he was Superman and jumped off the building. Jim looked at the bloody remains as he walked into the mall.

Jim walked into the shirt store and noticed that some of the shelves were almost empty. He wasn't sure if they were doing inventory or just had a big sale. He found the shirts he wanted and asked the salesman what was going on.

"You mean the shelves?" the salesman asked.

"Yeah," replied Jim. "I've been coming here for years, and never saw such poor inventory."

"They do look rather bare," admitted the salesman, looking at the shelves.

"That's what I said," spoke Jim further. "Why?"

"We're waiting for a shipment to come in."

"What's going on?" asked Jim, not understanding the lack of service.

"It seems the shipment has been fouled up in getting to us, sir," the salesman began. "The clothing arrived, as usual, from Taiwan or from Hong Kong to the port of Los Angeles. Unfortunately, a shipping and receiving clerk was, uh, stoned, so to speak. It appears he shipped the goods by rail to a foreign mail-order house in Durham, on the East coast. The foreign mail-order house recognized the mistake and called the shipping firm.

"Not taking any chances, the firm hired a trucking company to deliver the goods back to Los Angeles, but they think the truck driver took, or was given, some peyote, and lost control of the truck and died. There are rumors of an eyewitness who reported that the driver went crazy."

"So where are the shirts now?" asked Jim.

"No one seems to know," shrugged the salesman. "And this all occurred before the Drug Legislation Act started yesterday. Incredible, isn't it?"

"What a story," exclaimed Jim.

"Yes sir," replied the salesman and rang up the bill.

Jim left the store with the shirts. On the way home, he noticed that a lot of gasoline stations had "No Gas" signs. He didn't think about it too much because he had just filled his tank that morning.

Jim wondered about other consumer goods. He had enough clothing for a while and all the appliances and items he had at home still worked. He knew he had pretty simple tastes. He needed a few clothes, an apartment, someone to share his bed, and a little food and wine. "Food and wine," he said to himself. If there were ever a shortage of food, he knew people would stock up as much as possible.

Jim drove toward the supermarket. It was time to stock up on food for a few months, just in case.

The crowds at the supermarket were grabbing everything they could. Everyone was pushing and shoving.

"I better pick up a fire extinguisher in the morning," Jim reminded himself. He needed two box boys to help him to his car. He had bought three shopping carts worth of groceries.

Chapter Eighteen

One week later
May 1, 2028

Elaine was mad. She received a notice from Medi-Cal in Sacramento, stating that her government assistance would soon end. She depended on that check. The check provided food, clothes, and more importantly, medicines. Rent was taken care of by her managing job. She couldn't help it if she was always sick. She just had a low resistance to disease.

She was just getting over another sore throat and flu, and didn't feel well enough to get out of bed much. She felt feverishly hot all the time. She had the little fan on next to her bed, and took baths to keep cool. But as soon as she got out of the tub, she started to sweat again. She did try to relax and go out for drinks yesterday with a friend, Barry, but she didn't feel too well afterward. She felt fine when she was at the bar, but probably drank a little too much. The black Russians went down smoothly and by the end of the night she was pretty crocked. Barry didn't help much. He kept giving her drinks and they danced until the bar closed.

When they got back to her apartment, Barry gave her a Quaalude, and they danced some more. After a while, when the 'lude came on, they made love. She thought it was beautiful, and a little wild. She remembered part of the night, but her memory seemed to have gaps in it. During the lovemaking, she didn't feel any of the pain she had earlier in the day. And for a change, she slept like a baby.

The money she got from government assistance came in handy. Her psychiatrist, Dr. Mae Warren, after her first overdose when a teenager, said that she just wanted Elaine to have some money for food, since she had never worked and had no skills. She signed Elaine up for welfare benefits. Her psychiatrist wanted Elaine to feel safe so, hopefully, Elaine wouldn't feel the need to overdose on drugs again.

Elaine still hadn't worked much decades later. She did odd jobs from time to time. One boyfriend convinced her to do some nude dancing in the Valley. It was good money and no one hassled her much, but she got fired because she was sick and missed a lot of work.

According to the note from the government, recipients of government welfare benefits must work. The notice said that if she hadn't found a job by the end of a month, the government would assign her a job in a governmental agency at the end of the second month. If she didn't take the job at the end of two months, her benefits would be stopped.

She had to fill out a card with her name on it, and check off which job she preferred. Some of the jobs listed on the card were openings in the courts, police stations, hospitals, prisons, and even a juvenile facility.

Working with juvenile delinquents didn't interest her. She remembered what life was like when she was in high school. Students were only interested in showing each other how smart they were, and most of them were pretty stupid.

Prisoners were more of the same. The inmates might try to get into her pants or show her how tough they were. Besides the danger involved, she hated the thought of working in a place with bars on it.

Working with the police scared her. The police she met while nude dancing seemed all right, but others she had met had a macho problem. They were the 'protectors' of the people. They became 'somebody' when they put on their uniform. But once you take away their guns and their uniforms, they were just like everyone else. She knew that cops were the worst bed partners she ever had. They only cared about themselves and didn't care if she enjoyed sex or not.

The court job interested her. It might be easy to do clerical work, and she could meet lawyers and judges. She put a check mark next to the box for courts. It might be fun to be involved with legal dramas, just like the ones on TV soap operas. All the real life handsome attorneys would be there. With criminals, attractive lawyers, murderers, and arsonists, life wouldn't be boring.

Hospitals were interesting, too, she thought. Being sick all the time from one thing or another, she had learned a lot about medical treatments and how they affected her body. She suffered from herpes attacks, lower back pain, and crippling migraines. The migraines were always located on the right side of her head. They made her dizzy and kept her in pain for days on end. She always had at least one migraine a month, and they weren't even related to her period.

Of course, she no longer needed contacts at the hospitals or pharmacies to get drugs. She could just go and buy whatever she needed, if she had the money. Having money was the problem. She didn't know what the future had in store for her. It might even be an advantage to work in a hospital where she could get drugs at a discount.

Elaine felt hungry, but there was no food in the house, so she knew she had to go out. She began to dress, making sure her make-up was on right and her hair looked good. Her old car, a Dodge she had named Bertha, started up with a wheeze, but made it the four blocks to the store. The traffic was worse than usual. She passed two accidents on the way. She bought some fruit, Pepsi, milk, frozen food, and, as always, spent a long time in the medicine aisle. After picking up one or two items she needed, she took everything to the checker.

The man in line ahead of her was oblivious to everything around him. Elaine didn't notice him at first. She was too busy looking to see if she had enough money. When she looked up, she was surprised to see that the man was wearing a sleeveless T-shirt, shorts, and tennis shoes. He had broad shoulders, well-defined arms and muscular legs. He also had a small but muscular butt. She liked that in men. "Nice butt," she said to herself.

"Nice shape," she said flirtingly to the man in front.

He turned. He had a hard chin and ghostly cold eyes. "Thank you," he smiled.

"You must work hard at it," Elaine guessed.

"I do," he answered, looking at her. She wore a cotton blouse and her hair curled around her shoulders.

"Are you glad the drug bill passed?" he asked, looking at the medicines in her basket.

"Yes, I am," she admitted. "And you?"

"I am, too," he agreed. "It makes it easier to build up the bulk now."

"How's that?" she asked demurely.

"Now I can get all the steroids I want," he said with relief. "And nothing puts on muscle bulk like steroids."

"Oh," she said, remembering a friend of hers who took steroids. They gave him muscles but made him act weird.

"I'm Mike," he said, holding out his hand.

"Elaine," she replied, accepting his hand. His grip was deliberately painful.

"Nice name," he said, lying, then added, "Why don't we get together some time and we'll talk about weight lifting?"

"I'd like that," she commented, envisioning his arms and legs wrapped around her.

"Let me give you my number." He took a small piece of paper from his pocket and wrote his name and phone number on it. "Give me a call sometime. I'm sure we can get together."

"I'll do that," she smiled, looking at the card. She had some trouble focusing. It was the same feeling she had before the migraines started.

Mike took his bags of groceries and made his way to his car. Elaine stayed at the cash register and tried to ignore the pounding in her head.

She went to her car, took the groceries home, and then drove to the hospital to see if someone could relieve her headaches.

At the new hospital, things were crazy. The parking lot was full and she had to park in the back. Her head throbbed as she made her way to the emergency room. Every time she had a migraine, her vision constricted until it seemed like she was looking at the world through little pinholes, with everything else blurred in the periphery.

She sat down in the packed emergency room. People were moaning all around her. A ward clerk came by, took her name, asked about her complaint and then asked her for an insurance card. She gave the clerk the Medi-Cal card. He examined the card closely and said that there were many ahead of her and she'd have to wait.

Three hours later the ward clerk returned and said the doctor was ready to see her now. She felt unable to walk steadily to the examining room. She moved slowly and entered the examining room. She sat on the examining table. A young freckle-faced doctor came into the room. She thought he looked like a kid.

"I'm Doctor Browning," he said, holding out his hand.

"My head hurts, Doctor," she replied, after shaking hands.

"Let's talk about it," Doc Browning said, reassuring her in spite of his fatigue. Since the drug bill went into effect he had been busy. Emergency rooms across the country were full. They were all working overtime and all of the doctors felt the strain.

"Have you had these headaches a long time?" he asked, as he reviewed her medical history.

She nodded and told him how long her migraines had been, how they started and what she did for relief.

"So you take pills?"

"Yes," she said, indicating she only took aspirin for her headaches on the form she completed when she came into the emergency room.

"We'll take a CT scan to make sure everything is okay," Doc Browning said, noting that she had government aid and that the government would pay the large fee for the test. He didn't care where the money came from, as long as it was there.

"Well, Ms. Russell," he said to Elaine hours later, "the brain scan and encephalogram came out negative. You have a common variety of chronic migraines. The treatment of choice is Ergotamine administered every day to make sure the migraines don't return."

"Doctor," she said, slowly talking through the pain, "I've had Ergotamine before. It made me sick and didn't relieve my headache."

"What did help?" Doc Browning asked.

"Demerol," replied Elaine. "It didn't make the migraines disappear, but the migraines ended sooner with it than without it."

"Demerol?" asked Doc Browning. Giving demerol for a migraine was like giving a transfusion for a flea bite. He knew that the only thing stronger was morphine. "Still," he thought, "if she was given Demerol in the past, she might as well stay with it."

"Taking it twice a day?" he asked. She nodded, biting her lip as the pain coursed through her head.

The doctor left her for a moment and checked the dosage for Demerol in the PDR. He wasn't sure how many milligrams he should prescribe if taken twice a day. He felt strange writing prescriptions now. They didn't mean much, except in malpractice cases. He felt that writing prescriptions was an exercise in futility. No one needed prescriptions anymore.

The emergency room was hectic and he was hours behind in seeing his patients. He was almost caught up when someone on drugs lost control of their car and ran over the curb. The car smashed into a plate glass window. The man needed a hundred stitches. More doctors were needed than were available and he was burned out. He had done one too many double shifts.

He wrote Elaine a prescription for Demerol, then added p.r.n. at the bottom, and told her that she should take the pills as needed. He gave her the standard narcotic lecture, mentioning they could be addictive, and told her again that her blood test and brain scans showed nothing unusual.

Elaine's hands trembled as she took the prescription. She was happy there was nothing else wrong with her besides the migraines. She went back to her car and drove to her little duplex. She reached for the Demerol she already had left over from her last bout. She swallowed two pills, took off her clothes and got into bed.

Chapter Nineteen

One month later
June 1, 2028

Craig was bothered by people smoking marijuana at work. Although it was legal, he still didn't like it. He wondered if even a few marijuana cigarettes would confuse postal employees in sorting the mail. Craig hadn't heard anything about it yet, but felt he would. His bosses were always a little paranoid about losing their jobs, and often yelled at people when they felt nervous.

When Craig was in high school some kids wanted him to try marijuana. He did and it felt okay, but it was wasteful to him. He liked to relax, but only after he did something that deserved relaxing. "Idle hands are the Devil's playground," he remembered some of his elementary school teachers saying. And they were right.

Craig admired people who were fighting drugs. There were referendums for state control of the Drug Legislation Act, but it was a constitutional amendment, so it had to be approved by a majority of Congress. The state delegates were having little success introducing such bills which never got to the House floor in Congress. The one or two bills that were introduced were put down by John Jones and others, or sent to committee. Some of the dry states were trying to make their states drug and alcohol free, but getting seventy-five percent of the people to approve it was impossible.

Craig was appalled at the number of accident fatalities written up in the newspapers. Deaths were already over a million and the number of people crippled or injured was over a million also. Those on the streets were either dying, crippled, or getting themselves thrown into jail. Things were horrible.

Craig was sorry that the petition he signed to recall the President of the United States had not been effective. He felt the President was behind the legalization of drugs. A petition, supported by the M.A.A., finally got to Congress after taking weeks to get the signatures needed. The petition started immediately after the Drug Legislation Act got going. Once the millions of signatures were collected and proof of registration checked, the petition went to Congress to schedule a national election for the recall vote to be taken.

One of the women in Congress, Frederica Wright, on the Government Operations Committee, claimed that the signatures were illegal. They were obtained from sick people signing petitions in doctor's offices, thus people were not mentally competent at the time. Wright declared the bill illegal and slapped an injunction on the M.A.A. by means of a cease and desist order from federal court judges. A huge fine was levied against the M.A.A. for violating the antitrust act. The M.A.A. lodged a countersuit, but had to desist from active lobbying by the cease and desist order. No more petitions were allowed in doctor's offices, and the M.A.A. was furious.

For some strange reason, no challenges were made against the Import Act, Personal Rights Act, Drug Enforcement Act, or Drug Education Act. All of the federal court judges were quiet. Craig read that three judges came together to issue an injunction against the government on behalf of foreign interests, claiming restriction of trade, but the meeting was canceled before it took place.

Craig thought about his church work. Last week there was a massive letter-writing campaign to their representatives in Congress. He also spent some time helping at one of the hotline centers, being trained as a telephone counselor.

Craig detested delivering circulars from pharmaceutical companies touting the advantages of their drugs. A few were giving teasers of drugs to come in the near future. "A new high in highs," read one of the circulars he delivered, "without any side effects." The worst ones were the ones with the free samples included with the circulars.

When he went to the offices of Thalberg, Chaney, and Fairbanks, he saw Mary Lane, looking thinner than he remembered her looking.

"How have you been?" Mary asked then added, remembering his name, "Craig."

"Okay, Mary," he smiled. "How about you?"

"Fine, I guess," she murmured. "I need to lose some weight, though."

"Why?" demanded Craig, looking at the slight figure before him.

"I'm too damned fat," Mary replied.

"Oh no," he confessed. "You're beautiful, but you look like you need to gain weight, not lose it."

"Say that part again," Mary said quickly.

"About how you need to gain weight?" Craig asked.

"No," smiled Mary. "The part about I'm beautiful."

"Well," Craig admitted, tongue-tied. "You are."

"Thank you," Mary beamed.

"How did you get that cut on your arm?" Craig asked, looking at a bruised cut on Mary's left forearm.

"I was in an accident," she said.

"What happened?" Craig asked with concern.

"Some man three cars ahead of me on the freeway last week was hallucinating that he came to a sudden cliff. He slammed on his brakes, and we hit ours too late. My hand protected my head, but it got slammed into the windshield."

"I'm glad you're all right," Craig said, breathing a sigh of relief.

"There were fourteen cars involved," Mary remembered, "but we all walked away from it."

"Have you noticed the huge number of accidents around the town?" Craig asked.

"Have I ever!" Mary replied, swiping a curl out of her eye. Craig thought she looked cute. "Traffic is a regal pain. I haven't been able to get from one point to another without being stuck in traffic caused by an accident."

"I think it began when that drug law became legal," Craig said after a little thought.

"I think so, too."

"Some of the guys at work do some serious drug taking to pass the time away when they're stuck in traffic," Craig remarked. "And part of the time, they forget why they're on the job."

"Do all of the postmen take drugs?" asked Mary.

"Not all of us," Craig remarked, defending the department. "Some."

"Do you do drugs?" asked Mary, lowering her eyes to the floor.

"Oh no," Craig spoke slowly. "Do you?"

"No," she replied, still looking at the floor. She had tried giving up drugs for the umpteenth time last week, and made it two whole days before she went back. She gained three pounds and had a craving for food all the time. She was irritable without marijuana, and couldn't get her work done without uppers. She felt sluggish. She had to drink coffee and Pepsi or she would fall asleep.

"That was last week and this is now," she said to herself softly. She felt at this point that drugs weren't bad after all. They helped her through the night, especially when she was thinking about her ex-husband and the kids. It had been a long while since someone warmed her bed, and stayed until morning. After sleeping next to the same person for ten years before he divorced her, mornings were strange without anyone there. She thought about her children. They would be eleven and nine this year. "They're getting old," she thought, then added, "I'm getting old."

Carl Friedman, her old drug connection, would go to bed with her, but said he didn't want to stay all night. It occurred to her when she thought of Carl Friedman that she didn't know what Carl did for a living. She hoped that it wasn't pushing drugs, or he was going to be pretty upset about being broke. It didn't matter. They weren't serious about each other and she hadn't talked to him since she last needed drugs.

"What is your big plan for the weekend?" she asked Craig.

"I said I'd volunteer at a counseling center for people with abuse problems," Craig remembered. "And I have to study for a history exam next week. I'm going to school part time."

"For a doctorate?" asked Mary, always impressed by intellectuals.

"For a bachelor's," Craig said a bit ashamedly, "but mostly for my own knowledge. In History. History has always interested me."

"How would you write this period in the U.S. history books?" Mary asked inquisitively.

"I'd tentatively call it 'America gets its skeletons out into the open,'" said Craig. "And one thing I know is that America will never be the same."

"That's for sure," Mary agreed, thinking of the neighborhood gangs that were no longer on the street making obscene gestures at her to prove themselves to their friends.

"There are a lot of people dead," he surmised, "and it isn't over yet by a long shot."

Mary nodded.

Craig looked at Mary. "She's a caring woman," he thought, as he saw her pout. He was a bit discouraged. He was doing everything he could about the drug problem, but things were out of control. He didn't want to destroy her day more than he had already by being morbib about the drug deaths.

"Well, I have to be getting on," he smiled. "It was nice talking to you."

"Nice talking to you too."

"We'll have to do it again."

Mary nodded.

Craig lifted his satchel and picked up the mail. Mary watched him leave.

"Nice guy," she said, "but probably married. All the nice guys are married and usually to nice girls." She took a Librium from her purse and made her way to the water cooler.

Prescription for Mayhem

Chapter Twenty

Kevin stood next to his motorcycle in front of the hearse at the grave site. "It is a beautiful day," he thought. Some dew was on the grass and a chill was in the air. It was a good day to be buried. He watched the group of mourners who were listening to a priest. One of his fellow police came over to Kevin. They were waiting until the service was over to start their motorcycles and leave.

"Some funeral?" asked the other officer to Kevin.

"Yep," agreed Kevin.

"We've been so busy with funerals, we've had to cover them with you street cops," he commented.

"Yep," said Kevin dreamingly, looking at the cop and thinking, "Old motorcycle cops don't die, they get assigned to covering funerals, crowd control and working on movie sets."

"You've been busy, too," the other officer knowingly said to Kevin.

"Yep," Kevin tiredly yawned.

"Working traffic?" he asked, watching the priest sprinkle some holy water over the casket.

"Yep," muttered Kevin, wishing he had more time off. He had made many arrests for drunk and disorderly conduct, and he knew that he didn't even have to appear in court. All that was needed was a person's blood sample and the report from a laboratory.

The new court system radically decreased the time needed for a case to go through the bureaucratic mill. Cases that had taken five years to get to trial now took less than six months, and the reason it took that long was because lawyers needed preparation time. For people charged with possible substance abuse, it took less than two weeks for the case to be presented, tried, and convicted. Lawyers raised their fees to represent clients because once the verdict came down, there was no plea bargaining. A guilty person went to jail for seven years no matter what.

Kevin knew the person in the coffin had died when his car went over the divider and across the freeway into opposing traffic; nine others were killed instantly. A large number of other commuters were injured. When the autopsy report came in, it was determined that the driver had PCP in his blood.

When the ceremony finished, Kevin noticed an attractive young woman in black, sitting in the first row. Most of the other mourners were middle-aged. This young lady was in her early twenties and carried a baby basket.

"Pretty gal," said the motorcycle cop, observing Kevin's gaze.

Kevin nodded.

"New baby, I bet."

Kevin nodded.

"You can tell someone sure had money," the cop said to Kevin. All the cars lined up behind the hearse were fancy European ones.

"I wonder why a guy would do this to himself, with all these rich relatives?" Kevin asked. "Maybe he was broke."

"This guy was worth two or three million dollars," said the cop to Kevin.

Kevin couldn't believe it. "Maybe the guy couldn't get any satisfaction from life and took drugs to escape," Kevin argued, "or maybe he had a trust and couldn't get any of the money until he was twenty-five."

The other cop laughed softly.

"This guy didn't have to worry about that," he said. "He was way over twenty-five."

"How much?" Kevin asked inquisitively.

"He was fifty-seven."

"Fifty-seven?"

"Fifty-seven," said the cop.

"Then why did he take drugs?" Kevin asked.

"From what I've heard," told the other cop, "he was a stalwart member of the community. He had a perfect home life, and was even a member of the city council."

"Then maybe it had something to do with his wife being pregnant," Kevin theorized.

"That's not his wife," the motorcycle cop told.

"No?" asked Kevin, furrowing his brow.

"No," replied the motorcycle cop.

"Then, who the hell is she?"

"That's his granddaughter, and that's her husband walking toward her now."

"Why the hell would a guy take PCP, if he had everything going for him?" asked Kevin.

"Who the hell knows?" slowly spoke the motorcycle cop philosophically. "That's like asking why anyone would take a shot of booze if they already felt good. Maybe they want to feel even better? I'm still trying to figure that out, son," told the motorcycle cop, looking at Kevin.

Kevin felt strange under the gaze of an older, seasoned officer. Kevin had just gotten his sergeant stripes, but still felt uncomfortable.

"I bet funerals have been keeping you pretty busy," said Kevin.

"Yep," agreed the cop, "That hill you see behind us is full of headstones that weren't here two weeks ago."

"Business must be booming for mortuaries," Kevin joked.

"They're making a killing," the motorcycle cop replied quickly, smiling at the pun.

"Why did you do it?" asked the interrogator slowly. "Were you crazy?"

Luigi Devoy sat on a chair in the middle of the room, angry that he missed his mark. Luigi thought it was one of his talents to look harmless but some said he looked and sounded like Peter Lorre, the actor. He had gotten a contract from Julie Giuliano to take out all of the members of the *Guidance and Direction Committee*, starting with Samuel Bunker. He had been a contract assassin for fifteen years, and this was the first time he had missed, ever.

He finished up his existing contracts and then went to Washington, D.C., to case this Bunker guy. He followed Bunker around for three weeks, then he set himself up in a cheesy apartment house on the street where Bunker took walks with his collie, named Crapper. When Devoy had entered the Bunker residence to bug it one morning, Sam's maid told Luigi how Crapper seemed to have to go pee at least once every five minutes, and that Sam took the dog for evening walks in the neighborhood. When Devoy set up his automatic rifle and aligned the sights the day of the hit, his room door was broken in by Secret

Service agents and he was dragged off before he could cock the rifle and put his finger on the trigger.

Outside of the interrogation room, Sam Bunker was yelling at John Jones. "Do you mean to tell me that this guy followed me around for a week, planning to kill me?"

John Jones nodded. "Three weeks, not one week."

"Three weeks?" Sam shouted.

"I wanted to make sure that you guys had round-the-clock Secret Service men watching you," John Jones said. "In case your decisions weren't agreeable to the country."

"And?" asked Sam.

"They weren't," John told Sam. "Hell, Sam, as the head of the committee, I figured you were expendable. After all, who would miss you?" Jones smiled, telling Sam he was joking. "But, I do also admit that you were the best person to head the committee, Sam, and you're doing a great job.

"Do you know what's the worst thing about this?" Jones continued.

"What?" asked Sam, visibly disturbed.

"This guy's never voted in his life."

Sam's eyes opened widely at that remark. "Let's speak to him," Sam said, angrily.

As they walked into the room, Luigi stood up. When the guard leveled his rifle at him, Luigi decided to sit down.

"Luigi Devoy's your name?" asked Sam Bunker.

Luigi didn't speak.

"And the Secret Service says you were trying to kill me," Sam continued.

Luigi looked down at the floor.

"You know," Sam said, "I could understand this better if you were someone from the state I represent. I mean, it's considered normal for constituents to try to kill you. But you don't even vote."

"You don't even friggin' vote?!!!" Sam said again, venomously. "Now, boy, this is how we do things back home. I've been told that you'll be convicted of attempted murder, with premeditation and malice. Murder one! Do you know what that means?"

Luigi studied the floor.

"What it means is that I have a say in your punishment, according to the act I introduced. We're no longer talking about a life sentence, or five years with parole, boy. When they find you guilty, and they will, I'll make a decision about what to do with you. I won't spend the taxpayer's money and have them give you life without bail at hard labor. I won't even send you to jail."

Luigi looked up.

"You tried to kill me," Sam spat out between clenched teeth softly, remembering his first wife. "You're not on drugs and you don't even know me. That makes you a cold-blooded murderer. In my book, you deserve the chair and nothing less!"

Luigi searched Sam's face for signs that Sam was telling the truth.

"It might take two or three months to get you through court and another month for the appeal to fail," Sam said slowly through eye slits, "but three months from now, I'm going to watch you squirm and jerk as ten thousand volts runs through your body. I won't let you go to the gas chamber. I want it to be as painful as it can be!"

Luigi read Sam's face again. "A deal?" he asked softly, as he looked at Sam.

"No deals," Sam shook his head. "I don't care who hired you! You can tell us if you want to and make a clean breast of it, but you can also take it to the grave with you. In the next few months whoever hired you will try to kill you to make sure you won't talk. I hope he'll be successful. It'll save us taxpayers an electric bill."

"I'll talk," pleaded Luigi, hoping for anything less than the death penalty.

"Talk to someone else," Sam said. "I'm not going to have a good night's sleep until I see you in the electric chair and the doctor pronounces you dead. I also want an autopsy done on you afterwards to make sure you won't come back from the dead. I'll be there; count on it!"

Sam walked out of the room and closed the door behind him.

Kevin had covered a mass murder at a McDonald's restaurant yesterday. A crazed man took his shotgun outside and shot holes in his apartment house, babbling that he was killing the cockroaches that lived in the tenement. Then, he drove to the nearest McDonald's, took his shotgun from his truck, and killed thirty people before the police killed him. Investigation was still underway, because there were rumors that neighborhood teenagers had put some hallucinogens in his coffee pot.

Kevin had trouble staying awake. He drank one cup of coffee after another. After the mass murder at McDonald's, Kevin talked with Doctor Browning, the ER doctor, about drug detection.

"The point," Doc Browning said, "is that pupil size isn't always reliable. A blood test is the only definitive way of detecting drugs."

Kevin figured out that the best way to determine if a blood test was valid would be to draw blood as soon as possible. He mentioned that to the watch commander, who agreed and said that they should keep this in mind.

Hopefully, any suspected individuals could have their blood work done as quickly as possible.

After the watch report was over, Kevin went home. He was exhausted from doing a double shift. He fell into bed and was asleep within seconds.

Chapter Twenty-one

Six weeks later
June 15, 2028

"I'm tired," Sam Bunker groaned, as the Chaplain left the meeting of the *Guidance and Direction Committee*. "This hired murderer stuff has me sleeping less and less, the more I think about it."

"So don't think about it," Bob Emerson stated.

"Or make sure you attend more meetings of Congress," Tom Baker joked. "That'll make you sleep whether you want to or not."

"Well," said Sam, "that Devoy assassin is talking to us about anything we want to know. He's in with the FBI and CIA now."

"Who hired him?" asked Steve Harning.

"Some mafioso named Giuliano," Sam repeated. "You can tell that the Mafia is hurting because of lost drug business, so they put out a contract on me. And, I might add, there are contracts out on all of us."

"All of us?" asked Tom.

Sam nodded. Whenever Sam didn't talk, Tom worried.

"What do we do?" asked Bob.

"We keep on doing what we're doing as long as we can," said Frederica Wright with conviction, "And we depend on the Secret Service to protect us."

"Are they letting this guy off for squealing?" asked Steve.

"It's my choice and no one else's," Sam spoke slowly. "I'm the plaintiff for attempted murder. I'm going to make sure that man gets the electric chair, nothing less. He's talking right now in the hopes that he'll save his ass, but it won't work. I don't care what he says, he's a dead man."

Steve smiled slightly and nodded. His opinion of Sam had just gone up one hundred percent. He'd trust Sam with his life now.

"Anyway," asked Sam, "how is the rest of the nation doing?"

"About the same as the rest of us," said Tom wryly. "Some of the errors are being rectified, but there are always new problems opening up."

"Give me an example," demanded Frederica to Tom, starting to feel paranoid about snipers, and wanting to change the subject.

"People are trying to repeal the Immigration/Literacy Act to avoid deportation. They say the guidelines we set for literacy are too stringent."

"What are our guidelines again?" asked Bob.

"We want the people in school to be not less than two years behind their education level, and we want the adults to have the equivalent of a high school education. What's wrong with a twelfth grade high school education for all?" asked Sam realistically.

No one had any comments.

"I say we don't change our committee's requirements of literacy one bit," suggested Frederica.

Everyone nodded.

"This literacy law has put gang members behind bars until they upgrade their literacy level in our special schools," Tom reported.

"They're just a misguided bunch of teenagers," said Sam. "They need a firm hand and an occasional kick in the ass to point them in the right direction. I was a bit like that when I was young," he admitted.

"Hell, Sam," grinned Bob, "you're still a pain in the ass today."

Everybody laughed.

"I've been getting some pressure on the Import Act," Steve spoke up. "Big business is putting a lot of pressure to get an injunction against our act limiting all foreign goods coming into the U.S. Three federal court judges were preparing to grant an injunction against the act, but we took care of them."

"How?" asked Sam.

"We had warrants for their arrest charging treason against the government, and enough federal power to enforce it. We told them that if they made any effort to sit together and grant an injunction, they would be in jail before they had a chance to stand up. Then," Steve grinned slightly, "we did things the American way."

"What was that?" Frederica asked Steve, intrigued by his sly smile.

"We told them that if they told us who paid them the bribe money, as there had to be someone or some group putting them up to this, we would let them keep the money, match it, and make them heroes by not prosecuting them once they turned in their lobbying benefactors. All of them agreed."

"Naturally. I would, too," Tom concluded. "It's hard to turn down money being thrown at you from all directions."

"Who did it?" asked Frederica, always anxious to find out who was lobbying.

"We were expecting the Germans," admitted Steve, "since they're hurting from all of this, but it turned out to be the Japanese. I was betting on the Taiwanese or Koreans myself."

"What happened?" asked Bob, thinking about the international currency question.

"It was a cartel consisting of asian car companies. They gathered together and offered the judges each over seven million dollars to go for that injunction."

"That means that we have to pay those judges twenty-one million of the nation's money," said Bob. "I'm glad I don't have to explain this to Congress. I pity whoever does."

"Not quite," said Frederica smiling. "That was the rider you people had me draw up. We can confiscate each company's assets and prohibit any products from the companies from being brought into the country. The Securities and Exchange Commission is having a field day with them even as we speak. I assume that their stock has been taken off the market."

"Correct," said Steve. "These companies tried to bribe officials. They don't belong in America. Details of the bribe are being published in the *New York Times* and other papers nationwide. Their assets in our country alone reach into the billions. Twenty-one million dollars of their money we give the three judges is a drop in the bucket. And, as of now, it's our money. We can afford it."

"Speaking of big business," Frederica said thoughtfully, "How is the M.A.A. handling the Drug Legislation Act? Have any of you others been approached by their lobbyists? I sure have."

"I was, too," Steve remarked.

"Me too," Bob said.

"Ditto," Tom chimed in.

"I'm in," Sam raised his hand, nodding his head.

"They hired some big guns," Frederica noticed. "They have the cream of the lobbyists trying to get our laws changed. They even had a contingent meeting with me under the title of 'Making America Safe for Children.'"

"What did you do?" asked Sam.

"Once I caught onto their plans, I called security and the FBI after they offered me a campaign pledge of more money than I care to mention," spoke Frederica indignantly. "I had our security guards take these guys out and had them all arrested. They'll be talking soon, for I record everything in my office, and then they're off to jail. The M.A.A. is going to get another injunction from us the way they're going."

"The bad press is going to hurt them," Tom imagined, dreaming how thoroughly the news and wire services would crucify the M.A.A. before they were done with them.

"I wondered why lobbying stopped abruptly," said Sam in appreciation. "Thanks."

"All my friends in Congress are getting their asses kicked by those trying to get them to do something," commented Tom quietly. He had been giving counseling support to his anguished colleagues. But, the list was too long for him to be an effective listener, and was growing longer every day.

"Hold it," Sam said loudly, standing up quickly, and holding his arms outstretched. "Let's be civil about this. Is anybody arguing about the Personal Rights Act?"

"Just those bleeding heart civil rights activist types who say no one should be allowed the opportunity of harming another," said Frederica.

"Forget them," muttered Sam. "Anyone else have any gripes against the Personal Rights Act?" No one said anything.

"How about the Import Act?" Sam asked.

"Just those foreign powers we've been talking about," Steve replied.

"Forget them," said Sam. "As long as we stopped the federal court judges from taking outside bribes, we can look at the stock market and see first hand the evidence that America is paying its national debt for the first time in over a hundred years, and we know what we've done is right. Even our fellow Congressmen and women who are getting their fair share of gripes from their constituents know we're right. There is a lot of work yet to be done on producing our own goods, but we've made a start and will do more soon.

"I'm assuming there are no other complaints about the Drug Enforcement Act, Immigration/Literacy Act, or the Drug Education Act," Sam remarked in a tone that said he wasn't looking for a response.

The room was silent.

"So," continued Sam, "that leaves the Drug Legislation Act. How are the medical fields taking it?"

"Didn't I already ask that?" queried Frederica, looking at Sam and thinking how lazy he was.

"Pharmacists are doing business hand over fist," Bob commented. "Medical doctors are doing well, especially because of all the accidents that have occurred. They're not prescribing now, but their mean income is up."

"How many accidents have there been?" asked Tom.

"About one and a half million dead over the last month since the bill became law," Bob quietly replied, looking at a piece of paper. He didn't look up. He had been dreading telling this news to the group and was waiting for the right time. There was no right time.

The room was silent. Everyone thought about these deaths. Tom Baker asked himself if he were responsible for those deaths. Each of them asked themselves the same question: were they at fault?

"Holy shit!" Sam said to himself. "One and a half million people dead from drug-related accidents."

"How many are hospitalized?" he asked Bob.

"Two and a half million are in the hospitals at this time," spoke Bob after consulting papers in front of him. "I could sure use a drink now," he thought to himself. "Badly."

"I'm damn glad I asked you all to beef up the hospital system," Sam said, exhaling a big breath. "Without them, this place would probably look like a war zone."

"It is a war zone," said Tom, whispering. "And we helped kill them!" His eyes were closed. He made a sniffing sound with his nose, trying to hold back the tears. It didn't work. He folded his arms, lay his head on the table between his arms then started sobbing.

Sam's eyes grew watery. He had known that people would get hurt, but he had no idea that it would be so bad. All the work they had put into hospitals, courts, police, and prisons was getting a baptism as never before. With four million people dead or crippled, the laws had caused tremendous deaths all within two months. That meant to him that about one percent of all Americans were dead or hospitalized.

"We can deal with the Medical Association of America," Frederica soothingly said, ignoring Tom's crying, and bringing the meeting back to order. "They have an injunction against them for that petition they tried to shove down our throats. They've failed with lobbyists. Now, we just have to wait for their next move."

"They've thrown a lot at us," said Bob, looking up at the faces of his friends, "and we're still hanging in there. What can they do about it, refuse to treat patients?"

Sam's eyes opened wide. "They'd never do that," he blurted out in shock, as though his mind was touching the edge of something too horrible to think about. "They've taken the Hippocratic Oath. They're the healers we've always talked about, aren't they?"

Chapter Twenty-two

Sabrina sat in traffic school and cursed the officer for her speeding ticket. The officer gave her a lecture even though she was only driving ten miles above the speed limit. Then she got the ticket. Sabrina hated police. She thought them authoritative automatons. They didn't think, they just obeyed and served; mainly themselves.

"Life is funny," she said to herself. Yesterday she had received her first commission. She was going to paint a portrait of a clergyman for a library being dedicated to him. It was an important commission and she wanted to do her best. During the night she studied her books on the renaissance, on baroque and rococo art. She analyzed portraits of people to get a feeling for what she would be doing. It had to be as full of character as a Fuerbach, having the somberness and inner light of a Rembrandt, showing the outer light of a Vermeer and done with the precision of a Van Eyck. It was going to be great.

Sabrina got her sketchpad and went to the church. She sat down in a pew and studied the large room. She never went to church, but felt the buildings were all beautiful. There was something about a building created for an ideal rather than a utility. It was dimly lit and gothic arches reached to the high ceiling. Stained glass windows made shining rainbow patterns throughout the church.

She took out her sketchbook and made a few sketches inside the sanctuary. She sketched light streaming on the lectern, a cross-hatching for the altar and a huge cross with a figure of Christ crucified.

"Very good, young lady," said a voice from behind her. She turned to see a man dressed in white, with a crucifix on his side. He was smiling, a ringer for anyone's favorite uncle. His hair was white with a white beard. He wore wire glasses with bifocal lenses, and Sabrina liked him immediately.

"I'm not here to paint in your church," she smiled. "I've been commissioned to do a painting of Father Mahoney for the new library."

"The Lord does work in mysterious ways," said the man. "You did seek, and you found; you asked, and it was given; you knocked, and the door was opened onto you. I'm Michael Mahoney, Father emeritus of this parish. You must be the person doing my painting, though Lord knows why! People will have to look at my miserable face every day that the library is open. A Blessed Virgin Mary would have been more appropriate, in my opinion," he said smiling.

"My name is Sabrina, Father," she said, shaking hands. "I can paint the Virgin Mary, and then add on a white beard to pass her off as you," Sabrina grinned, testing the priest. "We can see if we can sneak it by the elders who commissioned it."

"Your shenanigans remind me of a choir boy I used to know," remembered Father Mahoney. "Are you Catholic?"

"No, Father," Sabrina told straightforwardly.

"Well, God bless you anyway," he laughed. "Where should I go to pose?" asked Father Mahoney.

"We could go to the library that will be dedicated to you and pose you surrounded by books," Sabrina said, thinking about images. "That might be appropriate, and I would like to see where the picture would be hung. That would give me some idea of the composition."

"This way," pointed the Father, taking her to a huge library located next to the Sanctuary. The library contained books that were both religious and secular, with histories of the Irish people in the Western United States; reported by the man commissioning the work to be one of the best and most complete libraries imaginable. The main reading room was three stories tall, with a skylight mosaic of St. James and the caption "Faith without works is not the work of the Holy Spirit."

It was an impressive room, with old oak bookcases and wall tapestries. Despite its large size, it had a comfortable drawing room feeling. She knew immediately where the painting would be hung. There was a blank area of wood paneling, flanked on either side by bookcases, above the central fireplace.

"Not exactly the art museum," she said to herself, "but it's suitable." The painting would be about six feet at its lowest point above the floor, to twelve feet tall at its highest, and four feet wide. She knew the church elders and ruling bodies wanted a portrait of a man's head in the spot, but a landscape would have been better.

"Somehow," the priest confessed, "I can't imagine a portrait of me looking down at the library patrons with my scowl of a face. I'd like something religious and uplifting. Am I making myself clear?" he stated, hesitantly.

"How about a landscape?" she asked, not knowing what type of landscape she would do. "A forest scene, perhaps."

"I was thinking more about the holy family," admitted Father Mahoney slowly.

Sabrina looked down at the sketch she had made of the interior of the church.

"How about one inside the church?" she asked.

"That might be fine," the Father compromised. "And you can show the Sacred Heart and some other sacred icons."

"The church elders who are paying for this want you in it. But I'll do my best to please you."

"That would be fine," smiled the priest, fingering his rosary beads.

"Maybe I should stay for a service," Sabrina remarked. "After all, I've never been to one."

"That would be wonderful," agreed the priest enthusiastically. "You can see what we do during a service, which we call a 'mass.' If we're lucky, the Holy Spirit may descend upon you and touch you."

The Father gave his sermon. It was about how only Christ can fill the holes in one's soul. When he served communion, she saw the pleasure it gave those who received it. When one man turned toward her after receiving communion, his face shined. Sabrina looked at the face and the light around it. She quickly sketched the man's face in her sketchpad.

After the mass, Sabrina told the priest an idea that had come to her.

"I'd like to do a portrait of you serving the church members communion in the foreground, with the church and the cross in the background," she said, making a quick sketch to show him the composition.

"That would be perfect," he replied as he studied the sketch. "See, my child. You have been touched by the Holy Spirit." Then, his eyes looked upon her sketchpad at the face of a man she saw in the congregation.

"Do you know that person?" he asked.

"No, but his face came to life when you served him. I was planning to use him in the portrait."

"I'd rather you didn't," the priest quietly said. "Many church members have helped this young man through some bad times. I believe he's redeemed himself, but some of the parishioners aren't ready to forgive him yet."

"What did he do?" she asked.

"I'm afraid I'm not at liberty to say," he replied.

One of the choir boys was walking by and glanced at the picture. "That's Bruce," he said, "isn't it?" recognizing the face. "He was on heroin for a long time. He had the shakes and still needs treatment."

"How old are you?" asked Sabrina to the boy.

"Nine," the boy said, "but I'll be ten in a month," he added proudly.

"You know a lot about drugs for a young lad," said the priest proudly.

"We have to learn it in school," the boy replied. "We get tested on it and everything."

"The kid knows more about drugs than I do," Sabrina thought.

"I'll work on the portrait and get back to you within a week," she told Father Mahoney. "I made enough sketches of you during the service for a good first cut."

"God bless you," he prayed as she took her sketchpad and walked out of the church.

When Sabrina got home, she worked at her easel with vigor. She painted into the night using her fine control of detail to make a mirror image of what she had seen during the service. At the bottom of the painting, she drew the backs of a family of four: mother, father, son, and daughter on their knees, with the priest in front, offering a communion wafer to them.

Something was missing, thought Sabrina. Something was needed to make the picture come alive, to show the spirituality on the priest's face and the holiness in the church, or it would be technically good and nothing more.

Sabrina looked for hours at what she had blocked in on the easel, not painting. She fell asleep in the chair, brushes on the armrests, and woke the next day, still dissatisfied. She called in sick at work, then went for a walk to clear her head. She'd only gone two blocks when she met a classmate from art school. They talked and decided to have lunch together.

"I've got a problem," confided Sabrina. "I've started a painting. It's pretty good, but it needs something. Something inspired. Something....more."

"I know the feeling," agreed Sabrina's friend, "I've found out that when I need to go beyond myself, I have to do something special."

"What's that?" asked Sabrina.

"I take acid or peyote," he admitted.

"Drugs?" she asked.

He nodded.

Sabrina sat and thought about it after her friend left. She had to do something. On her way home she stopped at the pharmacy and talked to the pharmacist. A woman in a laboratory coat stood behind the pharmacy counter.

"I have a problem?" Sabrina said, gathering courage.

"Yes?" the pharmacist asked.

"I'm an artist," she said.

"I see that," she replied, looking at Sabrina; examining her flannel shirt, jeans with paint stains, stringy hair tied off in a pony tail in back, and no make-up at all.

"I want to try a drug for some new concepts, different approaches to a subject," she pleaded softly, feeling that she had committed herself to something daring and horrifying.

"I'd advise some LSD," the pharmacist said with sympathy after a long pause. "It could cause birth defects or mental problems in years to come, but it would be the psychedelic of choice. We have different dosages available. I'd recommend the smallest. It shouldn't last more than a day, but you could have flashbacks and recurrences of your 'trip' in the future."

"I'll take it," Sabrina said without hesitation.

The pharmacist took a sugar cube, and the LSD solution; dropped one drop of the solution on the sugar cube, put it into a pill vial and gave it to her.

"That'll be two dollars seventy-five. Please pay at the front, and I'd advise you not to do anything for the next day after you take the pill. Also, please remember that it is a felony to drive under the influence of psychedelics...good luck."

Sabrina took the vial with the sugar cube. She called her boss and said she also might not be in the next day. She sat in front of the easel with the painting. Her hands trembled. The thought of birth defects and mental problems from a drop of liquid on a sugar cube was frightening. Examining the painting, she saw an ordinary portrait, not at all what she had planned to do. She grew angry at her ineptness.

She started pacing in front of the painting, glaring every few seconds at it. Suddenly she said angrily to the painting, "You son of a bitch, I'm going to jump on your saddle, ride, and tame you if it kills me." She swallowed the sugar cube, sat across from the easel, and waited for inspiration.

Prescription for Mayhem

Chapter Twenty-three

Mary was bored and craved excitement. Thank God it was the day she was going out with Craig, who had finally asked her out earlier last week. She couldn't remember which day, but it had to be either Monday or Tuesday that Craig had asked. Wednesday evening she went to a bar with some friends, got drunk, and woke up Thursday morning in bed with some guy who was snoring. When she looked at him, she didn't know his name. She couldn't remember when he picked her up or if they had sex. She just put on her clothes and left.

The day got worse. She didn't have her morning joint, so she started the day grouchy. Then she got a call from Carl Friedman, who said he had some wild new drugs not yet approved by the Food and Drug Administration, but if she wanted to try some, he'd come over. She said that she was busy, and to call her in a month.

"I'll keep in touch and you'll hear from me soon," Carl said caustically as he abruptly hung up.

She hummed a song to herself as she prepared for her date. She liked Craig. He seemed like a nice guy. He wasn't built like Charles Atlas, but he wasn't overly fat either. He had a nice smile, which made up for the fact that he wasn't terribly attractive.

She took out her evening wear and prepared for the evening. Craig said that he was planning to take her out for dinner and a play. No one had ever asked her out to a play before. She was sure Craig would be considerate, unlike Carl. Carl expected her to have sex for a few pills and some wine. This was going to be a good evening. Mary wanted to look glamorous for Craig, and for everyone else she'd be seeing during the evening. She knew that she looked good with make-up and her hair done. The diet pills she took were keeping her weight at an all-time low. Tonight she didn't even feel fat.

She didn't expect Craig for another half hour and smoked a joint to mellow her out for the evening. She thought it would just be a play and dinner, nothing more. Craig didn't seem the type who wanted to jump in bed with her. He probably wanted a relationship. Mary didn't know if she was ready for such a thing again. She went into the kitchen for a Pepsi. Coke or Pepsi were guaranteed to make her mouth fresh and get rid of the marijuana smell, and she put in a few eyedrops to get the red color out of her eyes that smoking marijuana always caused.

She went over her list of things. Her face was fine, so was her hair. The evening outfit fit well and she had on new tinted hose. Her nails were perfect, her teeth brushed. The shoes were fancy, but she knew that she could walk in them if she needed to. Her keys and wallet were in her clutch bag, as were some drugs if she needed a little pick-me-up during the evening. She had Kleenex and Maxipads in case her period came, and some make-up to touch up her face during the night. She remembered money and put some in her bag in case she had to walk home or take a taxi, should something go wrong. It hadn't crossed her mind to take money to pay for the play or dinner. After all, Craig asked to take her out; she hadn't asked him.

The doorbell rang.

"Hello," Craig smiled, as she opened the door, and joined him outside.

"You look lovely," he spoke with awe.

"Thanks," she happily said, turning full circle with arms outstretched.

"My pleasure," he remarked, then remembered to close his open mouth. He saw her hair toss and bounce as she made the pirouette. She was very pretty.

"Where are we off to?" she asked. "I'm starved."

"What type of food do you like?" he questioned.

"Anything, as long as there's a lot of it," she said.

"How about Japanese?" he asked, since he knew a great little restaurant near the theatre.

"Mexican would be a little more like it," she responded, loathing Japanese food with a passion. At least she was glad he didn't suggest raw fish.

"Italian?" he countered, knowing that Mexican food always gave him gas and he had a sensitive stomach.

"Fine," she said.

"My chariot awaits."

Craig's car was a quiet Oldsmobile, not new, but in good condition. Mary hoped for a sports car like the one Carl drove, so she was both a little relieved and peeved as she got in. The seats were comfortable, the car smelled clean, and the radio was on a rock station.

On the way to the restaurant, Mary watched Craig drive. She felt that men drove as they really were in life. Craig drove without error, not in a hurry, conscientious and not a showoff. He didn't drive much over the speed limit, but kept up with traffic. He was extremely courteous towards pedestrians. She felt safe in the car.

In the restaurant, she went to the ladies' room to check her make-up and then joined Craig at the table.

During dinner, Mary selected the wine and drank two glasses although Craig barely sipped his.

"I don't much like to drink if I have to drive," he stated flatly, but he smiled to show that he didn't care what she had to drink.

Mary had another glass of wine with dessert, finishing off the carafe, and returned to the restroom to freshen up. Her heels were a little wobbly and she monopolized the conversation in the car. She talked about herself, her earlier marriage, her kids, who were with their father, her goals and work, and brought Craig up on everything important to her in life.

Mary laughed, and overcompensated a bit. She wanted to make a good impression on Craig, even though she seemed a little buzzed from the dinner alcohol and the grass she had smoked before leaving home. Her brain was a little sluggish and she felt nervous. The first thing she had to do at the theatre was to take an upper so that her brain would clear for a while. It was important to have her act together for Craig.

They passed a three-car accident on the way to the theatre.

"My church is having us help people who are overwhelmed by drugs," he said in passing, thinking of the accident he just passed. "A lot of people out there are having problems handling alcohol, let alone drugs now that they're legal. I had over thirty calls myself last Saturday night from people who were seeking help on the drug hotline."

"Let me ask a question," Mary asked. "Which was worse, the people strung out on drugs or your having to spend a Saturday night answering phones when you could be out partying?"

"I didn't really have anyone I could party with," he admitted shyly.

"Do you hate drugs?" she asked hesitantly.

"Not hate; fear. I know that they can be addicting. There are people who can't live without them. Drugs to wake them up, drugs to help them eat, drugs to help them through the day, drugs to calm them and drugs to put them asleep at night. It sounds awful, doesn't it?" asked Craig.

Mary nodded. Craig had just described her life.

"And do you know what's the worst part of it all?" asked Craig.

"No," said Mary very quietly.

"Think of all the glasses of water those people must take to get all those drugs down their throats," Craig said and started to laugh. He couldn't stay serious too long. He enjoyed life and knew that a positive outlook in everything was important. "Rejoice in everything," from Philippians chapter four, verse four, was his favorite Bible verse.

Mary laughed too, and seconds later they arrived at the theatre.

As soon as they were inside, Mary excused herself, went to the bathroom, and took an upper.

As the play began, Mary began to fidget. Craig wasn't sure if it was the murder mystery with a lot of gunfire in it or that she just didn't like it. Craig didn't like it that much and wanted to leave at the intermission. Mary claimed it was charming and she had to know how it would end.

During intermission, Mary had a cup of coffee and a cookie and Craig settled for punch.

"I love going to plays," Mary happily remarked.

"I do too," he replied.

"This one is very dramatic," concluded Mary.

"I know," replied Craig. "It's supposed to be a comedy, a tongue-in-cheek one."

"I wonder how it'll end."

"I guess I won't be walking out," Craig told himself. He settled back into his chair as the house lights dimmed for the third act.

During the third act, Mary kept moving about. Craig knew the seats were uncomfortable, but not enough to squirm so much.

"It's probably because she's skin and bones," he thought. He remembered she had very little padding on her.

Mary, wired from the upper and coffee, was feeling the alcohol. She felt electrified. Her arms and hands were tingling. The play seemed to be moving slowly and every few seconds she looked at her watch to see how much time had elapsed. When the curtain fell, she went back to the bathroom and smoked a long joint. She straightened her hair and took a breath mint. After she squirted some perfume behind her ears, she took a drink of water and met Craig outside.

"The place smells like an opium den," she lied, looking askance at Craig.

"I know," agreed Craig. "The men's room does, too. I guess some people have to have their cigarettes or they'll go crazy. Some people have no control."

"Well," Mary asked, "what did you think of the play?"

"I usually try to see the good in things," he said, "but I really didn't enjoy it."

"I liked it a lot," Mary said with enthusiasm, watching other theatergoers make their way out toward their cars.

"I know you did," Craig noticed. "To me it seemed a bit shallow. There didn't seem to be much content."

"I know what you mean," Mary said, not knowing what he meant.

"How do you feel?" asked Craig.

"Great," Mary smiled, feeling that she was still wired. "Where to now? For some cocktails, or dancing, or..."

"I think back to your place, and then home for me," Craig said. "I have to be at the office at five o'clock tomorrow. If I don't get home and get some sleep, I'll be a basketcase."

Mary was quiet all the way back to her apartment.

"Would you like to come in for a nightcap?" she asked, expecting him to be coaxed in.

"No thank you," Craig smiled, "but I'll see you to your door and grab a quick hug or two."

At her door, Craig hugged her, and she hugged him, molding her body close to his. It felt good, and it felt right. After a few seconds, they separated. Craig smiled at her. "I'd like to see you again soon," he said.

"Are you sure about skipping that nightcap?" she asked.

He nodded, then turned around, putting his hands in his pockets, and made his way to the elevator. "I'll call you tomorrow," he voiced softly before the elevator doors closed.

"It was a wonderful night," Mary thought, closing the door behind her. She hummed all the way to bed, closed her eyes and fell into a wonderful sleep.

She was so happy, she forgot to take her sleeping pill.

Prescription for Mayhem

Chapter Twenty-four

Doc Browning sat in the hospital cafeteria, barely tasting the bland food. He opened his monthly medical society newsletter. In it was an article stating that the Food and Drug Administration had just been granted more money by Congress to fund testing and evaluation of new drugs by the drug industry.

Doc grumbled as he sipped his coffee, turning the page of his newsletter. He wondered if he should change from family practice to something surgical. Of course, it would be a longer residency and the staggering costs for malpractice insurance wouldn't be worth it. But, he knew his hands weren't steady enough for surgery, and he enjoyed his lifesaving efforts in the emergency room. Emergency rooms were wonderful, since most people coming in weren't going to argue with whatever procedure he wanted to do.

"The most compliant patient is an unconscious patient," remarked one of his instructors during his first year at medical school. And that still held true.

Doc Browning skipped to the next article about lobbyists indicted for bribery. Petitions going to Congress weren't successful. No federal court judge would grant an injunction against the law, no matter what the M.A.A. did. All legislation entering Congress was being buried in committee. The M.A.A. didn't seem to be doing too well, and the article concluded by stating that if legislation wasn't possible, another method would be needed. A march on Washington might be effective, or even a day where all doctors refused to work.

Doc Browning read between the lines and thought that the medical society was hinting of a strike if things didn't reutrn to normal.

He didn't know if he would participate in a strike. When he took the emergency room job, he had signed government forms stating that he wouldn't strike. There was also the question of his student loans. He had a student loan deferment because of the emergency room position and his residency at the university. The government could stop that at any time, and he had over a hundred thousand dollars of student loans outstanding. This was typical for medical students, and he knew he wasn't through going further in debt. He'd have to take out more loans before he completed his residency.

He was also concerned about patient compliance. Yesterday, a man came into the hospital with a swollen hand. Doc Browning concluded it was a spider bite, and suggested that the patient take a few aspirin and come back in a week. The man started to shout and said he didn't come in to find out what caused it. He wanted to know what to take to make his hand better and make the pain go away.

Doc Browning felt pressured and prescribed a light analgesic for the pain. He also prescribed an anti-inflammatory agent to decrease the swelling and a mild antibiotic in case of a secondary infection. The patient said that wouldn't make the pain go away.

Doc Browning suggested the patient talk to the pharmacist and wrote on the chart, "Triage, PIA," which told the pharmacist the patient was a "pain in the ass." When the pharmacist came in later, he said the patient was most cooperative. The pharmacist gave him a codeine compound and told him to return in eight hours if the pain didn't decrease. The pharmacist said he would give the man a shot of penicillin and some Ibuprofen for inflammation if he came back in. The pharmacist said that all the guy really needed was some concern, compassion, and a shot or two in the butt.

Doc Browning did sign a petition yesterday being circulated by the clergy, stating that drugs should be outlawed again, but he wasn't sure it would be effective. It would take months to collect enough signatures, and then the petition had to go to Congress.

He threw his magazine in the trash and walked back to the emergency room.

"We have a patient who is having vaginal pain and eye problems," said the nurse practitioner, "It's probably some bacteria, but could you take a look?"

"Let me review the chart and see if it's a patient who has been here before," he replied, knowing that a nurse must be present for every vaginal examination.

The chart was huge. The patient had been there many times even though the emergency room had been open just a few months. One doctor indicated that her symptoms weren't consistent with the findings, intimating she was a hypochondriac or malingerer. Browning realized that he had seen her once himself for headaches and that she seemed tense. He walked into the examining room.

"Doc Browning," he said, holding out his hand. "Good to see you again."

"Elaine Russell," she replied.

"How are the headaches doing?"

"Better, but I have this burning sensation in my vagina, and my eyes feel as if they've been sandpapered. I've also been sick for the last few days."

"Well," he told her, looking at her vital signs for the day on the chart the nurse practitioner gave him, "your temperature is up a bit and your left eye is a bit inflamed. We'll have to wait for the blood tests to see if the white count is affected." The leukocyte test and bacteria/viral/parasitology evaluations were already checked off on the lab request form. "That nurse practitioner is really on the ball," he mused. "She ordered the same tests I would have requested."

"Let's see what we have here," he said, placing Elaine's legs in the stirrups and putting on rubber gloves. He took a speculum and rubbed it between his gloved hands with a sterile towel, to warm it a bit. "This shouldn't hurt," he said, inserting the speculum inside her vagina, "but it might feel a bit cold."

"Looks red and inflamed all right," surmised Doc Browning, looking at the vaginal mucosa and the cervix. "A culture will probably confirm the diagnosis." The nurse practitioner had a swab ready for a sample for the laboratory staff to analyze. Doc Browning took the swab, obtained a sample of the cervical mucosa, and handed it to the nurse.

Upon removing the speculum, he took a look at Elaine's face. A pretty woman, he thought, aside from that red eye. He took her over to the biomicroscope for the eye exam. He noticed that the cornea of the eye and surrounding area resembled any other conjunctivitis he had ever seen.

"Where is the eye pain?" he asked, removing his head from the eyepiece of the microscope.

"It hurts right on my eyelids when I blink," she related, pointing to her upper left eyelid.

"I'm going to flip your eyelid to get a better look at the inside," he warned. "This won't hurt a bit."

Flipping the left eyelid, there was a blood red color on the inside of it.

"Gonorrhea," he thought, knowing that only gonorrhea could cause a red eye like that. He looked at the nurse, signaled for another swab and took a culture.

"It's going to take a few minutes for the results, so have a seat in the waiting room. We'll put some hot packs on the eye while you're waiting."

Elaine dressed, took the hot pack to the waiting room, waited a few minutes until a seat became vacant, then sat down.

"Have the lab check for gonorrhea," he told the nurse, as he went to the *PDR* to see if it was Penicillin G or Penicillin K for the treatment of gonorrhea. He couldn't remember which. He knew the pharmacist would prescribe for it, but he felt better when he noted a tentative medicine treatment regimen with his diagnosis.

An hour later, after treating some patients who had been injured in a car accident and sending for an orthopedist to set their fractures, the lab results came back; "Russell, Elaine. Gonococcal infection."

"I was right. A classic presentation of gonorrhea," he thought.

"Young lady," he spoke to Elaine, "please come with me." He took her to a separate room.

"You have gonorrhea," he said matter-of-factly, as though he didn't approve of her. "We'll send you to the pharmacist for a shot, but you'll have to notify the people you made love with in the last few months."

Elaine began to cry. The doctor seemed so cold and impersonal when he talked to her. She had pain in her vagina, and her eyes were burning. She felt ashamed for getting VD. She didn't know who it was, and it could have been any of five or ten men she knew.

"I'm sorry for crying," she apologized, "I just need some sympathy, and maybe an injection. I know I'll get better, but I sure feel like dirt."

"Some compassion and a shot in the butt," echoed in Doc Browning's mind. They were the same words of the pharmacist. "If I treated her so shabbily because of a VD infection, how much more would I demean her if she was an addict coming for heroin?" he thought. "I don't know," he told himself. "I don't know anything anymore."

"I'm sorry, also, for my actions," apologized Doc Browning, after being silent for a few moments. "You're going to be all right. I promise you are. A shot of penicillin and some later dosages should have this problem settled in a few weeks. Don't worry. Please refrain from sexual activity until it is over, and let your partner know the situation so it doesn't spread."

"I need a vacation," Doc Browning tiredly thought. He had been working almost day and night since the Drug Legislation Act was announced. What little sleep he had been getting was interspersed with emergency patients. Right now he was taking uppers to stay awake. In six more hours he was going to have a whole day off to himself. Maybe he'd spend some of the money he had been making. But he knew he'd probably spend the day catching up on sleep.

Yesterday, in a rare lull between patients, Doc Browning had talked further with a nice motorcycle sergeant. Sergeant Manila was writing his report in the hospital waiting room. He was supervising a gridlock at Normandie and Melrose. Some lady on uppers and downers started the whole incident.

"Busy?" asked Kevin.

"It hasn't let up," Doc muttered.

"Same here," voiced Kevin. "I'm wearing out tires with all the miles I'm putting on the motorcycle. I'm so tired when I get home, all I want to do is sleep."

"As long as you don't get too tired and have problems sleeping," Doc Browning said in a fatherly tone.

"Funny you should mention that," Kevin answered, looking into the cool eyes of Doc Browning, "I've been having problems sleeping."

"Maybe you need an occasional sleeping pill," suggested the doctor.

"Maybe a pill now and then might help," Kevin thought, not really sure about taking pills.

"Who knows?" Kevin uttered. "We may wake up and this'll be over, huh?"

"Wake me when it's over," Doc Browning awoke from his daydream, breaking into a run as he heard sirens outside the emergency room.

Prescription for Mayhem

Chapter Twenty-five

Two weeks later
July 1, 2028

"You have too many contracts out," related the accountant to Julie. "We're having trouble meeting our obligations."

"You mean we're broke?"

"Not exactly. As you know, most of our assets are liquid but we do have some permanent funds in the family portfolio."

"Can we support the family?"

"At the current payroll, without investing in new drugs or marketing the drugs now in storage, we can support the family for five years."

"And then?"

"And then we have to be in another business. We can't make it in drugs anymore."

"What do you have in mind?" asked Julie.

"Expanding our current facilities in gambling and prostitution," said the accountant with confidence.

"It might work," Julie agreed, "or kill us in the process. Anything else?"

"We could expand the assassination sector of the family business. Maybe we can contract our services to terrorists or those fearing terrorists."

"Good," Julie said, always liking assassinations. "Do it."

"Very well," agreed the accountant. "But with so many family members unemployed, if all the current contracts are met, there won't be enough funds to support the family for more than two years. That's hardly enough time to switch product lines."

"You don't mean you want us to give up open contracts?" asked Julie, knowing that a family contract was never reneged. Once the order for a hit went out, it was never changed. That created respect among the family members, insuring that no one got out of line. And it created fear with the outside people the family dealt with. Open countracts couldn't be cancelled. They were one of the family cornerstones.

"Have you heard that Luigi Devoy was taken into custody?"

"No! When?" asked Julie nervously. Luigi had been his main assassin for the last fifteen years. He never missed a hit and he had always gotten away clean. Not this time.

"Well," demanded Julie, "did he get the man responsible for the mess we're in?"

"He missed his target," quietly reported the accountant.

"He what?" bellowed Julie, standing up from his easy chair, clenching his fists. He started pacing. "My best man screwed up!"

"He missed," the accountant told. "He was picked up in an apartment house with his gun pointed at Bunker, the Chairman of the *Guidance and Direction Committee.*"

"I can't believe it!" Julie said to the walls. He began thinking desperately about who needed to be killed. Someone had to die. Someone had to die!

"And," added the accountant, starting to worry about stories of messengers carrying bad news, "you may want to put out a contract on Luigi Devoy. He's been with us for years and if he talked, he could sink us worse than Pete Alonso."

"Peter, 'the Dick,' Alonso," growled Julie, fuming. "He started it all, and we're still not any closer to removing the problem by killing that bastard! Or the guys who made the Drug Legislation Act, either!" he screamed at the accountant who was cowering.

"I do have some good news," the accountant reported. "The godson of your sister's daughter, Carl Friedman, from the Los Angeles area, just phoned to tell his Uncle Giuliano that even though business is bad, people won't be forgetting him that easy. He went to a client's apartment who had been putting him off since the drug law passed. Some dame named Mary Lane. When she said she didn't want to buy drugs, he beat her up and raped her. She paid him her usual monthly amount."

"I'm proud of him," said Julie a bit quieter, daydreaming. "He'll be a credit to the family yet, mark my words."

"What do we do about Devoy?" asked the accountant once he saw Julie was calmer.

"Put out a contract," said Julie quietly. Julie didn't know much about Devoy. He knew that Devoy was good, and usually did his job efficiently and silently. What he didn't know was if Devoy would squeal in a pinch. That was the question. If Devoy talked, he knew he was good as dead.

"I'm as good as dead," wailed Luigi Devoy, talking to the Attorney General. Devoy remembered the look on Sam Bunker's face. Sam looked exactly like Julie did whenever he ordered a kill.

"I don't want to die," Devoy whined and sniveled. "I've told you all I know," he wailed.

The Attorney General knew Devoy was beaten. The man who had killed so many people was now squirming to save his own life. It was up to Sam Bunker to grant him a stay of execution or not.

"I'll talk to Sam Bunker," promised the Attorney General, knowing that he would do no such thing.

"Ashes to ashes, dust to dust, we bury and consecrate the souls of our dearly departed brethren in the name of your son, Jesus. For we know that with Christ, and through Christ, in His name, all things are possible, for the glory of God. Amen."

The Chaplain looked at the five committee members. The Chaplain had been asked by his fellow clergy to speak up in Congress. His eulogy for the dead he had just given did that.

"Thank you, Chaplain," said Sam Bunker added sarcastically, slightly pissed at a eulogy for the souls of the millions who had died since the Drug Legislation Act began.

"You know, Chaplain," Sam added, very peeved, "we're trying to do the best possible job we can. The best we can, for everybody. Everybody. For you, too. Before you start treating us like we're pieces of crap and the lowest sinners, you'd better take a good look in the mirror. We're all suffering as much as Christ did when we hear of the deaths we've caused. Maybe even more than Christ did. Suffering; inside and out! I want you to remember that you're a guest here. You might want to begin acting like one. Good day."

The Chaplain walked out knowing that he had tried his best, as asked, to get the powerful people on Capitol Hill to change their minds. He didn't feel good about this. He knew that the five people in the room were the ones for the job. He knew there was a reason for what they did, and that they were concerned about the ramifications of what they enacted, but he didn't feel good about complaining about their actions in their midst.

"I know the feeling about looking in a mirror," said Bob Emerson, nervously. "Every time I look in the mirror, I see the face of a man who sentenced millions to death. A murderer..." he whispered softly. It was anything but a sobering thought. He hadn't been sober much in the last few months.

"I understand how you feel," agreed Steve judiciously. "But remember, all we did was return to the people the power of choice over their own lives."

"I have some good news," said Sam.

"You've given up booze," quipped Bob wryly, trying to lighten up the somberness of the room. He didn't want to look inside himself for answers. Every time he looked inside himself lately, he was sickened at what he saw. He was drinking more, and did not want to face himself, or others. His wife of twenty-two years mentioned at the dinner table yesterday that a trial separation might be good for their marriage.

"You've thrown out the girdle you wear to show everyone how trim you are," Tom Baker remarked, smiling. He too was trying to change the subject. He was so depressed by what was going on, and that it was his fault, that his wife suggested he consider a long vacation, or therapy. She said their marriage was falling apart.

Last week, Tom spanked his young daughter for no reason at all. He found himself crying hours later when he went to her to ask for forgiveness. She gave him her favorite Barbie doll to keep him company and to cheer him up. Even after he stopped crying, Tom found he couldn't pry the doll out of his hands easily. And when he finally did, his hands were bruised from how tightly he held onto the doll.

"You're allocating us an increase in salary for the work we've done beyond the call of duty," asked Steve.

"You've done such a good job that they're thinking of using you for the next election as a presidential candidate," flippantly chimed Frederica, also happy for the levity. Her private life had fallen to pieces. No one wanted to be with a person with one eye that was depressed and depressing to be around.

"Gentlemen, and lady," laughed Sam, holding his hand over his heart. "You flatter me. I'd like to give you this document of over two hundred fifty pages. You've earned it."

"What is it?" asked Tom.

"Forget playing dumb," said Sam. "You're going to have to read the whole damned thing anyway. And you will want to. This is the confession of Luigi

Devoy, the Mafia's number one killer. It names everyone, with enough evidence for a conviction of the entire Mafia. This represents the death of organized crime in America. The icing on the cake we've presented to the American public."

"Devoy," remembered Frederica. "Wasn't he the one who tried to assassinate you?" she asked Sam Bunker.

"Absolutely. As if I were a member of the Kennedy family," said Sam Bunker. "The CIA and FBI are moving en masse against the people named in this document. We have the police force to arrest them and the court system to process them. They'll hang," Sam said with a finality to it.

"How much are you paying Devoy for this?" asked Frederica.

"Devoy is being tried and will be convicted of attempted murder. He's given us this information so that we'll let him off with something less than the death penalty," informed Sam.

"And?" asked Frederica.

"And, under the Personal Rights Act, I can have him electrocuted," said Sam thoughtfully, "and I will."

"But think about what he's given us," Tom said defensively, hating any further loss of life. "Haven't we had enough of this killing?"

"He gave us the Mafia, that's true," summarized Sam. "But he has killed well over five hundred people during the fifteen years he's been a hit man. That's almost four people a month. If you had the power of life and death over him, would you sentence him to hell or give him a pardon? Remember, he is the murderer of hundreds."

The room was quiet.

"I believe that answers any questions," Sam said flatly.

"Say," asked Frederica, "What did any of you think about this morning's march on the Capitol? Over thirty thousand M.D.'s attended. They were dressed for the march in white coats and stethoscopes."

"It sure impressed me," said Tom. "They looked like a commercial for laundry detergent. Those coats were really white."

"Tell me this," urged Sam. "Did the M.A.A. seem genuinely concerned for the people, or were they just out to protect their own interests?"

"It seemed that they weren't genuinely concerned for the people," Tom reviewed in his mind what he saw, "but I'm no expert."

"But I am," Frederica voiced authoritatively. "I think their next step is to stop giving services and go out on strike."

"They'd never do that," Bob cried with a look of horror on his face. He was from a small Nebraska town where the doctor did everything from delivering calves to delivering babies. Once, his hometown doctor stayed up all night with him when he came home from the service with cholera. This gave him a lot of faith in physicians.

"Some will, some won't," Frederica said nonchalantly.

"They'll never get away with it," said Sam. "They're supposed to heal lives, not threaten us by using people as a bargaining chip."

"If police, firemen, and postmen can do it," asked Frederica, "what's to keep doctors from doing it?"

The room was quiet. Minutes later, Sam slid his chair back from the conference table, stood up, and spoke.

"We have to stop this," he ordered firmly.

"How?" asked Steve.

"I was just wondering that," admitted Sam as he sat back down at the conference table.

"If we don't stop this, we'll have the death and hospitalization statistics going up," remarked Bob, thinking past the alcohol in his body to the finances it would involve.

"We will," Sam added dramatically. "Anyone have ideas?"

"None," Frederica observed, seeing that they were at an impasse, "but if you give me a while to think about it, I may be able to come up with something."

"I don't have anything," Tom added bitterly, "Not even a good joke I can throw in. Good jokes are a rarity in these trying times."

"Amen," agreed Steve. "I don't have anything off the top of my head, but whatever we should do, it damn well better be quick."

"Meeting adjourned for assessment of the situation and possible solutions," Sam stated, without asking for any motion of any kind.

"And God help us," Tom cried to the heavens.

"If God doesn't help us," stated Steve, "He may be calling back a lot more of his fold quicker than we thought."

Chapter Twenty-six

One week later
July 8, 2028

"We pray for peace for the souls of the people in turmoil, in their lives, their weaknesses, and those yielding into temptation and possible separation from God, and the life He would have them live. May He grant them strength to fight the adversary, and return to a glorious life. Through Christ our Lord we pray; Amen."

"Thank you, Chaplain," happily smiled Tom.

"Thank you," said Sam. "And have yourself a good day. You hear?"

The Chaplain exited, feeling a little better than last week, knowing that he was praying for God to be in control of things.

"Well?" asked Sam, "It's been a week, and we've all had a while to think about this tentative doctors' strike."

"Not tentative," corrected Steve. "I'm convinced by my studies the last few days that this is an absolute certainty."

"Seconded," added Frederica. "And if you foolhardy people would have listened to me in the first place, you wouldn't have had to work your tails off."

"Does everyone believe Frederica about the strike, without a shadow of a doubt?" asked Sam.

Each nodded.

"Well, what do we do about it?" asked Bob.

Bob was hung over, slightly sick from withdrawl and trying to go to Alcoholics Anonymous meetings again. His wife left him three days ago, saying she was going to be visiting her mother with the kids for the rest of the summer. He cried, collapsing on the den floor, pleading with her not to leave. She held his face in her hands and kissed his forehead.

"I love you," she said, "But there's not enough room for me and your other love in this house!"

"What other love?" he said between sobs.

She didn't say a word. She walked over to the bar, took each liquor bottle, and smashed every one to bits. When she was done, she looked at him with tears of love in her eyes, and walked out.

"We have to stop them," said Sam. "If those doctors strike, they'll kill more people, uh, figuratively speaking."

"We have to prepare for this extremely thoroughly," said Bob slowly, thinking about his strategy for the situation. He was glad to be thinking about something beside his misery.

"I have something to start with," spoke Tom.

"The floor recognizes the practical joker of Washington, D.C.," said Sam, glad that the ball was rolling.

"Most M.D.'s are in college for a long time," Tom began.

"Tell us something we don't know," Frederica yawned.

"The average education for a doctor costs about a hundred fifty thousand dollars," stated Tom.

"Which means?" asked Steve, trying to figure out what Tom was getting at.

"Which means that most of the education is funded by *government* student loans," said Tom, smiling.

"That means," interrupted Bob, "that the interest and the principal payments are probably a good chunk of their salaries each month...."

"...Which also means if we decide to change policy, we would have to deal with doctors who have been out of school less than ten years," jumped in Steve, rolling with the thought. "These people might want to cooperate with us."

"Twenty years!" Bob said knowingly. "Some of their student loans are so large that it probably takes twenty years to pay them off."

"But," asked Sam. "If we can hold that debt over the heads of doctors who graduated within the last fifteen years, it would take care of most doctors under the age of forty-five.

"And," continued Sam, "we can state that in a time of national emergency, they have to repay their student loan in one lump sum as designated by the government."

"Who's talking about a national emergency?" asked Bob.

"I am," Sam blurted out, brainstorming. "When these doctors strike, the President is going to have to declare martial law and do something about the strikers."

"Steve," continued Sam, "you're the judicial wizard. Write us an emergency medical act in case of a national emergency. Have the President sign it after you run it by us. This states that any doctor who does not fulfill his duty in time of a national emergency must repay, in full, all of his outstanding student loans within thirty days of notification.

"Any problems with that?" Sam asked the group.

"I'd also like to see that these doctors face the possibility of having their medical licenses revoked for a period of no less than seven years," Frederica added quietly but thoughtfully. "That ought to take the wind out of their sails."

"So moved," Tom said, angry that doctors would hold their power over the heads of their patients.

"The vote?" asked Sam.

"Seconded," said Frederica.

"Ayes?" asked Sam.

Everyone raised a hand.

"It's in your ball park now," Sam told Steve. "Make it a good law, and make it unbreakable."

"I have a rider," said Bob, thinking further about the business of financing a medical education. "Regarding universities, we can make it mandatory that any medical student or resident who strikes would automatically be expelled from school. We have enough government funding to make our request law in the universities."

"And in the veterans' hospitals nationwide," added Frederica, remembering her experiences when she got out of medical school.

"It sounds good," agreed Tom. "No medical student would throw away his medical education and years of internship and residency. So moved."

"Seconded," said Steve, making a note to amend the bill.

"Ayes?" asked Sam.

Everyone agreed.

"Done," said Sam. "Steve?" he asked.

"Already ahead of you," Steve, smiled. He had already made a note for a trailer to the bill.

"How about doctors in the government and county hospitals we built a few months ago?" asked Bob.

"That's taken care of. We already have a 'no strike' clause in them," remarked Steve. "The doctors knew what they were getting themselves into when they signed the initial contract. Damn, I'm glad I put that in the contract. Is that foresight, or what?"

"All right," Sam cajoled. "Steve; one pat on the back for you."

"You know," Tom solemnly said. "This may cover the university, county, and government agencies, and the doctors under forty-five years of age, but that still leaves about half the nation's doctors free and clear, according to my information. Also, there are M.D.'s from well-to-do families who didn't use student loans. There must be some of those!"

"What do we do?" asked Sam.

"There's only one thing to do," stated Frederica, slowly. "We have to do the same thing as the military. In an emergency, if the person isn't available, then the job goes to the next person in line, whether they're able to handle it or not."

"That means..." spoke Bob to the group.

"That means that the law would have to include nurse practitioners and pharmacists doing the diagnosing and treatment regimens," related Frederica Wright, interrupting Bob Emerson. "It would also have to include the use of ancillary help like X-ray technicians to spot and set fractures, lab technicians and physical therapists to keep the blood work and physical therapy under control, and the like."

"But," Bob asked nervously, "that still leaves out the surgeons and other specialties. There's no replacement for them."

"That's true," Sam answered after some thought. "But, as surgeons aren't as involved in the daily doling out of medications, and are happiest when they're doing surgery and making money, I sure hope that they will realize that it's not in their best interests to strike."

"And if they don't?" asked Bob, softly, soberly, begging the question.

"The smart American will not have surgery done," added Sam quickly and then hesitantly continued, "and those needing surgery immediately will take what they can get. It will be a dark day for America."

"Sam," quietly said Tom, "Bob hasn't said it, but we haven't had a chance to talk much about the nation. We're supposed to be the 'land of the free and home of the brave.' With all these restrictions, the deaths, the possible loss of humanity from this doctor strike, shouldn't we stop and let this one go by?"

"I've thought about it all these last few months," Sam confessed. "I've felt guilty knowing I've had a hand in constitutional amendments that have led to deaths. My sleep has been troubled. I don't take enjoyment from many things now. But I'm convinced down to my bones that any doctor who would place the drug issue ahead of saving someone's life should not be allowed to practice medicine.

"I'm an old man," Sam uttered tiredly, "with over thirty years in Congress. When I was young, people going into medicine only cared about helping others. They were the missionaries of the home front, the healers caring for the sick. Money wasn't an issue to them. Today, that has changed. Most doctors are greedy and enter medicine mainly for the money they'll make. With Medicare and government spending to doctors almost as much as the defense budget, it's time that the greed stopped.

"I'm as sick as anyone at having to legislate against doctors," Sam admitted. "It means to me that another ideal we've looked up to has fallen and is tarnished. So far, we've only had to worry about pushers. We have done more good for the world in the last two months than ever before. And we've been proud of it, even though there is a high cost. Every morning when I look at this wrinkled face in the mirror, I tell myself that it has been worth it.

"None of us expected this number of deaths. Deaths in the millions, and millions crippled. However, I'm convinced that America is stronger than ever, even with the infirm. We have reversed some of the wrongs that were prevalent in this modern society. It has cost us, and cost us heavily. Folks, if we let the doctors take control of the drug world again, America will die as surely as if we strangle her ourselves. Hopefully, we won't need to do this to doctors," remarked Sam, then realistically added, "but I'm afraid we will."

"Good speech, Sam," Tom said, clapping, cutting Sam off.

"Excellent," voiced Steve.

"Daniel Webster the second," said Frederica, grinning.

"But I wasn't done...," Sam said.

"Yes, you are," stated Tom. "When they said that old politicians never die but keep talking until every else does, they weren't fooling."

"I have a point that needs clarifying," asked Bob. "What are we calling jails these days? Are we calling them prisons, or correction facilities?"

"Depends..." thoughtfully stated Steve. "If they're for juveniles with learning problems, they're educational facilities. If they're for people who have been arrested because of drug problems, they're correctional facilities. If it's for pushers and people convicted by the Personal Rights Act, prisons."

"John Jones is making certain that we have power, but it may be rough for him and us when elections come around on November eleventh. I'm up for re-election," said Frederica realistically.

Sam swore, "I'll never complain about a Special Session again in my life."

"You don't now," told Steve. "You're always asleep for them."

"I'm not asleep," Sam smiled. "I'm resting my eyes."

"Well," prayed Steve. "I sure hope that we never have to put this Medical Emergency Act into effect."

"So does everyone else," said Sam, "and the President, as well. He's the one to declare martial law if the strike hits. As long as we get the information to the doctors, clinics, hospitals, and the like before the strike hits, maybe we'll come out of this smelling like a rose."

"Smell? They always say a big stink clears the air," Bob said philosophically.

Chapter Twenty-seven

Two weeks later
July 23, 2028

Doc Browning was miserable after he opened his mail. One letter, from the university, stated that under the new Medical Emergency Act, he would be dismissed if he were not available to work during a national emergency. Another letter from the government stated that if there were a medical emergency and he was not available to see patients, he would have to repay all outstanding student loans within thirty days, and would face a seven to ten-year suspension of his medical license.

Doc Browning figured his current student loan balance was $155,342.75. The seventy-five cents seemed funny. That part he could pay, and the three hundred and forty two dollars as well. But the rest was impossible. The fact remained that he wasn't even finished with his residency.

The third piece of mail was a handwritten note from the medical society, stating that a strike would take effect the following Tuesday, and that all members were expected to participate. To top it off, a fourth letter arrived from the hospital reminding him of his contract and the no-strike clause he signed, indicating that if he violated the contract he would be prosecuted to the full extent of the law.

He thought about it when he got to the emergency room. He didn't know what to do. He had been reminded by Elaine Russell that he lacked compassion for the patients and that he should do what was right for them.

"Is it right for patients to suffer and die while I am striking?" he asked himself. "But, do people deserve the right to heal themselves, or do they need to be protected from themselves?" If he went on strike, he might be dismissed from the residency program, lose his license, and be faced with a huge student loan with no means to pay for it. If he didn't strike, he faced ostracism from the medical community, and he would have to work with these people and their criticisms in the future.

By Tuesday morning he still had no answers. The strike was to begin at twelve noon Eastern Standard Time. He had the day off, so he could think about it a little longer.

At nine in the morning, Western Standard Time, half of the doctors in the private hospitals finished up with the patients and walked off the job. Private practitioners throughout the country closed their offices. The M.A.A. held a press conference, stating that until the doctors' requests were met, they would maintain the strike. Their demand was simple. They wanted the government to return to the medical doctors the right to prescribe drugs.

Half an hour later, the television and radio programs were interrupted by a special news break. It was a message from the President of the United States.

"My friends," he began. "I have received a note from the Medical Association of America with a set of requests which are really demands. The doctors are on strike. They want the power that was placed in your hands returned to them. Unless we, the people, return the control over prescribing pharmaceuticals to them, they will not return to work.

"I consider this action no different from any other terrorist act. I will not meet with demands of terrorists, nor will I give in to these doctors' requests.

"I am declaring a national state of emergency and martial law in the United States. All university, county, and state hospitals will continue to operate in their usual manner. Medical doctors have until midnight tonight to return to their jobs. If they don't, they will automatically have their licenses revoked for seven years. All doctors' vacations are canceled and they are ordered to return to their jobs. Any and all medical students who fail to attend classes will be automatically expelled from their medical school programs.

"Pharmacists will continue to prescribe pharmaceuticals. As of now, all nurse practitioners are empowered to take over the medical doctors' jobs of diagnosis and treatment, with the help of pharmacists. X-ray technicians and CT-scan technicians are empowered to analyze fractures, and set them. Laboratory technicians as well as physical and pulmonary technicians are responsible for monitoring patient status. In emergencies, surgery will be performed by residents or interns according to the situations.

"I urge all medical doctors to evaluate the situation they face.

"May God bless you all, and, despite everything, keep you healthy and well. Pray for your families and the nation."

Regular station programming was resumed. Right after his speech, the President left the United States to attend a conference in Moscow.

Craig was upset; he'd heard the news when he was at the postal station sorting mail. He couldn't believe that doctors would strike, but he knew that people were not in control of themselves.

Craig felt healthy, though. He was planning to see Mary on Friday, since he was off on Saturday and could sleep in. She sure was a pretty woman. She was kind and considerate, but most of all, she was enjoyable to be with. She had a wonderful smile, was quick-witted and not stuck up. He felt good with her. She seemed to have the same ideals as he did, with both feet planted firmly on the ground.

Mary felt that she was flying by herself among the clouds, with her feet high above the trees. The world disappeared as her mind soared up to the heavens while still seated on her couch.

"This is wonderful," she thought. The world was beautiful. It had rainbows and cloudy sunsets, a night sky gleaming around her with stars like diamond dust across a field of black velvet. She didn't want to remember Carl Friedman's forcing her to have sex with him. In the back of her mind, she knew she had to escape. She needed this. And all it took was a hallucinogen to get away from the world. Birds were singing in the sky and the forest smelled like every day was Christmas. There were no people around her, just the soft feel of the world at her feet and a quiet breeze cooling her skin and head.

She came slowly down to earth, then stood and looked at her reflection in a pond. Suddenly, she heard a clanging sound. The forest turned from green to gray. Her vision blurred. The world began to spin and she felt herself falling. She was falling, as though she would never stop. Just as her world became black around her she closed her eyes, hoping that the forest would appear again.

"Where am I?" she asked, opening her eyes. She saw a cot, with bars over a small window.

"Honey," said a female voice behind her. "Your ass is in jail."

"Why?" asked Mary.

"Honey," the woman in a police uniform said, "you were walking down the street naked. They say you even stood looking in a pool of oil for a while. No one could get through to you, so they brought you here and we gave you those prisoner's clothes."

"Am I going to jail for substance abuse?" asked Mary nervously, not wanting to go to prison.

"Naw," consoled the police officer. "Walking down the street naked don't do no harm to anyone but yourself. They do got an exhibitionism charge against you though. You'll probably get off with a warning. They understand that stuff. You'll be seeing the judge within an hour."

"Thank you," Mary said with trepidation, afraid in the thought of going into a courtroom. She hoped the judge would be a woman. She never wanted to bow down to any man ever again.

"But how did you ever get those welts and bruises?" asked the police officer, referring to the injuries from Carl's attack.

"I guess I bumped into a lot of things," Mary nervously said.

"You sure must have," admitted the police officer. "With all those drugs, it's amazing that your head is still screwed on straight."

"It will be straight," Mary resolved. "This will never happen again!"

"It's not straight," Sabrina told the workmen putting up her canvas in the church library. "Move it to the right."

One workman moved the frame slightly to the right.

"Now move the right corner up a bit," she showed them with her hands what she meant.

The picture was moved up a bit.

"Perfect," she said.

Sabrina looked at her work. It was glorious. She was so happy that she had found some inspiration from LSD. The drug had worked. The glow around the cross and the priest's face seemed to emanate from within. Yet the painting had the overall effect of spirituality and joy that she had desired to instill.

In the painting, Father Mahoney's face was radiant. He seemed to be the perfect happy uncle she had seen in him when they first met. The priest's face portrayed the same joy and spirituality that she had seen in the face of the drug addict that day in church. A face of redemption, of thanks, humility, and mostly, joy.

The composition of the picture was good. The colors were tranquil and were a perfect choice for the ambience of the library. She imagined scholars taking a break from their research, walking to the painting to look at it for a few moments, then returning refreshed to the task before them. She knew that the church elders might have wanted to see the priest in a conventional portrait, but she hoped the beauty of the picture would overcome their doubts.

"'Tis blessed by the Holy Virgin herself," Father Mahoney admitted upon seeing the painting. He smiled as he saw his painted image giving communion to the family at the railing before the altar.

"Inspiring, isn't it?" asked the priest.

"I hope so," said Sabrina. She planned to call up the art journals to view her painting. With any luck, it could be shown to the community at large, and then she might receive other commissions for her work.

"Which was first, the creativity or the drug?" she asked herself silently, thinking about the LSD.

Sabrina knew that she had to read more about LSD and its side effects. She didn't want to damage her brain cells, nor have chromosomal problems should she ever decide she wanted kids.

She was happy because she was going to be paid for the painting. She needed the money for painting supplies, a little stereo for the apartment, and some more house plants. "God knows," she thought, "I could be more creative in a happier environment."

"Stick with me," she thought to the empty LSD vial in her purse. "We're going places," as she went off to the pharmacy for a refill.

"Time to go," said the female police officer to Mary Lane as she was led out of the cell. "The judge will see you now."

"Drugs are miserable," Mary confessed, still trying to think what she was going to say to the judge.

Prescription for Mayhem

Chapter Twenty-eight

Elaine was nervous. The M.A.A. strike had her scared. She knew she was sensitive and might be sick at any moment. If she took drugs and got worse, she'd have to go to the hospital and be seen by a nurse practitioner. She believed in doctors. If something happened, there was no one to go to for help. The penicillin had cleared up her gonorrhea, and her eyes were feeling better. If she was sick, there was a chance she'd end up in a hospital.

Television was no help. The news was horrible. An ex-congressman, Emil Wardlaw, had been murdered and disfigured. His body was hung in the center of Grand Central Station in New York. And a man named Julie Giuliano was apprehended attempting to murder Congressman Samuel Bunker just last night.

This morning, she thought she heard noises outside. She called '911,' but was put on hold by an answering machine for five minutes before an officer came on the line.

After switching channels a while, she was feeling motion sickness and had to go to the market to pick up some Dramamine. Dramamine made her stomach feel better whenever she took heroin and she felt it might do some good now.

She got out of bed to change clothes. Since she was tired, it took a while to dress and a while longer to put on her make-up. She had hot flashes and cold sweats through it all and her stomach was queasy. She reached the store, got a shopping cart and started down the aisles to see if there was anything else she wanted to buy. As she wandered down an aisle, there was a crash, and she jumped with fright.

"It's okay, Miss," calmly said the shopper next to her. "It's a few aisles over. Some kids must have crashed into a display in the middle of the aisle."

"Thank you," Elaine replied. "I'm a little nervous with all the craziness going on these days." She looked down at the shopper and saw a younger man, with shoulder-length hair, five feet five inches or so, with a mustache and a cute smile. He was a good six inches shorter than she was. "My name is Jim," he said, holding out his hand. "Jim Auchstetter."

"Elaine Russell," she smiled back, taking his hand and shaking it.

"I guess with the drug business and the doctors' strike, everyone is feeling a little bit tossed about lately," he observed.

"I certainly know what you mean," she admitted.

After some small talk, Jim asked her if she'd like to join him later that evening for dinner.

"That would be nice," she agreed, knowing that she wouldn't need to spend that much money on food at the store.

"Great," Jim enthusiastically said, then realized he'd better call his steady girlfriend, Karen, and let her know that he wouldn't be seeing her until tomorrow night. "Give me your address and phone number, and I'll give you mine. And, look, I'll pick you up at six, okay?"

"That would be fine," she smiled, writing her name and number on a piece of scrap paper.

Jim was at her door promptly at six. When she opened the door, he was impressed. She wore a white dress which accented her hair and complemented her pale, sleeveless arms. The curves of her breasts were very enticing, as was her flat stomach. Her legs looked good, even though she wore flats to be closer to his height.

"You look great," he admitted. There was something about tall women that he found exciting.

"That's nice to hear," she replied, smiling.

At the restaurant, he ordered two huge wine glasses filled to the brim. Elaine felt that she wasn't going to be drinking, but sipped the wine as they talked. It seemed they had a lot in common. The more they talked, the more she drank. Jim refilled her glass as soon as it was below the half-way mark. He hardly touched his drink.

"I'm getting a little buzzed from the wine," she commented.

"I know what you mean," smiled Jim. "So just take it easy and relax."

"I do feel better," she said.

When they got back to her bungalow, Elaine was a little drowsy.

"I don't feel too well," she told Jim.

"Why don't you take one of these?" he said, holding out a special mixture of a hallucinogen.

"What is it?" she questioned.

"A general drug guaranteed to knock out everything from cold viruses to venereal disease."

"Is it new?" she asked. "Oh, hell, I'll take one." She took one, then put an old record on her small record player, and sat down next to Jim to talk.

After a few minutes, Elaine began to feel light-headed. She went into her medicine chest to take a Valium to calm down. It didn't seem to come on instantly, like Valium usually did.

"I still don't feel too good," she said, slightly addled.

"It might be the wine you drank," suggested Jim. "Why don't you take a Quaalude or two to bring you down and relax you?"

"I'm out of Quaaludes," she said. She had taken the last ones when she had a friend over last week.

"Use one of mine," he said.

"Do you have anything smaller?" she looked at the pill.

"Sorry," he said, smiling.

She took half the pill, and he suggested they dance to get the circulation going. After dancing a few minutes, the room looked more colorful.

"I feel better," she said aloud to herself.

"Then you ought to finish up the pill," Jim advised, changing records.

She swallowed the second half, and they started to dance again.

"You know," she noticed, "it's getting hot in here."

"Why don't you take your dress off?" he suggested.

She looked at him, not realizing that the hallucinogen was distorting her vision. She was feeling a bit less inhibited.

"I don't know," she laughed coyly.

"I have it," he said, snapping his fingers. "What you need is a Quaalude to cool you down."

"Do you ever get a feeling of deja vu?" she asked, taking the pill, downing it with some wine, and thinking that all this felt very familiar. She didn't remember taking the first Quaalude.

"All the time," Jim agreed, watching her swallow the pill.

She looked at him with a look of complacency and with bedroom eyes. "I've got her," he said to himself.

Later, they were making love in her bedroom. Jim felt like he was on top of the world, having all that womanhood doing exactly what he wanted to, but Elaine had some weird feelings from the hallucinogen Jim fed her. The mixing of the Valium, hallucinogen, wine, and Quaaludes made her feel very strange.

"I feel strange," she muttered, slowly.

"I feel great," Jim retorted.

"I don't," she started crying. "And I haven't peaked yet. Can you do something to make me feel better?"

Jim felt angry. Here he gave her all these pills, bought her dinner and drinks, took her to bed, and she didn't even feel like it was worthwhile. "You're just frigid," he snapped. She started to feel angry, even though she couldn't see him too clearly. She yelled back at him. When she hit him, he hit her back. He began pummeling her as she tried weakly to defend herself.

Moments later, Jim had vented his hostility, leaving her beaten. He put his clothes on and walked out, not looking back.

Elaine felt miserable. Her body hurt from the beating, and her head felt like it was floating in a fuzzy sea. She sat on the bed, and turned on the TV, but she couldn't focus on the screen nor understand the sounds.

"I've got to get to sleep," she thought. She went to the cabinet in the bathroom and took out the strongest sedative she had; Nembutal. She took a handful of them, making sure she was going to get some sleep and get rid of that fuzzy feeling in her head. Seconds later, she took a handful of aspirins. She sat down on the edge of the tub.

"If I feel sick after this nap," she told herself, "I'll go to the doctor." Then she sat down, leaning against the bathtub, closed her eyes and peacefully went to sleep there on the bathroom floor.

Her heart stopped an hour later.

After slamming the door and hopping into his car, Jim sped toward home.

"Bitch," he thought, as he remembered back to their lovemaking. He had given his all and then he was told that it wasn't good enough. "Screw her! There's more babes in the woods just waiting to be chosen."

Suddenly he saw flashing lights behind him and heard a siren.

"Just what I need," Jim swore as he pulled over to the right side of the road.

Kevin Manila got off his motorcycle, a bit tired from his double shifts. The sports car looked familiar as he went around to the driver's side of the car.

"Sir," Kevin said tiredly, placing the car, "You were the one that I let go for making an illegal turn a few months ago. This time you were speeding. May I please see your license?"

"I'm sorry, officer," said Jim, handing him the license after taking it out of his wallet. He knew full well that he was speeding. "But I just had a fight with a girl, and I'm pretty pissed."

"Being angry isn't an excuse for speeding, sir," Kevin remarked with the usual recording he told speedsters, writing out a ticket for driving fifteen miles over the speed limit.

Jim looked at the ticket, noting that he was going fifteen miles over the speed limit. The ticket was going to cost him a couple hundred dollars or more before everything was done. Then again, he knew that he could attend traffic school and get it taken off his record.

"You know," Jim said, as he signed the ticket forcefully, "You police don't understand that people need compassion. You're always holding the law over our heads. Sometimes I wonder if you guys are human?"

"We are, sir, but we have to protect everyone. No one person comes before the law, and that's why we have tickets."

"So you say," Jim snapped back, taking the ticket and driving away from the scene at the posted speed limit.

"Asshole," Jim thought, as he drove off. "Just let that guy come to me for some plumbing work. I'll show him."

Prescription for Mayhem

Chapter Twenty-nine

One month later
August 23, 2028

Sabrina was inspired. In a month, she had completed fourteen oil paintings. Each painting was a different subject, and painted while taking the smallest dose of LSD available. She was pleased, and an artist who examined them said that she had developed a quality that would make her as marketable as a Wyeth, Rockwell, or a Picasso.

Sabrina didn't care about the fame. One of her friends had convinced an art gallery to give Sabrina a showing. On the first night of the showing, all the art critics who came were enthusiastic about the pictures. Happily, each picture sold, even for the ridiculously high prices the gallery listed.

"Now that you've made more than thirty thousand dollars, what are your plans?" the gallery owner asked, handing her a check.

"I don't know," she said, feeling that she had finally carved herself a niche in the art community.

"I know you will continue painting," the art gallery owner said. She was an elderly woman who had devoted much of her life to art. "I have seen many paintings in my day and your pictures touched me. They have a quality that's missing in art today."

"Thank you," Sabrina acknowledged, grateful for the compliment.

"Don't forget that when we print the lithographs, there will be more money for you," reminded the gallery owner.

Sabrina deposited the check and went for a walk. Her sketchbook was in hand. She felt that her success was because drugs were no longer taboo. She knew that drugs were only to be used when she hit a creative block, not for any other reason. LSD use was like playing with fire. The possibility of addiction was always there. She was concerned because she wasn't sure how much LSD she could use without causing serious harm to herself.

It happened when she saw a marquee around a pawn shop. The flashing lights and strobes made her feel as if she had taken LSD. She started hallucinating. She felt she was looking at a canvas at home. She spotted a rainbow and began to walk toward it. At the bottom of the rainbow there was a door covered with the colors of the rainbow. When she opened the door, all of the lights flashed around her. It looked as if she were caught in a war between the sun and the rainbow, using colors as their weapons. When her vision cleared, she saw her canvas infused with the colors, making the picture come alive.

Suddenly, she came back to reality. She now saw the marquee, fixed to the spot. She looked and saw colored lights around the marquee and remembered her 'trip.' There were letters amidst the colors which read "Watches, $5.98 and up." She realized that she was at a pawn shop and the world became solid once again.

"A flashback," she thought to herself. "A goddamn flashback!!" Having only taken acid for a bit more than two months, although many times, she had no idea that she would be getting flashbacks so soon. The books she read generally agreed that flashbacks occurred when people had been taking hallucinogens for a long time. She walked hesitantly to an outdoor cafe across the street, ordered some capuccino and sat down. Her hands were shaking. She looked at the marquee across from her, flashing to her the challenge to her sanity.

"Damn you," she cursed as she sipped her drink. She wasn't sure what was happening, but she was scared. Her hands twitched as she held the warm cup, which felt reassuring. She knew that she needed drugs to make her art come alive, but she didn't want to be a slave to them.

She rose from the chair at the cafe and walked aimlessly. By the time she looked around to see where she was, she realized she was across from the library where she did her portrait of Father Mahoney. She walked inside and stood before the painting. She smiled as she looked at it. "It's truly beautiful," she whispered. Then she turned and walked away. She walked aimlessly again. The world was a gray wash. There was nothing vibrant around her. Nothing colorful. Nothing worth looking at. Nothing alive. She felt she was transported back to the life she had, not the life she wanted. She had the eyes of a Van Gogh for a brief moment, and she felt they might have been ripped loose from their sockets. "Life has no meaning now," she said to herself, as she came to the edge of Pacific Ocean, and found herself gazing into the water.

"Come look at this," said Mary, looking at a painting in the gallery they passed. "It's beautiful."

"It is," Craig echoed, looking at the picture before him. It was a forest scene, with darkness in the foreground. In the sky above the forest, birds were in flight. One set of birds chased another. The sun, a goldish-red orb, was seen coming through the surrounding clouds which haloed the sun.

"Such a beautiful sunrise," Mary said.

Craig smiled. It was the most beautiful picture he had ever seen.

"Isn't that the perfect name for a painting?" Mary asked, directing Craig's eyes to the card below the frame.

"Victory," said Craig. "A perfect name for that painting."

"And by an artist named Sabrina," Mary read, taking Craig's hand in hers.

Craig smiled. It was a magnificent painting, but he noticed that it was sold. His smile waned. "But it's probably too expensive for me anyway," he thought.

"Let's go in," said Mary.

They walked into the gallery and looked at the fourteen canvases before them. All were wonderfully done, with pictures portraying different subjects, each with an ability to inspire the viewer to feel joy while looking at it.

"Aren't they wonderful?" asked the gallery owner, who was sitting at a desk.

"They are," agreed Mary, gripping Craig's hand more firmly.

"But all are sold," Craig said with sadness in his voice.

"Yes, they are," admitted the woman slowly, "but there will be a set of lithographs of four of the paintings available in the next few months. She lifted her hand and directed them to a wall of paintings.

Craig and Mary walked over to examine them. The paintings were all beautiful. There was one in particular that Craig liked. It was a painting of two children skipping rocks across a pond. It reminded him of his youth and the good times he once had.

"I'd be interested in the lithograph of the two children," he remarked, making up his mind. He took out a business card from the US Postal Service and handed it to her along with a credit card. After taking his deposit, Craig and Mary walked out, holding hands.

"That was a good choice," Mary agreed.

"Thank you," Craig smiled as he thought about the painting. He knew he had made the right decision. "Let's go and celebrate with some lunch," and they walked to a cafe a few streets down.

"It's nice to relax," Mary said as she sat down at the table, taking off her heels and getting comfortable. A waiter took their orders. "I bet those guys in Congress aren't relaxing, especially with the murder attempts on their lives. It's been on TV. Haven't you seen it? You must have. I bet that Samuel Bunker guy must be watching his shadow every moment, according to the news coverage he's been getting. You know there were two attempts on his life, don't you?"

"The ones who want to kill him were probably parents who lost their children to drugs," Craig guessed.

"Maybe the news was right, when they said the attempts were hits by the Mafia. They were upset because they are losing billions of dollars from drug trafficking," Mary repeated what the TV told her.

"You know what else? This medical strike isn't going as bad as many predicted," Craig said. "Although the doctors in private practice are out on strike, the government doctors aren't striking and have to treat their patients. The thought of revoking licenses and other measures are probably making some doctors reassess their hopes and responsibilities. I pray they realize they're supposed to care for people."

"What would you do for people on drugs?" asked Mary.

"I'd offer them religion," Craig said softly after giving it some thought. "Religion would make them feel useful and worthwhile, give them purpose, make them feel loved, and make them feel there is a constant they can depend upon."

"You're telling them that they need to have their souls saved?" asked Mary.

"Not exactly," said Craig. "Christianity gives me a sense of joy and purpose that nothing else does. I dunno. It seems to me that Christians have something others miss, a deep and personal relationship with God. It's fulfilling. Drugs can't give you that. Who needs drugs when you have God? I sure don't. Although Christianity is a religion, it gives me something more than that. It's a lifestyle."

"You're not trying to drag me to church, are you?" questioned Mary, with her eyes looking him over to see if he had hidden motives.

"I respect you," Craig told her, "and I'm not trying to influence you. I like you just the way you are."

"You sound so philosophical," Mary observed.

"I'm sorry," Craig said sadly, "It's a difficult subject for me to talk about, because it covers a lot. Kind of like this lunch," he groaned, looking at the food just placed in front of him, knowing that he couldn't finish it all.

"I'm full," Mary confessed, after stuffing herself.

"Me too," Craig said.

"How about a walk to get rid of this feeling?" she suggested.

"Sounds good to me."

"And who knows," she hinted, "we might see something worth while."

"Something joyful?" asked Craig.

"Something wonderful," Mary smiled.

"I know where there's a pond," Craig remembered, pointing in a direction with his hand. He thought of the lithograph he had ordered, one of children happily skipping rocks over a pond.

Mary took his hand, then walked arm-in-arm with him in the direction he indicated.

Prescription for Mayhem

Chapter Thirty

"He makes me lie down in green pastures, leads me besides restful water, and revives my soul. He leads me in paths of righteousness for His name's sake. Though I walk through the valley of death, I will fear no harm for You are with me; Your rod and Your staff protect me. You make a banquet in the presence of my enemies. You have anointed me with oil such that my cup overflows. Surely goodness and unfailing love will follow me all of my life, and I will dwell in the house of the Lord forever. Amen."

"Chaplain," asked Frederica. "Are we sheep? After all, this was written by David when he was a shepherd."

"You've read the Bible?" quipped Sam to Frederica. "I'm amazed."

"You should try it, Sam," Frederica countered. "Who knows, it might do you some good." She looked at Sam from his feet to his head and then said, "But then again, maybe not."

Frederica had noticed in the last few months that she felt empty inside much of the time, and wasn't as happy as she used to be. She picked up her bible to check a passage someone told her, and found herself reading it cover to cover. It was the first book she had read in over twenty years that wasn't directly related to government operations. She found herself thinking a lot lately about what was really important to her in life, and what wasn't.

"We have turned every one to his own way, as George Frederic Handel put it," wryly said Tom Baker. Tom was doing a Bible study on the obstinacy of man.

Tom felt great. He felt like the weight of the world was taken off his shoulders. In a long talk with his wife, he had decided that to keep his family together he wouldn't be running for re-election next year. He knew he would be happier giving up his Senate seat.

"How about you, Chaplain?" asked Steve Harning. "What do you think about these last four months since the Drug Legislation Act took effect?"

The Chaplain looked at Sam, who signaled the Presbyterian minister to take the empty chair at the end of the big oak table opposite him. The Chaplain and Sam had gone back a long way. After the murder of Sam's first wife, the Chaplain stood by him. It took years to piece Sam's life back together. Many nights the Chaplain heard knocking on his door at home, and found a drunken Sam Bunker, leaning against one of the Virginian columns. The minister usually put him to bed and woke him when it was time to get ready for Congress. Sam never forgot his kindness and was amazed that the Chaplain never asked him to stop drinking.

"Sam?" the Chaplain asked, opening his eyes after a fast prayer for guidance.

Sam nodded his head for the Chaplain to start.

"The hardest thing for me to evaluate is the Drug Legislation Act," said the Chaplain slowly, folding his hands against his chest. "I have so many feelings. I have compassion for the addict, knowing that I could be weak myself. I am saddened for those falling under its spell, and I pity the children who must grow up in this environment. I would have to ponder long and hard, researching what the Bible would have to say about the Drug Legislation Act, before I could begin to pass judgment."

"However," he added, "I do believe in all of you, for I know that you are doing your best. I would put myself in your care as surely as Daniel put his trust in God when in the lion's den. It is my hope that the country will turn out as you want it to."

With that, the Chaplain stood up, pushed in his chair, smiled a silent benediction at the people seated at the table and then walked out.

"Good man," observed Frederica.

"One of the best," Tom agreed.

"Changing topics to the worst," Bob said quickly to Sam, slurring his words slightly, "did that hit man you caught get sentenced yesterday? You know, the second hit man."

Steve looked at Bob, squinting as if to see him clearly. To his trained eyes and ears, Bob appeared to be drunk.

Sam nodded. He was there yesterday when the judge sentenced Julie Giuliano to death by electrocution, with the appeal being denied. Hours prior to the execution, he went to see Julie Giuliano.

Julie's arms and feet were handcuffed to metal bars. Sam ordered Julie gagged by marine guards, who then stepped outside the cell to leave them alone.

"I wanted to talk to you," spoke Sam slowly and quietly. Julie glared at him, but couldn't talk. "Peter Alonso claimed that you were the head of the Mafia. I believe him. But it's inconceivable that you would personally try to put the hit on me. Especially after Luigi Devoy spilled his guts about your whole organization before he was electrocuted.

"Didn't you find it strange that no one asked you for information about the family? We already have everything on every family member that we need for convictions, and we are busy getting subpoenas ready. We can expect that in six months, your family will be hanging from ropes around their necks. Your evil family line will go to hell to keep you company there. Don't think anyone will escape. You won't, that's for sure! Within an hour, you'll be dead anyway. There's no escape. And don't worry about dying alone. I'll be there to watch you twist and turn until you die.

"By the way," Sam said, reaching into his coat pocket, "I wanted to show you this picture. It's of my first wife. She was killed about twenty-five years ago in a hit and run accident, when you were about twenty-five or so. The coroner said that it was a professional job, and that she was injected with poison to make sure she was dead. As I cried for years afterwards, I asked myself, 'Who would want her dead?' It took me a year to remember that I had received a strange phone call from one of my constituents shortly before my love died. They urged me not to push through a bill I introduced in Congress against child prostitution. All I wanted was strong punishments for those people who forced children into child prostitution...I did it for the children. It took a while for the FBI and me to piece together that the Mafia had organized the hit.

"Now that you are where I want you, look at this picture. It's of a woman you never knew, who was guilty only of loving me beyond compare. I love her more than you will ever know. My present wife is a good person and I love her, but she could never replace my first love. So, as you have condemned my love to death, I am returning the gesture.

"By order of the judge, I am the last person you will speak to. Your family will not visit you, as you have already had the last rites. I wanted to see you bound and gagged, like the pig you are. You cannot answer back, nor spit on this picture and defile it.

"Die slowly," Sam flatly spoke as he turned toward the door to admit back the marine guards. "Die slowly," Sam said again.

"No," Sam reminisced, correcting Bob. "He didn't get sentenced. He got electrocuted!" Sam remembered the instant before death. He had taken the picture and held it up against the glass observation room window so Julie could see it in his last moments of life.

"You know," Steve diplomatically changed subjects, looking at Bob, "Utah almost had a fifty percent turnout of their voters on an initiative to repeal the Drug Legislation Act and make Utah a dry state again."

"If anyone can do it," Tom said knowingly, "a state with a lot of religious voters could. Still, they have to get seventy-five percent of the total people in the state, not just the voters, to repeal the law."

"You know," Sam said, unusually softly, "I'd like to adjourn the session for today. We'll continue at our usual time a week from now. I'd like to go put some flowers on my wife's grave over near Arlington, and have a chat with her. Any problems with that?"

Everyone looked down.

Tom shivered. He never knew Sam could be that quiet.

"Thank you, my friends," Sam said. "Meeting adjourned."

They didn't look at Sam as he left the room, eyes filled with tears.

Mary had the day off. There was a convention in New York for the personnel from entertainment public relations firms, and she wanted to catch up on some overdue shopping.

When she got to the mall, it was pretty empty. This was unusual for a weekday. The mall was usually packed all the time and impossible to shop in on the weekends.

She selected a blouse she wanted, and found a second one at another boutique. The stockings she needed proved more difficult to find. When she arrived at a major department store, she was told that stockings were two weeks behind in delivery.

"Why?" asked Mary.

"Because the production changes the country is going through have changed everything," said the clerk. "Stockings used to be made in the Orient, or wherever it was cheapest. Now they have to be made here. But, don't worry, the back order is only two weeks behind, while a month ago, it was five weeks behind. Within a few months, everything will be back to normal."

Mary knew the clerk was right. Some things were getting better. People weren't half as crazy as they seemed to be a month ago. It was as though the country was recovering from a cold. Accidents were getting less frequent, and the mortality rate had dropped. Mary noticed that when she drove from her house to the mall, she wasn't stuck in traffic due to an accident.

She knew there still were a lot of police cars on the road, but they didn't seem to be chasing anyone. A traffic policeman she once dated had said that half their job was to make themselves visible. The other half of a policeman's job was pulling over careless drivers.

She got home and threw off her shoes. She sorted and put away the things she bought. Exhausted from shopping all day long, she sat down and had a martini. She wondered what she was going to do that night, being bored. She thought about phoning Craig, but she didn't want to appear to be too interested.

As she swirled her martini around, she thought of something that would take care of the evening. She had a pill left over from a party she attended months back. The person who gave the pill to her said that it was guaranteed to blow the user's head apart. "Why not indulge myself?" she thought dreamingly, using any excuse she could find to forget her rape by Carl Friedman a month ago. That nightmare stayed in the back of her mind; burning with such a flame that she wondered if it ever would go out. "I deserve it," she rationalized. She went to her medicine cabinet and took the pill with a healthy sip of her drink.

She sat back on the couch, turned on her clock radio to a mellow softies station and sipped the martini. Somehow, the room got hazy. She looked at her drink and swirled it around gently until it began to look like a whirlpool. She felt that her body was being directed down the whirlpool, until the darkness surrounded her. She began choking. She started to scream, but with the darkness all around her, she couldn't hear herself.

Suddenly everything became light. She woke up. There were white walls all around her covered with linoleum.

"Doctor," alerted the nurse practitioner to Doc Browning, "she's out of it, I think."

"Hello," Doc Browning spoke, smiling at Mary. "Just relax, and let me tell you what has happened."

Mary tried to sit up, but felt too weak to move. She looked around her and knew she was in a hospital bed, wearing a hospital gown.

"Your neighbors heard your scream and called the police," he said slowly. "They broke into your apartment and found you screaming. There were all these drugs on the coffee table. They brought you here to the hospital and we pumped your stomach. The contents are being analyzed right now. Your throat must be feeling pretty raw, I guess," he said.

Mary nodded.

"Because of your uncontrollable screaming, we put you in this soundproof room," Doc Browning told her. "You were wailing for two hours. How are you feeling?" he asked.

Mary just nodded.

"My guess from your symptoms is that you took a pill that was part upper, part downer, and part psychedelic. A 'designer drug.' It is possible you might have a relapse. You have a one in three chance that the psychedelic will affect you again. I'd advise you to have someone stay up with you tonight, waking you every two hours to make sure you're all right."

Some hours later, Mary had a taxi take her home. She went inside to get cabfare and felt weak after paying the cabbie. The door was ajar from the lock being broken, but she latched the door at the top after the cabbie left. She took a list of referral agencies and crisis hotlines the hospital had given her. There was no one else for her to turn to. She didn't know anyone she trusted to stay with her for the night. If she asked an office mate, she knew it would be in the gossip mill the next day.

"This has got to stop," she said with determination, as she dialed the first number on the referral sheet.

"Referral service," said a friendly voice.

"Hello, my name is Mary," she said quickly. "I took a psychedelic this afternoon and ended up in an emergency room. The doctor said that I should have someone stay with me tonight to wake me up every few hours to make sure that I'm all right. I don't have anyone to turn to! I've been trying to get off drugs for a long while. Can someone please help me?"

"Mary," said the voice quietly after a long pause, "This is Craig Osborne. This is my evening to monitor calls on the hotline. I recognized your voice. I'll come on over within the hour if it's okay. I'm due to be relieved soon. If you'd prefer, I can arrange for another person, perhaps a woman, if you'd rather I do that."

Mary held the phone away from her and looked at it. She couldn't believe it. She just told Craig, the guy she was dating, that she was hooked on drugs and trying to come down from a psychedelic. Now Craig would not want anything to do with her. It was good to hear that he wanted to help her out, but she didn't want him to see her like this.

"I don't know," Mary said quietly, confused.

"I understand," Craig replied.

A few seconds later, a female voice came on the line. "My name is Susan. Craig said you needed someone to stay with you for the night. Is there anything you'd like me to bring over that will help you?"

Mary thought about it for a second, then said, "Can you please put Craig back on?"

Craig returned to the phone. Mary started to sniffle, "Craig, please come over when you can. I need you badly."

"I'll be there shortly," Craig said. "Keep in mind that picture we saw together if things start going out of control."

Craig came over with a bag of groceries. Mary sobbed in his arms, told him she was an addict and that she would probably have a relapse before the evening was over.

Craig smiled at her and brushed her hair from her face. "Don't worry about it. Just get some sleep. Everything will be fine in the morning."

He took her into the bedroom, told her to put on pajamas and get into bed. He went into the living room while she changed. Once she was in bed, he returned and tucked her in. He kissed her on the forehead and said that he would be in the other room. He said he'd return every two hours to make sure she was okay.

Mary didn't remember much that night, except that she had a good night's sleep. She awoke at seven o'clock the next day, feeling wonderful. She walked into the living room and saw Craig asleep on the floor. He was sleeping next to an alarm clock.

Mary walked into the kitchen and looked through the bag of groceries. She knew all men liked to have breakfast in the morning. She smiled as she looked over at Craig and started making him breakfast.

Prescription for Mayhem

Chapter Thirty-one

One week later
August 30, 2028

"Thank you again, Chaplain, for those words," began Sam Bunker, starting the meeting. "Thank you also for letting me sleep off my drunk at your house last night. You know, no one makes breakfast quite like you do. If you were a girl, I'd marry you."

"If I were a girl and you had proposed to me, I would probably be a nun by now," said the Chaplain, smiling.

Sam reminisced, "It's been a long time since I've done that, sleeping off a drunk at your house."

"Over fifteen years, I think," said the Chaplain, scratching his head as he tried to remember the date.

"The way I feel this morning," Sam groaned, nursing a hangover, "it'll be another fifteen before I try that again."

The Chaplain left the committee chambers.

"We'll hold off a few more minutes until Bob gets here," Sam said. "He must be on that damned beltway, going in circles around Washington. Funny, we all seem to be going in circles here at the nation's capitol."

"Sam," Frederica said with care, "Bob won't be showing up today."

Sam looked up slowly. Frederica's voice didn't sound right. Something was wrong! "Is he all right?" Sam asked anxiously.

"He's in jail," Steve related. "He was stopped by the police for driving under the influence of alcohol. The blood tests came back positive. With all that alcohol he had in his blood, I'm amazed that he was still breathing."

"Can we get him out of jail?" asked Tom. This was news to him.

"I've known Bob Emerson for a long time, junior," Sam said, thinking about the situation. "He's one of the nicest men I've ever met. I'd be willing to bet that if we went to him, he'd tell us that it was none of our business. He'd say that no one is above the law. And he'll probably plead guilty before the judge. I think he'd castrate us if we tried to change anything."

Steve smiled. "No bet, Sam. I already went to talk to him. With my judicial pull we could get him off one way or another. He did say we should mind our own business, that the law is greater than any one man, and he was planning to plead guilty. You were wrong, though. He didn't say he'd castrate us if we tried anything. He said he'd impale us if we tried anything."

"See," Sam agreed, raising his hands in resignation, "I really do know him. It is sad when the drug wars hit home. I'll miss Bob....I really will."

"Me too," Tom seconded.

Steve and Frederica just nodded their heads. Not only had Bob Emerson saved their reputations many times, but they depended on his steadfastness in times of stress.

"It's a crying shame," whined Frederica. She liked Bob a lot, and there weren't many people she liked these days. "We're the ones to blame for it! We put him there. And we're the only ones who can get him out."

"Bullshit!" Sam spat. Her words hit a nerve. "The moment Bob decided to drive a car while drunk, he put himself behind the eight ball. Remember; he broke a law. And of all the people to break the law, he was one of the people who wrote it. I believe he knows it. If you think anyone is going to take him out of prison, make him an ambassador for seven years in some third world country, you're mistaken. He won't do it. I'll bet my career on it. And he'll kick sand in the face of anyone who tries.

"Any other comments?" asked Sam. "I don't want to hear anything about Bob again. Let's forget about him. Case closed," he spoke, as he pounded his hand on the table. He sat down and wrote himself a note about seeing Bob later to ask if he needed anything.

"Let me take over the business and finance part of our committee for Bob temporarily, if you'd like," Steve volunteered diplomatically, "although I do have enough to do as it is."

"Thank you," Sam said quietly.

The room was quiet for a few moments.

"Have you heard the joke about the Senator and the chorus girl?" asked Tom, breaking the silence.

"That joke was bad when Teddy Roosevelt was in office," Sam Bunker said dryly, "and it hasn't improved with age."

"That's it," Tom cried, jumping up from his chair, "That's why you look so familiar. It's Teddy Roosevelt...that's where the similarity lies. You two look so much alike."

"You mean I look like Teddy Roosevelt?" asked Sam in amazement. No one had ever told him that.

"Not quite," said Tom. He paused, then told Sam, "You look like his horse."

Everyone started chuckling. Even Sam did; and he thought he had heard them all before.

"You win," laughed Sam. "I guess some of the old jokes are still pretty good."

Tom bowed graciously, then sat down again.

"Next?" asked Sam. He was grateful for Tom's joke, but anxious to get back to work.

"The M.A.A. strike is losing ground fast," spoke Frederica. "Doctors who are on strike have lost their university privileges. We have some government agencies monitoring those who are on the job and those who aren't. The independent doctors are getting tired of supporting the movement, and many of the others are starting to bicker among themselves."

"But is the public getting good service," asked Sam, "or are we adding to the number of deaths we've accumulated so far?"

"So far, it's been pretty good for the patients," said Frederica. "Nurse practitioners seem able to handle over eighty percent of the problems, and everyone is cooperating.

"And," continued Frederica, "the students have faithfully attended classes and clinics. The veteran's hospitals haven't dropped a bit, nor have the government funded hospitals. Of the fifty percent that went out on strike the first day following the President's message, only ten percent of the doctors stayed away the next day."

"I hate to be a pest," interrupted Steve.

"Well?" asked Tom.

"I've been going crazy with all the additional drug advertisements on television. New ads for hemorrhoidal preparations, for cramps and for damn near everything under the sun. They're using pretty girls, old ladies telling us they're our mothers and we should do what they say and buy their products. It's annoying," Steve grimaced bitterly, "and I wish there were an end to it."

"We can fix that," stated Sam in a threatening voice.

"We can, can't we?" Tom said, smiling.

"Well?" asked Frederica, grinning from ear to ear. She had also been sick of the increase in ads. She felt there was something inherently wrong with doctors who spent thousands of dollars advertising on television for patients to visit their medical offices.

"The vote?" asked Sam.

Everyone nodded.

"Good," Sam sighed. "Steve, start thinking of ways that the drug industry and medical groups can begin developing tasteful ads and cut down on those incessant commercials. The drug industry has done well by our legislation, but we can come down hard on them if we have to."

"I've got it down," Steve underlined the note, "and this makes my day," he added, hoping that he'd be able to watch TV again with fewer interruptions.

"Anything else?" Sam asked.

No one replied.

"I'm beginning to like this," Sam said. "Steve is the only person who has anything to do."

"I'll help on the drug industry question," volunteered Frederica, seeing how tired Steve looked. She didn't like the life she had outside of work.

"In that case," said Sam, "I'll rest and relax three times the usual amount to make up for everybody else on the job. This meeting is adjourned."

While on duty, Kevin Manila got a call from his mother, telling him that his little brother had died from an overdose of drugs. Because of the drugs, his brother tried to wrestle control of a bus from the driver, overturning the bus in the process. He killed himself and thirty people on board when the bus careened down a hill into a ravine. Kevin tried to get the day off for the funeral but the captain said he could only have the morning and afternoon off. He'd have to come in for the swing shift.

Kevin looked at the casket. It was closed because the body was mutilated. There was a little skirmish outside the church. There were dozens of relatives from the accident, throwing rocks at Kevin's family. At the grave site, the priest said the liturgy quickly and then walked away.

For the rest of the day, Kevin took turns reassuring his parents. He made certain that someone would be near them for the rest of the week.

It was barely ten minutes after his shift started when he saw a car weaving down the street. He turned on the motorcycle siren and started in pursuit. The person pulled off the road and he approached the car.

He looked at the driver. She was a stringy haired woman in a flannel shirt. She had a dazed look in her eyes. He called for an ambulance and took her out of the car. She slurred her words and was incoherent. Minutes later, the ambulance arrived and prepared to take her to the hospital for a blood test and observation.

As the ambulance started up, another driver who was trying to give up amphetamines, turned his head toward the ambulance. He didn't notice that his car was heading into the policeman. He knew he was fighting with all his might to keep awake but it was no good. He had been awake for four days, nervous from the amphetamines in his system.

Kevin was looking at a sketch pad on top of the car. "The driver is a pretty good artist," he thought, as he put the pad back on the seat to wait for the tow truck to arrive. He saw the signature on the bottom of one of the pictures: Sabrina. Suddenly he looked up and saw the other car's headlights were inches away. He was frozen for a second. The car rammed into the impounded car, smashing Kevin's left hand between the two cars.

"Officer Manila down, corner of Carlos and Gower," he said into the lapel radio. He passed out as the ambulance drivers ran toward him.

The ambulance drivers turned off the engine, and ran out of the ambulance. "That cop's lucky we didn't leave ten seconds earlier," one of the ambulance drivers said to the other. They left Sabrina restrained in the ambulance and concentrated on Kevin.

"Where am I?" he asked, when he awakened.

"You're in an emergency room," the nurse practitioner said, studying the X-ray again. "Pretty lucky, too. That car that rammed into you just missed making you a sandwich between the two cars. The only thing that's pretty messed up is your left hand."

Kevin couldn't move his left hand.

"I can't feel it," he exclaimed nervously.

"I sure as hell hope not," said the nurse practitioner. "I put anesthetic in it to deaden the pain of the surgery. The nerves were compressed, but they weren't severed. You'll be able to use your hand again."

Kevin breathed a sigh of relief.

"It's going to be weak, though, for the rest of your life, young man," Doc Browning remarked, walking into the room, looking at his chart. "That means no baseball, lifting heavy things, shooting with it..."

"I'm right handed, so I don't have to worry about using it to shoot with," Kevin told.

"But you're not going to have the strength to steer or pull the clutch on that motorcycle of yours any more," stated the doctor.

Kevin thought about it. His life as a motorcycle cop was finished. "How about the guy who hit me?"

"He's in the morgue," said the doctor. "He wasn't wearing a seat belt and the windshield decapitated him."

"Doc, level with me. Do you think I'll be able to use the hand again as it used to be?"

"It won't be deformed, but it'll feel like it's asleep for a long time," the Doctor said. "Nerves are capricious, and no one can know if or when they will regenerate. Certainly, I don't. You will be able to use it, but by no means will you be able to lift or twist anything much more than about five to ten pounds worth for a long while. I estimate a year to three years to recover whatever usage you'll have."

In the next bed over, behind the curtains, Sabrina heard the doctor talking as he left the recovery room where Kevin Manila was lying. One of her hands was handcuffed to the bed railing.

"The kid's arm's going to feel miserable when the anesthetic wears off," he stated with sympathy, "so make sure he gets something to put him to sleep. He'll be fine. He's pretty tough and he should make it," observed Doc Browning, who figured out that he was going to make plenty when he billed whoever was at fault for this.

Sabrina sat quietly in the bed. On the way to the hospital she had recovered some of her faculties. The first thing they did in the hospital was to draw blood for a drug/alcohol assay. She knew she had had a few drinks with some friends who applauded her successful show at the gallery. She thought she had the beginnings of a flashback but then everything went black. The next thing she remembered, she was in an ambulance going to the hospital.

"Make sure you're covered up, Miss," a voice said, tapping lightly on the drape before entering. "I'm Doctor Browning. Let me see that armband of yours. Yes, you're Sabrina. Well, I have good news. The lab test came back and the alcohol content in your blood was just below the legal limit. You're allowed a tenth of a percent in your blood, and you had just a hair under that limit. I think you'll have no problem getting off with just a reckless driving incident instead of driving under the influence."

A woman police officer came in and unlocked the cuffs. Sabrina was thoughtful as she put on her clothes. She knew that she had to go to a hearing and possibly have her license suspended. If the judge wanted, he could consider her drunk and sentence her to seven years in prison. She knew she'd never had blackouts before. When she thought about it, she realized that LSD flashbacks wouldn't appear in a blood test. It was a mental state that arose from previous drug use. "It's that damned drug that did this," she thought the police officer watched her dress. "It wasn't the alcohol. The LSD has got me. It's reeling me in and I can't do anything about it!"

The policewoman put Sabrina's arms behind her back, and handcuffed them together.

Prescription for Mayhem

Chapter Thirty-two

Doc Browning sat in the cafeteria, resting after assisting with the police officer's surgery. He was sorry about the young officer with whom he had talked once or twice. He was sure it was going to take the office a long time to recover from the injury. He felt better, having had a chance to sleep more every evening. The emergency room had slowed down. He was able to take a day off yesterday.

He felt good about a letter he had written, resigning from the M.A.A., stating that if a strike occurred, it shouldn't involve the healing arts. He also indicated that each person had the right to make his or her own decision about drugs and how they live their life. He felt a little nervous about it at first, but realized that the more he wrote, the better he felt.

Doc Browning had been thinking about life when they brought in the corpse of Elaine Russell last month. He examined the body and remembered the attractive young woman. He remembered a poem he had heard in high school by Edward Arlington Robinson, about *Richard Cory*, who people thought had everything in life; money, looks, and all that people imagined a man could want. He had to memorize the poem. It went:

Whenever Richard Cory went down town,
We people on the pavement looked at him:

He was a gentleman from sole to crown,
Clean favored, and imperially slim.

And he was always quietly arrayed,
And he was always human when he talked;
But still he fluttered pulses when he said, "Good morning,"
and he glittered when he walked.

And he was rich—yes, richer than a king—
And admirably schooled in every grace;
In fine, we thought that he was everything
To make us wish that we were in his place.

So on we worked, and waited for the light,
And went without the meat, and cursed the bread,
And Richard Cory, one calm summer night,
Went home and put a bullet through his head.

He had looked at Elaine's body, pronounced her dead and sent it to pathology for them to determine the cause of death.

Doc Browning needed a vacation. He wanted more out of life than treating patients. He wanted a social life, which was impossible with the schedule he was keeping now. And he wanted that Ferrari, the one whose down payment he could not have afforded five months ago. He could afford it now. A red one. He wanted to drive with the top down, the wind in his hair, not traveling anywhere in particular, and stopping wherever and whenever he liked.

He was paged over the intercom and ran to the emergency room. A young man was on the table, his left knee almost severed from his thigh. Browning called for help, and hoped that the orthopedist hadn't left. The nurse practitioner had some plasma in the patient's arm, and was sending off a blood sample for typing and replacement.

Doc Browning went to work. He observed that the main femoral artery and branches were still intact, with the nerve similarly so. The bone was exposed and the knee was badly damaged. He learned that the patient had been at a bar, trying to pick up a girl when her jealous boyfriend attacked him with a knife. By the time the people in the bar broke it up, the man's knee was partially severed.

The nurse noticed that the patient was attractive. He had a nice body, long hair, and a mustache. The ward clerk took the man's wallet for information, writing the name "Jim Auchstetter" on the report form. She noticed a medical insurance card was in the wallet.

"That's all I need," the ward clerk said, "he's okay for treating."

The orthopedist showed up and said that the leg could be repaired. "Let's take him to surgery as soon as he's stabilized," he said, getting approval for preparation of the operating room, and waiting for the blood typing. Just to make sure he could administer an anesthetic, he asked for a drug analysis on the blood.

Jim lay on the gurney in the pre-operative room, with a bag of dextrose and sterile water in one arm and plasma in the other. Someone came by and changed the dextrose and water for a pint of blood, changing the blood every time it ran low. Jim was given three pints, and color came back to his cheeks.

Within the hour he began to moan, and a woman volunteer was told to stay with him until he awakened. After a few more minutes, Jim's eyes opened.

"Where am I?" he asked.

"In the hospital," said the volunteer, a retired senior citizen. "You were in an accident."

"I don't feel dead," he said. "I've got feelings in my hands, and some in my legs." It then dawned on him, "I can't feel one leg."

He sat up and look at the leg with the wound and screamed.

"You crazy old bitch," he shouted out. "What happened to my leg?"

At that moment, Doc Browning came in with a portfolio of X-rays.

"Thank you. You can go now," he said to the volunteer, who walked out. She stuck her tongue out at Jim. "Ingrate," she muttered under her breath.

"I'm Doc Browning," he told, pushing gently on Jim's chest to get him to lie down.

"Am I dead?" Jim asked.

"Certainly not," laughed Doc Browning. "You were in an accident."

"What happened?" asked Jim.

"As I understand it, you were in a bar, and tried to pick up on a young lady. Her boyfriend was angry and was stoned. He attacked you. He had a knife, and I guess he was trying to remove your penis or testicles. He was stopped before he did, but he did manage to get to your leg and knee and do some damage."

"How bad is it?"

"Bad enough," Doc Browning said grimly. "The experts say you'll walk again, but with a pretty good limp. Elevator shoes might help the poorer foot, but we'll have to see."

"So I'll have a limp the rest of my life?"

Doc Browning nodded.

"Will I need a cane?" asked Jim.

"Maybe," Doc Browning said analytically, noting that Jim was taking it pretty well. "You probably will be an inch or two shorter when we're done with everything."

Jim frowned. "What'll happen to the other guy?"

"That's up to you," Doc Browning advised. "You've got control of that."

"Well," Jim said bitingly, "they say that what you sow you reap."

"They do at that," agreed Doc Browning, who heard his name paged and ran out.

Chapter Thirty-Three

Two weeks later
September 13, 2028

"And, after it was all over, they walked with the man to Emmaus, and when they walked in, He was hesitant to walk in, thinking of leaving. But, the two men convinced Him that He should sup with them. And, they walked in, and when they broke bread, they knew who He was, and their hearts burned inside from all the glorious news He gave them. May all of us have that burning to make sense out of the material world, in order to feed the spiritual."

"Thank you, Chaplain," said Tom.

"Thank you," agreed Sam.

The Chaplain exited the chambers.

"Well," said Sam with enthusiasm, "let's get started."

"Well," admitted Steve, "I've had fun putting the screws to advertisers in the drug industry to limit advertisements. We didn't even have to create a bill, thanks to Frederica here."

"It was easy," Frederica said dotingly. "We just made it a government stipulation, from a dictate by the head of the Food and Drug Administration, that no pharmaceutical agency dealing with the government can advertise in anything except professional journals. They've all complied instantly. I guess they knew they were overly enthusiastic."

"How about the rest of the country?" asked Sam.

"Good, and not so good," said Tom. "It seems that drug-related incidents, overdoses, traffic incidents, hospital stays, and the like, are shooting down each day."

"That must be the good part," said Sam, knowing that more was coming. "What's the bad part?" He braced himself.

"There are two million dead and four million injured," said Tom softly. The room was quiet.

"Damn straight the cost is high," Sam spoke after a while, solemnly. "We've cured some of the ills that have plagued the country for so long, but at a price. A most precious price. The most valuable thing our country has to offer is its people."

"Sam," said Tom wearily, lifting his head up. "Get off the soap box, already."

"Sorry," said Sam, smiling weakly. "I was thinking of a national congress of the P.T.A. I am going to address tomorrow."

"Are we planning to rescind any acts we've passed?" asked Steve.

"I don't think so," Sam thought out loud. "But there's nothing more for our committee to do. We did it all, didn't we?"

"We should keep the laws on the books," said Frederica. "That way, if any need comes up, Congress can always repeal them. But it might act as a control of sorts if it stays."

"It sounds as though you're talking about disbanding this committee," Tom concluded.

"We've done what we set out to do," Sam surmised. "Haven't we? We've given the country a kick in the pants and caused Lady Liberty herself to stand up straight again. I am thinking of disbanding, but I'll have to talk to John Jones about that. When I look at those acts we wrote, I feel that they're good acts. Don't you?"

Everyone nodded.

"But we should get together in a few weeks and see if there's any other business to take care of," Sam said. "You folks don't know what a pain in the butt it's going to be to have to write up the goals, findings, and an implementation of this committee for the *Congressional Record.*"

Everyone smiled, thinking that Sam deserved it.

Sam banged his hand on the oak conference table. "Meeting adjourned for two weeks," he said, and reminded himself that one day he was going to have to buy himself a gavel. Banging his hand on tables hurt.

Kevin hit his hand closing the drawer. The hand still hurt, but the constant throbbing in it was worse than the sharp pains he had from time to time. He had been promoted to a desk job until his hand was sufficiently healed to go back on the streets. He was temporarily assigned with helping the transition of officers from traffic detail to vice and gambling.

Things were slowing down at the police station. People were getting an idea of how drugs and their new liberties could affect their lives. For some it was a bitter lesson. Others took to it like a kid in a candy store.

Sabrina smiled as she read in the morning *Los Angeles Times* that she was now considered one of the best new female artists in the country. She worked at a furious pace and completed another set of ten paintings for the gallery. Some thought she was overworked but she knew she was making up for lost time. The set of ten paintings had something fresh in them, even though she did them without drugs. She dreaded the day when she would get artist's block. She feared for the future.

Craig was worried a bit about Mary. She had found a new job with better pay after Thalberg, Chaney, and Fairbanks fired her. Mary seemed to be doing well, but he knew that she had gone cold turkey off all drugs and it was going to be hard for her.

While viewing a picture at a gallery, Mary felt a little dizzy and had to sit down. Her stomach was rumbling, and she knew that unless she took a diet pill, her mind was going to fight her body. An upper would also help to make her feel better. When she told Craig about it, Craig mentioned that maybe they should go get a small bite to eat.

Mary smiled, forgetting the problem with drugs, and walked out with Craig. She was happy that Craig was in her life.

Prescription for Mayhem

Chapter Thirty-four

Two weeks later
September 27, 2028

The champagne flowed into the glass.

"You know, Chaplain," Tom blurted out between sips. "You sure make opening a champagne bottle an art. As interesting as a sermon. Maybe you missed your calling?"

"It's easy to get to the best things in life," said the Chaplain, smiling.

"Help yourself to food," Sam Bunker shouted above the noise, pointing to the table in the committee chambers. "There's plenty to go around."

"What slush fund did you get this from?" asked Frederica suspiciously, but serving herself a huge chunk of beef.

"Nowhere," Sam told, his mouth full. "It's my money. We're celebrating the end of the committee. I didn't want to chair this committee in the first place. Thank God it's over."

"We're officially disbanded," Sam said loudly so that it could be heard in every corner of the of the room. "Did you hear that, Mr. Speaker of the House, John Jones? You shouldn't have picked me to do the job in the first place. You only wanted to get even with me for falling asleep in your moment of glory. Hell, I wasn't any different from all the others who start to listen to you and end up daydreaming. It's the listening that puts me to sleep every time!"

"You don't have to yell! I heard you," said John Jones between gulps of champagne. "And although I hate to admit it, you all did an excellent job."

John Jones then lifted his glass in a silent toast to his dead ten-year-old daughter. "Honey," he thought, "we did it for you."

"This illiteracy rate of thirty percent will be history within a few decades," dreamed Frederica. "That's something in itself."

"I don't know," said Tom Baker, jokingly. "If people are literate, Frederica, then they might have the intelligence not to vote you into office again."

Tom didn't fear the future. He had something lined up for when he left Congress. There was a consulting job waiting for him in his home state government's education and welfare department as soon as his Senate term ended. He knew it was going to be perfect for him and his family.

Frederica smiled good-naturedly at Tom's remark. She was feeling better about herself these days. She thought that maybe it had something to do with her starting to go to church.

The chamber doors opened, and three men came into the room. One was handcuffed.

"Thank you," Sam Bunker said with true gratitude in his voice. "Please undo the man's cuffs and please wait outside. As you can see, there are no windows or doors and no way out. You'll be able to take him away shortly."

Once the men walked outside, closing the doors behind them, everyone slapped the uncuffed man on the back.

"You look great, Bob," said Sam Bunker said, handing Bob Emerson a very full glass of champagne once Bob stopped rubbing his uncuffed wrists.

"Thanks," replied Bob Emerson, looking at the champagne for a second. Then he slowly put the full champagne glass on the table, not touching a sip. He hadn't touched a drop in almost a month, and wasn't going to start now.

"I feel good, too," Bob said. "No booze and prison food sure makes you lose weight, even at the minimum security facility." His wife almost lived there, visiting him as much as she did once she found out what happened. He felt closer to her than he had in years.

"What do they have you doing?" asked Frederica.

"What else would they use the Chairman of the Banking and Currency Committee for, but to handle the bookkeeping of the facility," Bob said good-heartedly.

"You know," said Sam, "we've disbanding the committee. I never told you how well you did, Bob."

"I know," said Bob proudly. "But you're the ones who deserve the credit..."

"Not true, Bob," interrupted Tom, spearing a chicken leg with his fork. "Without you, we wouldn't have done what we had to. You gave us insight that no one else supplied."

"And we did want you around at our official disbanding. You're as much a part of this as I am," Sam stated.

"Wait a minute," corrected Steve. "We did the work, as I remember it. You did the assignments, if I remember correctly."

"Well," said Sam. "If I wasn't the clay pigeon for all those marksmen, do you think you'd be here today?

"You know," Sam confided to John Jones, "If anything happened to me, I made arrangements for you to be willed my pet dog."

"That's very considerate of you," John Jones said. He thought that it was a loving person that made sure that their pets were protected. He liked dogs.

Sam smiled as though he knew an inside joke. "You'd find out first hand why he's named Crapper...he goes everywhere."

"I don't know how you ever made it possible," Bob interrupted Sam in talking to John Jones. "It must have taken an act of God to get all of us to agree to this committee."

"It just took a little something," smiled John Jones, thinking of his daughter, his little girl, who had made his life so joyful.

"I feel good knowing that we did what Congress had been trying to do for centuries," proudly said Steve.

Steve knew that his part in writing the bills was going to leave a mark in history. He felt just like those who signed the Declaration of Independence. Leaving a mark was important to him. He didn't tell anyone that he was going into the hospital for open heart surgery the next day. The previous bypasses hadn't worked and chances were three to one against his surviving the next week. He reached for the turkey, but then changed his mind and reached for the ham. "You only live once," he thought, "and I've accomplished everything I wanted to. Death can have no sting."

"You know," Sam said, after choking on an olive, "this pill for America was pretty hard to swallow."

"What pill is that?" asked John Jones.

"This drug legalization," said Sam, selecting another olive. "It didn't go down easily."

"No, it didn't," stated John Jones. "Well, you're officially disbanded now."

"Great," Sam slyly said, "because there's one more thing our committee was supposed to address, but didn't. I thought I'd wait until I wouldn't have to handle it to tell you."

"And what is that?" John Jones asked, narrowing his eyes.

"Yeah, what?" asked Tom.

"Well?" asked Steve.

"The environment. Ecology, pollution, and ozone depletion. All that stuff. But that's a can of worms for a different committee," said Sam. "If we fixed everything, what would Congress do?"

"The same thing you do most of the time, Sam," Tom jumped in. "Nothing!"

"You know," observed Bob, "It's hard to believe that it's only been a year and a quarter since we penned our first bills. And can you believe it's only been five months since our drug legislation bill became law? What a time it has been. I feel like I've been on a merry-go-round."

"It felt like a roller coaster to me," Tom reminisced, "and I got sick along the ride." He was worrying about the increase in babies being born by women on drugs that either had birth defects or were born addicted to drugs.

"We turned the world upside down," commented Frederica. She knew that being on the committee was a proud chapter in her life.

"You know," sadly voiced Tom, "I sure hope the church will pick up the pieces of humanity that we left behind. Someone has to." He prayed a Christian would be filling his vacant seat when he left.

"We're always looking for someone to help us clean up the room after a party," said the Chaplain subtly. "But the Lord provides. May His will be done."

"Amen," said John Jones.

"Amen," agreed Sam Bunker, smiling.

"Amen," Tom Baker said.

"Amen," added Frederica Wright quietly.

"Amen," said Steve Harning, thinking that there could be no finer eulogy than that.

"Amen," finished Bob Emerson, grateful that the world was almost back to normal.

Craig sat at home that night after a long day's work. He felt tired. Mary was working late and said she'd call him in the morning to say hello. There were still a lot of people out there who needed healing, spiritually and physically. Craig made a note to include healing for the nation to his prayer list before he went to bed.

His mind drifted to a story he had heard when he was young. It was the story of Pandora's box. In this box were all the evils of the world. Craig realized that not all evils had escaped from the box. There was one last evil recently let loose; the evil of addiction. According to the story, there was only Hope left in the box. Hope; frail, strong, and at times inconsequential. Craig prayed it would be enough.

He sighed, then opened his Bible, and suddenly changed his mind. He turned from his Bible study over to the start of Revelations, and began reading.

Prescription for Mayhem

Afterword

I wrote this book for several reasons. I had to deal with the fact that many people I knew (especially those listed in the dedication) had drug problems. These were or are good friends. Very good friends. People I accepted, who accepted me as I am. They had various drug problems. Some were small. Some big. Some had drugs under control, while others were being controlled by drugs.

There are many reasons why people do drugs. Some want to escape reality, some want to flaunt authority to make themselves seem bigger than the system, some want danger, some find individuality through drugs, and some use drugs to forget something that happened to them. I am sure that there are other reasons and nuances of why people take drugs.

I asked myself how the drug problem could be solved? How could this state of affairs be settled for all my friends? How could this sticky drug situation be cleared up, once and for all?

I started thinking. And, when I do, I usually go to the Bible. I made a word search of the Bible (both the New and Old Testaments) to see what the words "force," "power," "strength," and "authority" meant.

The Bible is an interesting book. But, crucially, it was written for believers, not as a introduction to nonbelievers. It was written as a handbook on how to live, think, and act for people who were Jews believing in God, and to

Christians believing in God through Christ. It was not written to or for people who were not "religious."

So, when we look in the Bible at the words force, power, authority, or at the commandments, these laws, rules, and powers are "given" to people who are believers. They do *not* state that nonbelievers are *commanded* or *forced* to behave as believers. Perhaps that is the way other cults or religions believe, but not Judaism or Christianity. The Bible gives commandments and directives only to those who follow under their banners.

So, how do the words force, power, strength, and authority relate to the drug question we are wrestling with today? Are we religious folks supposed to use our strength and authority to force people not to drink alcohol if they want? I don't think so. But is it wrong for us as believers to drink alcohol or take drugs? Absolutely! Booze or drugs take our minds off God and ultimately separates us from God. According to the Bible, that separation is a pretty bad thing to happen to us believers.

Now, I'm not saying I'm holier than anybody else. I admit that every so often I go out with my baseball buddies and get very drunk. Plastered. Or, if the world is going crazy around me, I may decide to get drunk and forget the world for a while. I do not know why I do this, but I do. (Sounds like Romans seven, doesn't it?) I know it's wrong, but it seems like the very thing to do at the time. Thankfully, it only happens a few times a year, but it makes me acutely aware that I'm in the same mess that everyone's in. I'm no paragon of virtue, although I'm constantly trying to be a better person in God's eyes.

For a Christian, the greatest gift God gives us is salvation. But, God also provides us with free will. We have the ability to decide for God or against God, to follow God's rules and authority or to ignore the rules and break them. Although some people may argue that we are "elected" or "predestined" towards religiousness, I still contend we have some free will. Free will is our greatest gift next to salvation, and free will helps us accept God and helps us to develop a lifelong relationship with God.

So, if we use our position of authority to command others, to force them to give up their free will with regard to drugs, it seems to me that we are putting ourselves up to God's level. We're judging them. Now, I'll argue with anyone about currently accepted morality, but with the Bible as my standard. "It's right for me, because the Bible says so..." or "...It's not right for you, because the Bible says so."

But, it is up to each of us to come to our own conclusions regarding drugs. It must be an individual decision, not a corporate or legislative decision. It is not biblical for me to judge your use of drugs. Judgment or vengeance is not mine to control or dispense, especially when the drug question is raised. If someone feels drugs are bad, what do you think gives them the right to tell someone taking drugs how to live? Nothing! As long as these people on drugs don't endanger others, is it okay?

What is the answer to the drug problem? Are we damned if we keep drugs illegal and damned if we make drugs legal? One thing that happens if drugs are legalized is that each person becomes responsible for themselves and their own lives. The question of "Who is my big brother?" becomes less debatable. People can only blame themselves for the way their lives turn out! Could society function if drugs were legal? Probably, but people taking drugs would have to be considerate and conscientious to others. There would have to be extremely strict and explicit legal penalties if drug users failed to be responsible and cognizant to others. Could society function as it does now, with drugs illegal? Possibly.

But is the solution to the problem to make drugs so illegal that no one can get drugs or that everyone is scared to make them? Absence of an item people are lusting for does not mean that the desire disappears. In many people, I've noticed that absence of drugs or making them illegal makes the desire for them *more* powerful. And, is more police control needed? If we need more police to enforce the drug laws to protect or intimidate the average Joe or Jane on the street, we might as well roll up our Constitution, toss it away, and turn our democracy into a monarchy or dictatorship.

How can we solve the problem? Not just patch the problem, or deal with the results of the drug problem so that we're always playing catch-up and not addressing the problem itself, but *solve* it. Some of the side effects of the drug issue are addiction, gangsters, and exploitation. But we also have to deal with the fact that some politicians legislated drugs illegal. Now, politicians made alcohol illegal in the twenties, and we can see how devastating that was to our nation's self-respect and sense of responsibility.

We have to *solve* the drug problem!! And this is my proposal.

I am not an anarchist, usually vote as a Democrat, and think that the political system we have in America is a working system capable of good. However, I believe some pretty crappy decisions have been made by legislators who are incapable of thinking about long-term problems and solutions. All recent presidents and politicians come to mind. Short-term solutions are NOT viable solutions. Any conclusive historical study of the drug problem can show you that.

Now, my friends, you have to ask yourself how you would solve the problem of drugs. Do you want to sweep this dilemma under the carpet and pretend it doesn't exist? Do you think drugs should not be legalized? And how would that solve the problem? Or, do you think there is any way that the drug problem can be solved any other way besides legalizing drugs?

I have thought about it for many a month. I can see no solution to the drug issue other than legalization. As you saw in the book, there would probably be a bloody price to pay for legalizing drugs, but I can see no other way to solve the problem. And, I have come to the conclusion that legislative controls and use of government force are not workable options in solving the drug problem. They have failed miserably *every* time they've been used in the past. Failed miserably...Terribly!

This afterword may help tell you where I am coming from. As I mentioned in the preface, your job is to think about the issues yourself. Don't just spend five minutes mulling over my text which is laid out for you so that you don't need to expend any effort. Take time to search for the drug problem, to define the topic for yourself, to wrestle with the subject internally, long and hard. Take enough time to dwell on the issues.

Think about people you know who have drug or alcohol problems. How about those you know with addictions; coffee, drugs, cigarettes...? How do they fit in? What solutions can you come up with that would be applicable to each one of them? Think of your conclusions to the drug question, taking everything, pro and con, into consideration. And I'm convinced that your conclusions will be the right ones.

God bless you as you ponder these questions.

B. Steven Mohnarke